1-15-45

Dear Reader,

Welcome to another [...]

Duets #29

Award-winning author Kristin Gabriel returns this
month with *Beauty and the Bachelor,* the last book
in the delightful CAFÉ ROMEO trilogy, about a
coffee shop that doubles as a dating service. *What
better place to find both lattes and love!* And talented
Gwen Pemberton delivers *Counterfeit Daddy,* the tale
of a sexy bachelor hero who poses as a family man in
order to impress his gorgeous female boss!

Duets #30

Author Julie Kistler teams up this month with
Colleen Collins to serve up BEDS & BACHELORS,
two linked stories about a romantic but unusual
B & B in San Francisco. Every bedroom has a
movie theme! Julie's tale, *In Bed with the Wild One,*
is a romp about a mousy heroine who sets off to have
an adventure with the bad-boy hero. Then B & B
owner Kate encounters her very own fantasy man in
In Bed with the Pirate.

I hope you enjoy both Duets volumes this month!

Birgit Davis-Todd
Senior Editor, Harlequin Duets

Beauty and the Bachelor

"Are you ready, Noah?"

He sat up in bed, blinking at the light shining in from the hallway. "Ready?" he asked groggily.

Sabrina held up the cordless phone in her hand. "It's time to make the call."

"Oh." Noah relaxed against the pillows, then studied her with half-lidded eyes. "I like your hair that way."

She laughed softly. "It's a mess. I just got out of bed."

"I know. That's what I like about it."

She moved closer to the bed. "Are you sure you're awake? You sound different."

He folded his arms behind his head, causing the blanket to slip away and reveal his bare chest. "I'm only half-awake, and I'm hoping like hell that this is a dream. Of course, if it was a dream, you wouldn't be standing there."

She took a step closer to him, her voice a husky whisper. "What would I be doing?"

He closed his eyes. "Oh, Sabrina, I can think of a thousand things...."

For more, turn to page 9

Counterfeit Daddy

"Okay, kids, family meeting time."

Chet herded the group out back onto the screened porch. "You three are up to something and I want to know what."

The children exchanged looks. "It was Brittany's idea," Sean said.

"I didn't tell you to make the vacuum explode," she said. "I only told you to make Chet look helpless...just a little helpless."

"But why?" Chet asked.

"'Cause she thinks women like doofus guys."

Chet took a deep breath. "Let me get this straight. You decided to make me into one of those doofus guys so women will like me?"

"Nope." Kevin grinned. "Just her."

"Ahh." At least they had good taste. "You wanted Ms. West to like me so I can keep my job."

"Not exactly," Brittany said. "We wanted her to really, really like you."

"We were kinda thinking of something else."

"Like what kind of something?"

"Something like a wife," Brittany said.

For more, turn to page 197

HARLEQUIN DUETS

ISBN 0-373-44095-2

BEAUTY AND THE BACHELOR
Copyright © 2000 by Kristin Eckhardt

COUNTERFEIT DADDY
Copyright © 2000 by Gwen Pemberton

KRISTIN GABRIEL

Beauty and the Bachelor

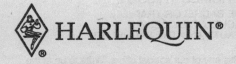

HARLEQUIN®

TORONTO • NEW YORK • LONDON
AMSTERDAM • PARIS • SYDNEY • HAMBURG
STOCKHOLM • ATHENS • TOKYO • MILAN • MADRID
PRAGUE • WARSAW • BUDAPEST • AUCKLAND

Dear Reader,

At last I get to tell Noah's story. He's the last of the Callahan brothers and he's just as determined as his siblings to avoid one of his aunt's bachelor traps. Only, by this point, we all know what happened to his brothers. And now, poor lonely Noah is about to meet his Waterloo....

This is the final book in the CAFÉ ROMEO series. I hope you enjoyed reading about the romantic misadventures of the Callahan men, not to mention their incorrigible aunt Sophie!

Wishing you a life full of lattes and love!

Kristin Gabriel

CAFÉ ROMEO TRILOGY

25—THE BACHELOR TRAP
27—BACHELOR BY DESIGN
29—BEAUTY AND THE BACHELOR

Don't miss any of our special offers. Write to us at the following address for information on our newest releases.

Harlequin Reader Service
U.S.: 3010 Walden Ave., P.O. Box 1325, Buffalo, NY 14269
Canadian: P.O. Box 609, Fort Erie, Ont. L2A 5X3

For my daughter, Chelsea, who has a way with words.

Special thanks to Shane Eckhardt for his mechanical expertise and for being a great brother-in-law.

1

NOAH CALLAHAN ITCHED everywhere.

Weddings had always made him uncomfortable, but he'd never actually broken out in hives before. An unusual reaction, but then this was an unusual wedding. Or double wedding, to be more precise. And the grooms were his two older brothers. Unfortunately, their best man was still in the chapel parking lot, sitting in the driver's seat of his classic 1965 red Ford Mustang and drenching himself in calamine lotion.

Huge red welts covered his arms and torso. After squeezing the last pink drop out of the bottle, he wiped his hands on an old towel he kept under the seat. Then he buttoned up his white dress shirt. Thankfully, most of the hives were hidden by his tuxedo. He did have one near the base of his thumb, and another behind his ear, but as long as he could refrain from scratching them, they shouldn't be too noticeable.

They itched like crazy though, since he hadn't treated them with the telltale pink lotion. His brothers already teased him unmercifully about his aversion to marriage. He didn't want them to know matrimony actually caused him to have an allergic reaction. Which was why he'd always avoided weddings.

Until now.

It might be understandable for the bride or groom to get cold feet, but the best man? Hell, he *wanted* to stand up for his brothers. Even if Jake and Trace were about to make the biggest mistakes of their lives. Not that Noah didn't like Nina and Chloe, their respective brides-to-be. They were great. He could hardly blame his brothers for falling in love.

No, the person to blame for all of this was Aunt Sophie, or Madame Sophia, as she was known to the patrons of Café Romeo, a matchmaking service fronting as a coffeehouse. Madame Sophia had developed a reputation for blending perfect coffee and perfect couples. A former fortune-teller with a traveling carnival, she now read her customers' coffee grounds and predicted their romantic futures.

Poor Jake and Trace had both fallen headfirst into her bachelor traps. Two strong-minded men who hadn't believed in Madame Sophia's abilities until it was too late.

He adjusted his bow tie. It was almost time to face the music. To Noah, Mendelssohn's Wedding March sounded like a funeral dirge. It was in a way, since it signaled the death of a man's freedom.

Hard to believe that six weeks ago Jake and Trace hadn't even met their prospective brides. Now they were ready to vow until-death-do-us-part. A cold shiver ran up his spine.

Because Noah was next on Madame Sophia's hit list.

Oh, she hadn't admitted it in so many words. But he recognized that calculating gleam in her eye. Knew she'd secretly confiscated his coffee grounds, along with those of his brothers. She thought she had him.

She was wrong.

No way would Noah succumb to one of her matchmaking schemes. He'd even gone so far as to arrange a job transfer to Cleveland, Ohio. He worked as an insurance investigator for a large, very respected company. Fortunately, insurance fraud happened just as frequently in Cleveland as it did in St. Louis. He hated leaving his hometown, but desperate times called for desperate transfers.

Besides, it wasn't as if anyone needed him here. Jake and Trace always handled every family crisis, elbowing him out of the way if he tried to help. He was twenty-six years old and a good inch taller than both of them, but they still treated him like their baby brother. They hadn't even entrusted him to hold onto the wedding rings until the ceremony!

The ceremony. He glanced at his watch. ''Damn.''

The last thing he wanted to do was reinforce their erroneous opinion of him by showing up late. With only minutes to spare, he reached into the backseat for his tuxedo jacket. The sound of screeching tires drew his gaze to the back windshield just in time to see a shiny black pickup truck racing out of the parking lot, taking the corner on two wheels.

The next moment his passenger door was yanked open and a strange woman jumped into the front seat. "Follow that truck!"

Noah gaped at her. "What?"

The redhead turned to him, her green eyes wide and frantic. "Move it, mister!"

She looked normal in her gauzy turquoise dress and matching sling-back heels. But the woman was obviously crazy.

"I'm not going anywhere. Except to a wedding."

"I don't have time for this," she muttered, fumbling frantically in her purse. Then she pulled out a narrow gray cylinder and pointed it at him. "Don't make me use this."

He'd seen the effects of pepper spray and he sure as hell didn't want it used on him. Now he just had to decide if he'd rather face down a tube of toxic spray or two irate big brothers. Then he took a closer look. "It's breath spray!"

"Please," she cried, desperation straining her voice. "My baby's in there."

That was all he needed to hear. Noah switched on the ignition, shifted into gear, then floored the gas pedal. The woman lurched back against the seat as the Mustang shot out of the parking space.

He pulled onto the busy street, ignoring the posted speed limit. "Why the hell didn't you tell me your baby had been kidnapped?"

"It just all happened so fast...." Her voice trailed

off as she leaned forward in the seat, peering out the front windshield for some sign of the black pickup truck.

"There it is," she cried, pointing as the truck barreled through a yellow light into the busy intersection five car-lengths ahead of them.

The stoplight turned red and Noah slammed on the brakes, the Mustang screeching to a halt just as traffic streamed into the intersection in front of them.

The woman whirled around to face him. "What are you doing? She's getting away!"

She? Noah wondered why he was surprised. He'd heard of women kidnapping babies before. He just didn't know too many who drove a one-ton, dual-wheel pickup truck with chrome mags.

"I didn't have any choice," he snapped, his heart still pounding at the close call. "We can't catch anyone if we're in a three-car pileup. In fact, I'd like you to put your seat belt on."

"Then what do you want me to do?" she asked, ignoring his request. "The hokey-pokey? *You're letting her get away!*"

Noah clenched his jaw as he leaned over and unspooled her seat belt. He caught the soft scent of lavender and felt her silky hair brush his cheek. From this vantage point, he also accidentally glimpsed the lacy top edge of her white camisole and thoughts of what lay underneath filled his mind.

He mentally shook himself, then cinched the seat belt into place, resuming his place behind the steering wheel just as the stoplight turned green. How could he be having lascivious thoughts about a woman in her desperate situation? He hadn't looked down her dress on purpose, but he hadn't looked away immediately, either. Some hero, he thought in disgust as he floored the accelerator.

He wove in and out of the two-lane traffic, searching avidly for any sign of the black pickup. Mile after mile, he scanned side streets and parking lots. His passenger did the same, her gaze glued to the window, the silence growing heavy and tense between them.

The truck was nowhere in sight.

His hands clenched on the steering wheel. Maybe he should have taken his chances and run that red light. If anything happened to that baby...

"You lost her."

His gut twisted at the dejection in her voice. He pulled off the street and into a crowded strip-mall parking lot, kicking himself for leaving his cell phone at home. "Look, don't worry. We'll find a pay phone and call the police."

"It won't do any good."

"Sure it will." He steered the car along the curb until he reached a phone booth. He shifted into park, then turned to her. "I got the license-plate number. The police will be able to track down the driver in no time."

She bit her lower lip. "You don't understand."

How could he? He didn't have a child. And since

he definitely planned to remain a bachelor, he'd never know the depth of her heartache and terror.

Or the depth of her love.

At the sight of one lone tear trailing down her cheek, Noah pulled a handkerchief out of his pocket and handed it to her. He wanted to do more. But what? "Look, I'm sorry. I promise to do everything in my power to help you."

"It's all my fault," she whispered.

"You can't blame yourself."

"Yes." She nodded her head vigorously up and down. "Yes, I can. I screwed up. If it wasn't for that stupid letter, this never would have happened."

Her remarks made him curious, but they didn't have time for long explanations. "What's your name?"

"Sabrina," she said with a sniff. "Sabrina Lovett."

His brows drew together. *Sabrina Lovett.* Where had he heard that name before? He panicked for a moment, wondering if he'd dated her once. Her lush green eyes did look eerily familiar. "Do you want me to call the police for you, Sabrina? We really need to report this as soon as possible."

She shook her head. "Forget it. They won't care."

"They sure as hell will care! We're talking about a kidnapping."

"I've been receiving threats for over a week, but the police couldn't be bothered. Now she's gone." Sabrina took a deep, shaky breath. "Who's going to give her tuna for breakfast? Or let her sit in a windowsill so she can watch the birds in the trees?''

He blinked. What kind of mother fed her baby fish for breakfast? Or even worse, let her sit in an open window?

''Who will check her for ear mites?'' She sniffed. ''And make sure she doesn't choke on a hair ball?''

He drew back. ''Wait a minute. Are you talking about a baby or—''

''A cat,'' she affirmed, drying her eyes. ''My cat. Her name is Beauty.''

He let her words sink in, still not quite able to believe it. ''You mean, I skipped out on my brothers' double wedding to chase after a stray cat?''

She looked up at him in surprise. ''Your brothers? That means you must be...''

''Noah Callahan,'' he clipped, wondering how he could have been duped by this woman. ''You just hijacked the best man.''

''You're Noah Callahan?'' She closed her eyes. ''I don't believe it. Madame Sophia told me fate would find a way, but I never expected to meet you like this.''

Prickles of alarm ran up and down his spine. ''Don't tell me, let me guess—she read your coffee grounds.''

''Well, actually...no.'' She opened her eyes and cleared her throat. ''Look, it's a little complicated and I've got other things on my mind at the moment. Like finding my cat.''

Her tone sounded stronger now, almost defiant. Which made him even more curious.

"Do you mind telling me who would kidnap a cat?" He whipped the car around and approached the exit lane of the parking lot. "And why?"

"It's a long story."

"It's a long way back to the chapel, so we'll have plenty of time."

"I really don't know where to start."

He waited impatiently for a break in the heavy traffic. "Why don't you start with the letter?"

She jerked her attention back to him. "How do you know about the letter?"

He eased into a turning lane, then waited on another red light. "You told me. If I remember right, you said, 'If it wasn't for that stupid letter, this never would have happened.'"

She shrugged, turning her gaze back to the passing scenery. "Well, it's true. I tend to be rather…impulsive. Sending that letter was a mistake. A big mistake. Madame Sophia told me fate would find a way to bring me together with my perfect match. Only I decided fate could use a little nudge."

The green signal arrow flashed and he made a left. "So this is all about finding a boyfriend? I just missed the most important day of Jake and Trace's lives because you have a lousy love life?"

"You're angry."

"Damn straight. But I'm not nearly as angry as my brothers are going to be when I finally show up at Café Romeo for the wedding reception. I'll be lucky if they don't feed me knuckle sandwiches."

She turned to him. "Surely if you just explain to them…"

"Oh, right," he interjected. "I can just hear it now. 'Sorry I missed the ceremony, guys. See, this woman jumped into my car and threatened me with breath spray if I didn't solve the case of the kidnapped kitty.'"

"Well, if you put it like that," she said with a huff, a flush on her cheeks.

He couldn't help but notice that Sabrina Lovett was beautiful when she was angry. Hell, she was beautiful, period. He normally preferred blondes, but he liked her sassy auburn hair and lucent green eyes. Even better, he liked the tiny freckles sprinkled over the bridge of her nose that made her more human than goddess.

Of course, a goddess implied perfection, and he'd yet to find a perfect woman. Although he'd had a damn good time searching for one.

"If your brothers want someone to blame," she continued, "they can blame me."

"Look, I'll handle them. Now tell me how you got into this mess."

"That's easy. I wanted to meet my perfect match."

"And he chose your cat over you?"

She frowned at him. "The person driving that pickup truck is *not* my perfect match. In the first place, she's a woman. And in the second place, she's a lunatic. I've got much higher standards for my future husband.''

Noah pulled into the chapel parking lot. "So who is this paragon?"

"You."

SABRINA BRACED HERSELF as the car lurched to a halt.

"Me?" he cried, looking at her as if she was nuts. "We've never even met before today."

"I know. But, as I said before, Madame Sophia told me fate would find a way to bring me together with my perfect match. I just never dreamed it would be quite like this."

"This isn't a dream, it's a nightmare," he said from between clenched teeth. "I thought you told me she didn't read your coffee grounds."

"She didn't. She doesn't even know you're the one. I read my coffee grounds myself. I'm trying to learn the trade."

"Oh, wonderful," he muttered. "Just what the world needs—another matchmaker on the loose. You people should come with a warning label."

Madame Sophia had told her to ignore the skeptics, so she bit her tongue as she scanned the deserted parking lot. "Looks like everyone has already left for the wedding reception."

His gaze never moved from her face. "My aunt put you up to this, didn't she? Hijacking my car, the phony story about the catnapping, the car chase.

None of it's real. It's all part of one of her elaborate bachelor traps.''

She hadn't expected him to immediately fall head over heels in love with her, but his attitude left a lot to be desired. ''I assure you, it's very real. And I already told you Madame Sophia doesn't know a thing about it.''

Sabrina intended to keep it that way. At least until she knew for certain that she hadn't made another mistake.

He stared at her for a long moment. ''Wait a minute...you're the girl in the picture. You're Aunt Sophie's goddaughter.''

She frowned. ''What picture?''

''The one on the mantelpiece all those years I was growing up. Except you had pigtails then, and braces.''

She suppressed a shudder. ''Don't remind me.''

''So what are you doing here? I thought you moved to Europe or Greenland or somewhere far, far away.''

It was obvious he wished she'd stayed far, far away. Too bad. Noah Callahan had better get used to having her around. At least for the next fifty years or so.

''I'm back,'' she replied, skipping her nomadic family history. Life in a traveling carnival was not conducive to putting down roots. Even if it was fun. As a child, she'd enjoyed her vagabond life. Until she'd learned that other children lived differently than her. They had houses. Pets. A school instead of a traveling tutor. They made friends and kept them for years. They had traditions.

A place they called home.

As Sabrina grew, her parents took on part ownership of the carnival and became even more absorbed in their work. They fully expected Sabrina to follow in their footsteps, never suspecting her growing discontentment. But Madame Sophia knew. Just like Sabrina now knew she could never go back to that life.

She wanted a home. A family. A husband. Was that so much to ask? "Didn't your aunt tell you I was coming to St. Louis?"

"No, she didn't say a word about it. She didn't mention your cat, either. Were you both invited to the wedding?"

She didn't like his tone. "I didn't want to leave Beauty alone, especially after all those threats. It's a nice day, so I decided she would be safer in my car. I certainly didn't expect anyone to tail me, or slash my tire, or steal Beauty right out from under my nose."

"Right. And you just happened to jump in my car. Quite a coincidence."

She clenched her jaw. "Look, I'm not exactly thrilled about it, either. I never knew fate had such a bizarre sense of humor."

He drove toward her disabled car. "You may not have noticed, but I'm not laughing."

"Neither am I. At this point, all I care about is getting my cat back safe and sound."

"Well, just for future reference, you might want to brush up on your flirting techniques, since the authorities frown on hijacking unsuspecting men in the name of romance."

Without another word, she popped the car door open and climbed out, telling herself not to lose her temper. She marched over to her twenty-year-old Nova, opened the trunk, then hauled out the jack and spare tire. Kneeling down by the wheel well, she heard the sound of Noah's classic Mustang still idling smoothly beside her.

He leaned his head over his open window. "What do you think you're doing?"

"First, I'm going to change this flat tire. Then I'm going to make an appearance at the wedding reception at Café Romeo. Then I'm going to find my cat."

He frowned at her, then at the jack in her hand. "Do you even know how to change a tire?"

"I'm sure I can figure it out." She turned away from him and set the jack on the ground. "Goodbye, Mr. Callahan."

Noah didn't reply. After what seemed an eternity, his car slowly pulled away. Sabrina breathed a sigh of relief. Despite all her fantasies about him, she hadn't been at all prepared for that handsome face or those deep blue eyes.

She must have made a mistake. Again. Sabrina Lovett could never win a man like that in a million years! Not that she considered herself ugly any-more. Over the years, her bright red hair had mellowed into an attractive auburn and her freckles had faded. Those ugly braces had miraculously straightened her teeth and once she'd quit indulging in cotton candy and funnel cakes, those excess pounds had fallen away.

An old boyfriend had once described her as wholesome. She grimaced as she loosened the bolts on the wheel. *Wholesome.* Not exactly the image to make men look twice, but it had proved invaluable in her career. Her *former* career.

Now she had a chance to start over, thanks to Madame Sophia. Her godmother was more like a fairy godmother. She'd sent Sabrina special little gifts throughout her childhood, helped out when she ran short on her college tuition, and even offered her a chance to someday take over at Café Romeo.

If she could master the craft of reading coffee grounds.

That was the hitch. Sabrina had excelled in all her business classes in college, earning her degree with honors. But she still had to prove herself as a coffee-grounds reader. So far she was batting zero.

Unless she was right about Noah. She gave the jack one last crank. She *had* to be right about Noah. Her future literally depended on it.

Sabrina straightened up and wiped her damp brow. Then she blinked in surprise as the Mustang pulled up beside her once more. Without a word, Noah got out of the driver's seat and rolled up his sleeves. Then he grabbed her by both shoulders and moved her gently but firmly out of the way.

"What do you think you're doing?" she asked, as he bent down and twirled the loosened bolts off in fast succession.

"I'm waiting to hear the rest of your story. You still haven't explained about the letter. Or why you've been receiving threats. Or why anyone in their right mind would willingly kidnap a cat."

So the man wasn't an animal lover. Just one more reason for Sabrina to fear her coffee grounds had given out the wrong message. "Why are you interested?"

He shrugged as he pulled the tire off the axle. "Riddles drive me crazy. It's one of the reasons I became an insurance investigator. I like searching for answers to perplexing questions."

"This isn't some riddle, this is my life."

He paused and looked up at her. "I know. And at the moment, it fascinates me."

His inquisitive blue eyes made her stomach flip-flop. "What exactly do you want to know?"

He turned back to the tire, rolling it toward the open trunk. "Everything."

That narrowed it down. Still, she had screwed up his afternoon, so maybe she did owe him an explanation. "The trouble started when Madame offered to read my coffee grounds."

"It usually does," he muttered.

"Only I wanted to do it myself," she said, ignoring his comment. "I'd had some training, and I was ready to prove myself."

He picked up a bolt off the pavement. "So your coffee grounds spelled out my name?"

"It doesn't quite work that way. The secret is—"

"No." He held up one hand, forestalling her explanation. "I don't want to know. It's bad enough that I'm the one who showed up in the bottom of your cup."

"Madame Sophia warned me that some people try to resist fate. But she said not to worry, because fate—"

"Would find a way," he finished for her. "Got it. That doesn't seem so unusual. A little frightening, but not unusual. She shanghaied Jake and Trace the same way."

Her brows drew together. "What do you mean by 'shanghaied'?"

His mouth tipped up in a half smile as he pulled the spare tire out of the trunk. "Dear, sweet Aunt Sophie staged a fake deathbed scene so she could trick us into leaving behind our coffee grounds. It's a long story. Suffice it to say that my coffee grounds were obtained against my will."

"You don't seem too upset about it," she observed. She also observed the play of muscles in his arms and back as he worked, and the way his sweat-dampened shirt molded to his body.

"That's because I don't plan to stick around to become victim number three. As soon as I tie up a few loose ends, I'm outta here."

I'm outta here. She tried not to let his words discourage her. "Where are you going?"

"Cleveland. I start my new job in two weeks."

Two weeks. She only had fourteen days to make Noah Callahan fall in love with her. Since no man had ever actually fallen in love with her before, she certainly had her work cut out for her.

He looked up at her, squinting in the sunlight. "Why are we talking about me? I'm still waiting to hear your story."

She leaned against her sun-warmed car. "I read my coffee grounds, then compared the results against the applications everyone fills out before a reading."

"I never filled out an application."

"Madame Sophia must have filled one out for you. But I didn't find it the first time. I...uh...made a mistake."

"What kind of mistake?"

"I picked another man as my perfect match. Niles Dooley."

His face brightened. "Really?"

"It was a mistake," she reiterated. "A big mistake. And I only made it worse."

He hoisted the spare tire onto the hub. "How?"

She licked her lips. "Well, I wrote him a letter." More like two hundred letters, considering the number of drafts that had ended up in the trash can before she'd finally been satisfied. "I thought it might be less intrusive than a telephone call from a total stranger. In the letter, I briefly introduced myself, then asked him to meet me for a date. I was hoping the mystery of it all would entice him."

Noah straightened to his full height, which was well over Sabrina's head. "Did it work?"

"Unfortunately, yes," she replied, preparing herself for the really embarrassing part.

"So what happened?"

"We met at the Vienna House for dinner."

He whistled low. "Impressive. That place costs a fortune."

"Tell me about it. The sausage platter alone is over thirty bucks. I almost maxed out my credit card."

"You paid?"

She nodded. "It seems Niles is employment-challenged. He's an inventor. His hero is Johan Vaaler."

"Who is Johan Vaaler?"

"The man who invented the paper clip."

His blue eyes twinkled in the sunlight. "Niles sounds like quite a catch. Maybe this mistake was fate *finding a way.*"

"I don't think so."

"Why not?" He turned to finish tightening the bolts on the spare, then removed the jack. He straightened up, brushing his hands on his dress pants. "Didn't Niles like you?"

"Niles was crazy about me, but his wife wasn't so thrilled."

He blinked. "What?"

"Niles Dooley has been unhappily married for the past three years," she informed him. "In fact, he brought his suitcase with him to the restaurant.

He was ready and willing to fly to the Caribbean for a quickie divorce, all expenses paid. By me, of course.''

Noah shook his head in disbelief. "What a jerk. I hope you set him straight."

"I did." She took a deep breath. "Shortly before our date, I had done another reading of my coffee grounds and realized my mistake. I told him my future is with you and that I hope to be married soon."

He froze. "Married?" Then he reached up to scratch behind his ear. "Well, I suppose a little white lie was necessary under the circumstances."

Sabrina hadn't been lying, but Noah looked jumpy enough already. She'd better wait awhile to tell him she wanted six kids. Besides, she needed to do another reading, just to make certain her coffee grounds were in order.

She watched him scratch at his neck, then the top of his hand. "Is something the matter?"

He scratched behind his ear again. "Nothing serious."

For the first time she noticed the light pink spots on his forearms. "You're not allergic to grease, are you?"

He shifted his weight from one foot to the other, then scratched his elbow. "Grease? No."

"The rubber from the tire?"

He shook his hand. "Nothing like that."

She didn't believe him. The man looked miserable. "Are you sure?"

"Positive. So how did Niles react? I hope he took it like a man."

"Not really. But he stopped crying when I bought him chocolate-truffle cheesecake for dessert." She sighed. "I just wish it had ended there."

Noah paused. "Wait a minute. Is this the guy who's been stalking you? Threatening you?"

"No. I haven't seen Niles since that night. Unfortunately, neither has his wife. She's the one who kidnapped Beauty. She found my letter and is convinced that I have her husband holed up in a love nest somewhere. She won't rest until she finds him."

"How will stealing your cat accomplish that?"

Sabrina shrugged, her heart clenching at the thought of Beauty at the mercy of that woman. "I don't know. But the woman is relentless. She's making my life miserable and enjoying every minute of it."

"Have you complained to the police?"

"Numerous times. Niles had mentioned that his wife is a security guard somewhere, so I guess she knows enough to stay just inside the law. Frankly, the police seem to find the entire situation amusing."

"So now what?"

Sabrina squared her shoulders. "Now it's time for Plan B."

2

NOAH HAD STOPPED itching by the time he walked into his brothers' wedding reception at Café Romeo. Physically, anyway. But an annoying mental itch still nagged at him. *What the hell was Plan B?* He'd left the church parking lot without asking Sabrina to explain. He told himself he didn't want to know, despite the fact that he'd thought of little else during the drive over.

The same thing always happened to him whenever he was on a particularly perplexing case. Only this had nothing to do with business. And he couldn't exactly call his encounter with Sabrina Lovett a pleasure. She'd annoyed him, intrigued him, and enticed him.

A hell of a combination.

"Just put her out of your mind," he muttered to himself as he looked around the crowded coffeehouse. He didn't see either of the newlywed couples. Despite his hives, it bothered him that he'd missed standing up as Jake and Trace's best man.

Sabrina Lovett bothered him even more.

It wasn't just her bizarre story or her entrancing green eyes. It was the way the curvy redhead had barged into his life as if she belonged there. No flirtatious come-ons or coy glances. None of the usual games he'd grown so tired of women playing. Instead, Sabrina had been remarkably direct. *My future is with you...I hope to be married soon.* Her words had made him break out in new and uncomfortable places.

He scratched behind his ear, wondering how she could be so certain. His father had been married for over eight years before he'd discovered the hard way that he'd wed the wrong woman. How could Sabrina possibly believe he was Mr. Right before she'd even met him?

The crowd parted and he saw the source of all his troubles. He folded his arms across his chest as Sophie Callahan glided toward him, her long gold caftan floating behind her and her bangle bracelets jingling in accompaniment to her graceful steps. She was tall for a woman, with bright orange-red hair that never seemed to fade to gray. At sixty, she still displayed the bouncy exuberance that had made it possible for her to keep up with three rambunctious young boys. Noah's throat still got tight when he thought about the way Aunt Sophie had stepped into their lives after their mother had run out.

Since Noah had only been four years old at the time, Sophie was the only mother he could really remember. And despite the chaos she could cause in his life, he couldn't imagine any other woman taking her place.

"There you are," she said, her blue eyes sparkling. "We missed you at the wedding."

"And you know why."

"Now, Noah, how could I possibly know?"

"Cut the innocent act, Aunt Sophie. It might work with Jake and Trace, but I'm not falling for it."

"Noah, dear, I'm a little rusty on mind reading, so if you wouldn't mind just giving me a little hint."

A muscle flicked in his jaw. "Sabrina Lovett."

Her face brightened. "You've met Sabrina?"

"Met her? She's the reason I missed the wedding!"

Sophie patted his arm. "No need to feel guilty about it. Jake and Trace were upset at first, but I'm sure all those comments about beating you to a pulp were just a case of bridegroom jitters."

Noah wished he could be as certain. Trace he could probably handle. Most of their tussles in the past had ended in a draw. But Jake, a former boxer, was another story. Noah had no desire to be on the receiving end of that powerful left hook.

"No use putting it off," he said with an air of resignation. His gaze scanned the room once more. "Where are they?"

"Right behind you, little brother."

Noah turned to see Trace, arms folded across his chest, legs wide apart. The tuxedo belied the fact that Trace had once been a tough hood.

"Where's Jake?" Noah scanned the crowd.

"He and Nina already left," Sophie chimed. "They had to catch a plane in time to make their cruise." She clasped her wrinkled hands together. "It was so romantic. Jake picked up Nina in his arms and carried her right out the door. Everyone cheered." She breathed a wistful sigh. "There's nothing like true love."

Noah's eyes narrowed. "Aunt Sophie?"

"Yes, dear?"

"It isn't going to work."

Her titian brows drew together. "What isn't going to work?"

"Your diabolical scheme to match me up with Sabrina Lovett."

"Diabolical?" She clapped a hand to her chest. "Me?"

Trace laughed, and even Noah had to smile at her theatrics.

"That's right," Noah said. "Dangerous, too. Remember the Bonecrusher? Jake almost got killed protecting Nina from that guy. And Trace's first date with Chloe almost landed him in jail for a crime he didn't commit."

"Hey, keep me out of this," Trace said, circling one arm around Aunt Sophie's shoulders. "I'm not complaining. Chloe is the best thing that ever happened to me. Even with Ramon in the bargain."

"Shhhh!" Sophie glanced around the room. "Keep your voices down. Ramon feels badly enough about all the trouble he caused for you and Chloe."

Ramon D'Onofrio, Chloe's younger brother, had been a waiter at Café Romeo since it opened two years ago. Neither Noah nor his brothers could understand why Aunt Sophie insisted on keeping him. But she was as loyal to her employees as she was to her three nephews. Even an employee who spilled coffee on the customers and hyperventilated under stress.

"Ramon's just lucky he got off with probation," Noah said. "And I know the guy is Chloe's brother, but I'm not sure he's done causing trouble."

"He's done causing trouble with us." Trace nodded toward a corner booth where Chloe sat with Ramon. She looked incredible in her formfitting, beaded white wedding gown and Noah felt an unexpected jab of envy.

Trace lovingly watched his wife. "Chloe finally decided to tell him he won't be living with us after we come back from our honeymoon."

Sophie clucked her tongue. "Poor Ramon. This just isn't his day. I also had to break the news that he won't be managing Café Romeo while I'm away."

Noah and Trace both turned to her, speaking in unison. "Away?"

She smiled. "Didn't I tell you? I haven't had a vacation since I opened Café Romeo, so my friend Hannah and I decided to drive down to New Orleans. A bunch of the old carnival gang is going to get together there for a reunion."

Trace frowned. "That sounds great, Aunt Sophie.

But this really isn't the best time to leave town. Neither Jake nor I will be here to watch over the coffeehouse for you.''

Noah bristled. ''*I'll* be here.''

Trace looked at him. ''I thought you were moving to Cleveland.''

''Not for two weeks.'' He turned to Aunt Sophie. ''In fact, this is the perfect time for you to take a vacation. I've got the next two weeks off, and there's nothing else I'd rather do than baby-sit Café Romeo for you.''

Her face lit up. ''Really?''

''Really.''

She clasped a hand to her chest. ''Oh, Noah, this is wonderful! Now you and Sabrina will have plenty of time to get to know each other.''

His stomach dropped. ''What?''

''Let me guess,'' Trace said with a grin. ''Sabrina is the woman who made you miss my wedding.''

''They met in the chapel parking lot,'' Sophie explained. ''Isn't that romantic?''

Noah barely heard them, still reeling from the fact that he'd just stepped voluntarily into one of Sophie's bachelor traps. Maybe it wasn't too late to back out. Maybe he could still escape.

Trace slapped him on the back. ''Don't fight it, Noah. Just accept the inevitable.'' His gaze fixed on his new bride. ''You'll be very glad you did.''

Noah watched him walk toward Chloe and take her in his arms. Their long, intense kiss drew applause and wolf whistles from the guests. His brother held onto Chloe as if he never wanted to let her go.

Noah turned back on his aunt, his heart pounding in his chest. A dozen excuses raced through his mind, each one dumber than the next. Then he made the mistake of looking into her clear blue eyes. He swallowed hard, realizing he couldn't disappoint her. Not after all she'd done for his family. Even if she had tricked him into this situation.

"Sabrina's my apprentice," Sophie informed him, "and a very quick study. She's new in town, so I'd really appreciate it if you could look after her."

"One baby-sitter at your service," Noah said, grabbing a champagne glass from the tray of a passing waiter. "Both Café Romeo and Sabrina Lovett will be safe in my hands."

And he meant that literally. He wasn't about to take any chances by indulging in a fling with a determined redhead. No matter how enticing the prospect.

Sophie reached for his hand. "I can't tell you how much this means to me, Noah. It's been so long since I've had a real vacation."

"You deserve it," he said, leaning over to kiss her cheek.

She looked around the coffeehouse. "The place pretty much runs itself. The work schedule is already done, and we're all stocked up on supplies. You'll just need to open and close every night, deposit the receipts in the bank, and please, be nice to Ramon.''

''Easier said than done.'' Noah drained his glass. ''Trace claims the counseling helped, but frankly, I have my doubts. The guy is a pain in the ass.''

Aunt Sophie reached up to straighten his bow tie. ''He's just sensitive. Promise me you'll be patient with him. It's only for a couple of weeks.''

Between Sabrina and Ramon, this promised to be the longest two weeks of Noah's life. ''All right. I promise.''

She patted his shoulder. ''Good. Since that's settled, I'll go tell Hannah we're on our way to New Orleans. In fact, there's really no reason we can't leave today.''

Noah set down his empty champagne glass and went in search of something stronger. But Trace waylaid him before he could reach the coffee bar.

''Chloe and I are slipping out the back.'' Trace shoved a piece of paper in Noah's hand. ''Here's a phone number where you can reach me in case any problems come up.''

Since it was Trace's wedding day, Noah refrained from punching him in the nose. But just barely. Did his brother really think Noah couldn't handle the little problems of Café Romeo? Did Trace really believe him to be that incompetent? That irresponsible?

''Gee, thanks,'' Noah said, crumpling the paper in his fist.

''Now, whatever you do,'' Trace admonished,

oblivious to Noah's reaction, "don't give that number to Ramon. Chloe and I are keeping our honeymoon spot a secret. But I'll be close by St. Louis if you need me."

"I won't need you," Noah assured him. "Just enjoy your honeymoon."

Trace grinned. "It can't start soon enough for me."

Noah watched as his brother practically sprinted toward the back of the coffeehouse, fooling no one. The crowd followed the groom, throwing rice and shouting congratulations as he and Chloe ducked out the back service door.

Noah turned and tossed the phone number into a trash can. Then he headed for the kitchen, needing something stronger than the Kahlúa he'd find at the coffee bar. If he was lucky, he'd find the bottle of vodka Ramon always stashed behind the microwave oven.

Then again, if he was lucky, he'd be in Cleveland right now.

SABRINA STOOD ALONE in the kitchen of Café Romeo, intently studying the soggy grounds at the bottom of her coffee cup. She'd chugged three cups of Madame Sophia's special Jamaican almond blend in less than thirty minutes. And they all told her the same thing.

Noah Callahan was her perfect match.

So, either he really was her perfect match or she was a complete failure as a coffee-grounds reader.

The shrill ring of the black wall phone beside her made her jump.

She set down the cup, then picked up the receiver. "Café Romeo. How may I help you?"

A husky voice came over the line. "May I speak to the home-wrecker, please?"

A caffeine rush helped her pulse kick into high gear. "This is Sabrina Lovett. Look, Mrs. Dooley..."

"Just shut up and listen," Doris Dooley interjected. "If you want to see your pussycat again, you'll do exactly as I tell you."

Sabrina twined the phone cord between her fingers. "Is Beauty all right?"

"Who the hell is Beauty?"

"My cat," she replied, trying desperately to hold on to her temper. Alienating Doris further wouldn't help her resolve this mess. "That's her name."

Doris snorted. "Boy, do you have a twisted sense of humor. This is the ugliest cat I've ever seen in my life. Of course, you also have the ugliest car I've ever seen. I tried to put it out of its misery today when I slashed that tire. It was nothing personal."

Her grip tightened on the receiver. "If you do anything to hurt Beauty..."

"I don't hurt animals," Doris clipped. "Home-wreckers, yes. Animals, never."

"Just tell me what you want."

"I want my husband back."

"I told you before, I don't have your husband. I don't *want* your husband."

"Did you or did you not send him a love letter?"

"That was a mistake. And how many love letters start out with 'Dear Mr. Dooley'? I think you're blowing this way out of proportion."

"And I think you're a low-life, lying husband-stealer."

Sabrina gave up. "Look, this isn't getting us anywhere."

"I agree. If you refuse to give me Niles back, then I want compensation. Then, if you're lucky, I'll give you back your ugly cat."

"Excuse me?"

"I want five thousand dollars in cash."

Sabrina choked, her hand going to her throat. "What?"

"What's the matter? You don't think Niles is worth five thousand? He might be a little on the scrawny side, but he's a relatively healthy, heterosexual male. What more do you want?"

She wanted her cat back. She wanted Doris to leave her alone. She wanted to start this day all over again. "I am not giving you five thousand dollars."

"So you want to play hardball? Fine by me. I want five thousand in small bills by the end of the week. If you don't come through, I may run out of money to buy cat food."

"Let me get this straight," Sabrina said slowly, still unable to believe she was even having this conversation. "You're holding Beauty for ransom?"

"Of course not," Doris said evenly. "That would be illegal. I've taken Beauty into protective custody. A woman like you is not a good influence on an impressionable feline."

Sabrina closed her eyes, wondering if she'd just entered the twilight zone. "This is ridiculous."

"I call it pathetic. There are plenty of men out there, so why go chasing after my husband? He's not that great a catch."

"Then why do you want him back?"

"Because he's mine. No one takes what's mine without paying for it, one way or another."

"This is extortion."

Doris snorted a laugh. "That's pretty good for a dumb floozy. Did my husband teach you that word? He's pretty well-endowed in the brains department, even if he's lacking in a few other vital places."

"Are you sure you want him back?"

"Now that you ask, I am becoming rather attached to your cat. Maybe we should just call it even. Nice talking to you..."

"No, wait," Sabrina cried, panicking at the thought of never seeing Beauty again. A few years ago she'd found the scrawny, homely alley cat scavenging for food on the carnival grounds. With the help of a little patience and several cans of tuna, she'd finally tamed her enough to hold her. Then she'd taken the cat home with her, naming her Beauty because she truly believed in the power of positive thinking. And it had worked. Beauty had slowly been transformed into a plump, sleek feline who liked to snuggle at the foot of Sabrina's bed every night.

But Beauty was more than Sabrina's pet. She was her family.

"I'm a busy woman," Doris said gruffly. "So I don't have time to sit here and listen to you whine. If you've got something relevant to say, then spit it out."

So much for her attempt at diplomacy. Sabrina decided to play her trump card. "If you don't give me Beauty back immediately, I'll go to the police."

"Be my guest," Doris replied, sounding much too confident. "It will save them a trip."

"What's that supposed to mean?"

"It means I've already filed a harassment complaint against you. They were very sympathetic. Especially after I showed them your letter and explained how you robbed me of my husband. I cried, too. Men are suckers for a few tears. They suggested I get a restraining order."

"*You're* the one who's been harassing *me*."

"Prove it."

Sabrina wanted to hit something. She couldn't prove it. Doris Dooley had conducted her harassment campaign with a cool and very calculated deliberation. She hadn't made a single mistake. Until today.

Sabrina took a deep breath. "I'm sure kidnapping a pet has to be some kind of crime. They'll believe my side of the story when they find Beauty in your possession."

"I'd call this more of a property dispute. Besides, what makes you think I have your ugly cat with me? Now, enough chitchat. I want my husband or five thousand dollars. You've got one week to figure out which you can't live without. I think that's more than fair."

"I think it's crazy! You can't..." Sabrina's voice trailed off when she heard the dial tone humming in her ear.

She slammed down the receiver. "Damn!"

"Problems?"

She whirled around to see Noah Callahan standing inside the kitchen doorway, looking like a model for *GQ* in his black tuxedo. His sexy smile knocked her off balance and she reached out a hand to the stainless-steel counter to steady herself. "Nothing I can't handle."

"Are you sure? Sometimes it helps to talk about it."

"Positive." She picked up her coffee cup and rinsed it out in the sink, letting the coffee grounds run down the drain. She could hardly think straight around Noah, much less confide in him. And she needed all her wits about her to figure out how to get Beauty back.

"Was that call about your cat?"

She pressed her lips together in consternation. The man was not only gorgeous, but intuitive. "Yes. It was the kidnapper."

He smiled. "Don't you mean the *catnapper?*"

She frowned up at him. "This isn't funny."

He walked toward her, then turned off the tap and took the coffee cup out of her hand. That's when she realized her fingers were shaking. Noah clasped her cold hands in his big warm ones, squeezing them gently.

"You're right. It's not funny." He looked into her eyes. "Tell me about Plan B."

His touch sent a tingle straight up both arms and the kitchen now seemed overly warm. Suddenly, she didn't feel so alone. Growing up an only child, Sabrina had become used to depending on herself. Especially since her parents had devoted all their time and attention to their careers.

Although, she'd always been able to count on Madame Sophia. Her godmother had been her confidant and a voice of wisdom during some turbulent years. Best of all, she'd given Sabrina a glimpse of a normal life. A normal family. The Callahans.

Sabrina had started falling in love with Noah Callahan when she was seven years old, after Madame Sophia sent her his picture. He'd had an infectious grin and an unruly cowlick and two front teeth missing.

Over the years, Madame Sophia had filled her letters with the escapades of her three rambunctious nephews. But Sabrina had always looked for Noah's name first. By the time she was a teenager, she'd fantasized about meeting him. Maybe even going out on a date. Then reality had intruded and she'd been forced to put her romantic fantasies on hold.

It seemed like a lifetime ago.

But now she was here and Noah was standing right in front of her.

She inhaled the subtle, spicy scent of his aftershave and for the first time noticed he had unusually long, thick eyelashes for a man. They framed a pair of breathtaking blue eyes.

She licked her lips, her mouth suddenly very dry. But before she could tell him anything, the kitchen door swung open.

"Stop!" Ramon D'Onofrio dropped the empty tray he was holding, and it hit the tile floor with a loud crash. He hurdled the tray and rushed to Sabrina's side, his puppy-brown eyes wide and beseeching. "Don't fall for it, Sabrina. Noah Callahan is a playboy. A womanizer. A philanthropist."

Noah still held her hands loosely in his. "I think you mean a philanderer."

"See," Ramon cried, "he admits it!"

Sabrina smoothly pulled her hands out of Noah's grasp, wishing he *was* a philanthropist. She could really use a donation of five thousand dollars right about now. What she didn't need was Ramon D'Onofrio flying into a jealous frenzy. The waiter had a huge crush on her. Unfortunately, he just couldn't understand why she didn't return his feelings. He was certain their love was written in the stars, if not the coffee grounds.

"Relax, Ramon," she said gently. "Noah isn't trying to do anything except help me. I have a small problem."

The waiter turned to her, his eyes full of concern. "What kind of problem?"

"It's...personal."

Ramon nodded. "It's your weight, isn't it?"

She blinked. "My weight?"

"We've all noticed you've added a few extra pounds since you started working here. But don't worry, I love full-figured women."

Okay, so maybe she had more than one problem. Turning to food in times of stress had always been one of her weaknesses. But she hadn't gained more than one, two, maybe six pounds since all this trouble started with Niles and Doris Dooley.

Her apron suddenly felt tight. She sucked in her stomach as Noah's gaze slowly traveled up and down her body.

"She looks good to me," he said with a lazy smile.

Ramon sniffed. "See? He's always tells a woman just what she wants to hear. Never the truth. Never the cold, hard facts. I believe in honesty. If a woman is getting fat, then I respect her enough to tell her."

"Gee, thanks." She picked up a tray of chocolate eclairs off the counter and shoved it into Ramon's hands. "I know you're off duty, but would you mind taking these out? They need to go on the buffet table right away."

He nodded. "I understand. It's hard for you to resist temptation." He headed for the door. "And don't worry, Sabrina. I'll do everything in my power to help you fight this weight problem."

She watched Ramon leave, then tore off her apron. She couldn't delay any longer. Beauty needed her. She'd hoped she could reason with Doris Dooley. Hoped this nightmare would end if she dealt with her calmly and rationally. Obviously, she'd been wrong.

"Going somewhere?"

"I'm leaving. It's time to take drastic action."

"As in Plan B?"

"That's right. I'm not going to let Doris Dooley push me around anymore."

He hesitated. "Are you sure that's smart? She doesn't exactly seem stable."

"I'll have to take my chances."

He stepped in front of the door, blocking her exit. "Aunt Sophie asked me to keep an eye on you."

"You've done enough already." Her words came out sharper than she intended and she saw him wince. Since she was planning to marry the man, the last thing she wanted to do was alienate him.

She forced a smile. "Look, I'm sorry. I didn't mean it the way it sounded. It's been a really rough day. But none of this is your fault."

He took a step closer to her. "I'm still willing to help. I think you could use a friend right now."

She barely noticed the way he emphasized the word *friend*, her mind distracted by other things. Like the shadow of whiskers on his square jaw and the naturally deep, seductive tenor of his voice. It curled inside of her, leaving no doubt that Ramon had been telling the truth. Noah Callahan definitely had a way with women.

Which just might be to her advantage.

"A friend, no." She smiled. "But I could definitely use a decoy."

3

"I DON'T LIKE Plan B." Noah parked his car near the entrance of the subdivision. The fading sunlight cast a peaceful glow over the neighborhood. He could smell steaks grilling and hear the muted roar of a lawn mower. Somewhere a dog barked, followed by the sound of children laughing. An odd feeling of contentment stole over him. For one brief, insane moment he wanted to belong here.

He quickly came to his senses. He could never be happy in a place like this, especially with neighbors like Niles and Doris Dooley. The Dooley house lay just one block ahead of them. He'd been ready to turn around and head back to Café Romeo until Sabrina informed him that if he did she'd just come back here without him. But that didn't mean he still couldn't try to talk her out of it.

"I mean it, Sabrina. It's crazy."

"Ith perfeck," she replied, the elastic hair band in her mouth impeding her speech. She sat in the passenger seat, finger-combing her silky auburn hair to the back of her neck.

He shook his head. "You can't just sneak into the woman's house. What if she catches you?"

Sabrina took the hair band out of her mouth and quickly flipped her hair in and out of it to form a neat ponytail. "She won't catch me because you'll be there to distract her."

"If she even lets me in the door."

"I think you're seriously underestimating your powers of persuasion." Her gaze flicked over him and he saw the approval in her eyes.

He'd made a quick stop by his apartment and changed out of his tuxedo and into a suit and tie. Now that he'd shed the wedding attire, his hives had begun to fade. The message seemed all too clear: stay single or suffer.

"Besides," she continued, "I doubt Doris will even be there. Niles told me she works the evening shift. If she is home, just keep her busy for ten minutes. If I don't find Beauty by then, I'll be out of there in a flash."

"And if you do find her?"

"Then I'll be out of there even faster. Believe me, the last thing I want is another confrontation with Doris Dooley."

He rubbed one hand over his jaw, still not convinced. "There's got to be a better way. What if she catches you? Or worse, what if she thinks you're an intruder and decides to shoot first and ask questions later? If she's a security guard, I assume she owns a gun."

"She owns seven handguns, a twelve-gauge shotgun and an Uzi," Sabrina informed him. "Niles told me about them. He's afraid of guns."

"Sounds like he should be even more afraid of his wife."

"That's probably why he's in hiding. Maybe he's hoping she'll forget about him, or find another man to take his place." She smiled. "That's where you come in."

Just how far did she expect him to go? "I think I should warn you that I'm not that kind of guy."

"Ramon said you are. So did Madame Sophia, and the waitress who works the early shift, and your brother Jake and…"

He held up one hand, knowing the list would probably be endless. He'd had more than his share of romances up until two months ago. Then his love life had come to a screeching halt. "All right. Maybe I should clarify. I'm not that kind of guy *anymore*. Ever since Aunt Sophie confiscated my coffee grounds, I've taken certain precautions."

She arched a brow. "Such as?"

"Such as steering clear of romance until I get to Cleveland, where it's safe. At least until Café Romeo starts to franchise."

"And here I thought you were a skeptic."

He shook his head. "Oh, no. I have a healthy respect for my aunt's abilities. Especially after what happened to Jake and Trace. I definitely don't intend to be victim number three."

She blinked at him, then turned and popped open the door. "See you in ten minutes."

Before he could say another word, she was gone. So much for trying to talk her out of this crazy scheme. He watched as she disappeared behind the long row of ranch houses lining the quiet suburban street.

"Damn," he muttered, as he shifted into gear, then slowly glided along the curb until he reached 401 Chinaberry Street.

The Dooleys lived in a salmon-pink house with white shutters on the windows and Christmas lights still strung along the eaves. The narrow driveway was empty and the white garage door closed. He couldn't see any sign of life either inside or outside the house.

Noah sank back against the seat and checked his watch. Eight minutes to go. He tapped his index finger on the steering wheel, wondering exactly how he'd gotten into this situation. At least Sabrina hadn't mentioned marriage again. Probably because she was too worried about her cat. Once she got Beauty back, she might decide to turn all her attention on him. Which meant he'd better develop a plan of his own to keep her at arm's length. Or even farther.

Because in the last few hours he'd learned that Sabrina Lovett didn't give up easily. He'd also learned that she had the most unusual green eyes. They changed color with her emotions. Sadness turned them jade green. Anger made them deepen to moss. When she laughed they shimmered with flecks of gold.

He wondered what color emerged with passion.

The honk of a car horn jerked him from his reverie. He looked in his rearview mirror and saw a familiar black pickup truck looming behind him. He cringed when he saw the woman sitting behind the wheel.

Time to sweep Dangerous Doris off her feet.

SABRINA KICKED OFF her shoes, then climbed over the chain-link fence separating the Dooleys' back-yard from its neighbors. She crept up the porch steps that led to the sliding glass door and peeked inside. The NRA sticker on the glass wasn't the only thing blocking her view. Vertical blinds pre-vented her from seeing anything else. She pressed her ear against the cool glass and listened.

Silence.

Maybe Doris really was at work. Or sleeping. Or down in Niles's basement laboratory trying to con-coct a personality.

There was only one way to find out.

She pulled a paper clip from her pocket, bent it open, then slipped one end into the keyhole. It was an old trick she'd learned from her father, an escape artist with the carnival. She'd been his assistant every summer during her teen years—until she'd moved on to other endeavors.

Sabrina gave the paper clip a couple of deft twists, hoping she hadn't lost her touch. At last the latch gave way, and she breathed a silent thank-you to her dad and to Johan Vaaler. Then she inched the sliding door open, straining her ears for the slightest indication of someone moving around in the house. After several silent minutes, she carefully separated the vertical blinds far enough to get a good look inside.

The kitchen had seen its glory days in the early seventies, when the avocado and harvest-gold color scheme reigned. An old Kelvinator refrigerator hummed in one corner and a newspaper lay open on the small Formica-topped table. The faucet dripped into the stained enamel sink with a steady tap…tap…tap. The room was small, but surprisingly cozy. Best of all, it was empty.

Her heart pounding in her chest, Sabrina stepped inside, closing the sliding glass door soundlessly behind her. She tiptoed across the faded yellow linoleum to the doorway that separated the kitchen from the rest of the house. She could now see the small, square living room and part of a hallway that must lead to the bedrooms and bath.

The living room was dark and empty. She released her breath in a long, relieved sigh. Maybe this wouldn't be so bad, after all. With Doris gone, she could make a thorough search of the place.

She wondered briefly about Noah, then decided he must be keeping watch from his car. Which meant he'd be ready and waiting when she sprung Beauty. So much the better. She didn't need him around to distract her.

But one thing was for certain. She wasn't leaving without her cat.

NOAH PASTED A SMILE on his face and leaned his elbow out the open window as Doris Dooley walked up to the driver's door of his Mustang. Walked might not be the right word for it. Her stride reminded him of a Sherman tank—ruthless and deliberate, able to mow down anything in her path. Which at the moment, was him.

"You're blocking my driveway," Doris announced when she reached his window. "Move it. Now." Then she spun on her heel and walked away.

"No problem," he replied, rolling his car forward. Now that he'd seen her up close, he knew Doris wouldn't ever be in any danger of winning a beauty contest.

Her ash-blond hair softened the angular planes of her face and curled around her jaw. She wore blue eyeshadow and too much blue mascara around her pale gray eyes. Her uniform, a shapeless khaki shirt and matching pants, concealed her figure. She was tall for a woman, at least five foot nine inches.

Ignoring the overwhelming urge to floor the gas pedal and make his escape, he shifted the car into park, then cut the engine. Doris had pulled her pickup truck into the driveway and was heading for the front door by the time he reached her.

"Mrs. Dooley?"

"No soliciting," she snapped, pointing to the sign in the window. The one next to the NRA sticker.

He checked his watch. Still three minutes to go. Cursing softly under his breath, he quickly closed the distance between them. "Your husband invited me to come here today."

She turned sharply. "Niles? You've seen Niles?"

He cleared his throat, improvising as he went along. "No, but I did speak with him on the phone a couple of weeks ago. I'm with Pinnacle Insurance Company."

He flashed his business card, flipping his wallet closed before she had a chance to notice his title was Investigator rather than Salesman. "We have several policies that I believe might interest you and your husband."

She unlocked the front door, then turned to him. "Do you provide coverage for stolen husbands?"

He smiled. "No, but I have several other options that might interest you."

She gave him a slow once-over. "I think you just might at that. Come in, Mr...I'm sorry, I didn't catch your name."

"Calhoun," he improvised, following her into the house. "Norm Calhoun. But you can just call me Norm."

"Okay, Norm. Have a seat."

Noah looked from the boxy puce-green sofa to the matching armchair, both at least thirty years old. He chose the armchair, hoping he wouldn't be here long. Hoping even more that Sabrina wouldn't make a sudden, unexpected appearance.

"Nice place," he said loudly to warn her of their presence.

"Niles inherited the house from his grandmother.

As you can see, she had a real flair for decorating.''
Doris flipped her keys on top of the television console. "Care for a beer?''

Noah held up one hand. "I can't drink while I'm on duty.''

Doris laughed as she walked into the kitchen. She returned a moment later with two beer cans in her hand, then tossed him one. "Life isn't any fun unless you break some rules.''

He caught it one-handed, then popped the tab. Foam fizzed up through the opening and he took a quick swallow. "Thank you, Mrs. Dooley.''

"Call me Doris. I'm not a Mrs. anymore.'' She plopped down on the recliner and rested one foot on top of the scarred walnut coffee table. "I lost my husband three weeks ago.''

He sat down on the sofa and decided to play dumb. "I'm sorry. This must be a difficult time for you.''

She drank long and deep, then wiped the back of her hand across her mouth. "Difficult, hell. It's been driving me crazy. If I ever get my hands on that floozy who stole him from me...'' Her grip tightened on her beer can until the aluminum collapsed under the pressure.

"You're probably better off without him,'' he said, trying to distract her from her lethal fantasies.

She fingered a blond curl behind her ear, as if suddenly self-conscious. "Do you really think so, Norm?''

Uh-oh. He'd seen that expression before. He'd

wanted to distract the woman, not encourage her. Now for some fancy footwork. "Of course, it will take you some time to get over him. Time to heal and analyze what went wrong with the relationship."

"I already know what went wrong," she retorted. "I married a worm. Now I want a man. A real man who knows how to love a woman."

He glanced at his watch, then rose hastily to his feet. Sabrina's ten minutes were up. "Well, I won't keep you any longer. I'm sure you're a busy woman."

She frowned. "But you just got here."

He moved toward the door. "I'm not one of those pushy insurance salesmen who overstays his welcome. They're the ones who give the rest of us a bad name."

"But you haven't even explained any of your policies yet." She set her beer can on the coffee table, then rose to her feet. "And I realize now that I do have something valuable that needs insuring."

He looked longingly toward the door. "You might want a few days to think it over. So many people over-insure these days."

Her eyes narrowed. "What kind of salesman are you?"

A lousy one. That's why he did investigative work. This debacle was also the reason he worked alone. Why had he ever offered to come along with Sabrina in the first place?

Because he'd felt guilty for losing her cat in the

car chase. And because his Aunt Sophie was depending on him. And because Sabrina's eyes fascinated him.

"Norm?"

He blinked, then looked at Doris. She stood directly in front of him now, with her hands on her hips and suspicion thinning her red lips.

"I'll ask you again," she said, her voice low and menacing. "What kind of salesman are you?"

He flashed a smile. "Okay, I'll confess. This is the first sales call I've ever made. I guess I need to work on my technique a little."

"I'd say more than a little."

He nodded. "You're absolutely right. I'll go home right now and study the manual."

"Not so fast." She grasped his elbow and took a step closer to him. "First I want to show you something."

Her grip was surprisingly strong. He tried to ease out of it, but she wouldn't let go. "What?"

She flashed him a coquettish smile that made his blood run cold. "Come with me. I think you'll like what you see."

He had to get out of here. Now. He'd agreed to be a decoy, not a sex toy. Despite his reputation as a playboy, Noah just didn't fall into bed with any woman who came along. And he definitely drew the line at married women. Especially married women who owned guns.

But Doris didn't give him a chance to escape.

She practically dragged him down the hallway to the last door on the left. "Here we are."

"Listen, Doris, it's against company policy for salesmen to…fraternize with clients."

"I like to break rules, remember?" She winked at him, then pulled a small key out of her pocket and unlocked the door.

He just hoped she didn't like breaking anything else. Specifically, the bones of men who refused to sleep with her. Not that she'd asked him yet, but a man makes certain assumptions when a woman drags him to her bedroom.

Only it wasn't her bedroom.

He blinked as the door swung open, wondering if he was seeing things. He looked at the beer in his hand, then back at the room.

"This is my hobby room," she announced proudly. "Like it?"

He followed her slowly through the door, taking it all in. The yellow-and-white gingham coverlet and pillows adorning the daybed. The matching window drapes. The plastic ivy plant hanging in the corner. And last, but certainly not least, the wide array of weapons showcased in a long display cabinet on the wall. Brass knuckles. Nunchakus. Stun guns. A veritable buffet of violence.

"What's all this?" he asked, unnerved by the combination of gingham and guns. He became even more unnerved when he glimpsed the pink pedicured toes sticking out from under the floor-length drapes. *Sabrina.* Her ten minutes had been up a long time ago. So what the hell was she still doing here? And what would Doris do if she found her?

"This is my collection," she said, pointing in Sabrina's direction. "Like it?"

Noah would have called it an arsenal, but why quibble? Some people collected stamps, others collected coins; Doris simply had a hobby that was a little different. Then he remembered that she liked to break the rules.

Time to make a quick getaway.

"I could really use another beer, Doris." He clasped her elbow, turning her away from the window before she could discover Sabrina's hiding place. "Why don't we go back in the living room so we can discuss which policy would be the right one for you."

"Not so fast." She kicked the door shut with one foot. "I've saved the best for last." Then she nodded toward the daybed. "Have a seat."

He clenched his jaw in frustration as he sat down. She unlocked the glass panel on the display cabinet, then reverently removed an old wooden gun case. "These are my pride and joy. Authentic dueling pistols from the nineteenth century. Believe it or not, they're still in perfect working condition."

"That definitely increases their value. Maybe we should take them out into the living room so I can have more light to examine them."

"I'll just open the drapes," she said, moving toward the window."

"No!" He jumped up and took the gun case out

of her hands. "That won't be necessary. Let's have a look at them."

They both sat on the daybed, the springs creaking with their combined weight. He breathed a silent sigh of relief that Doris kept her distance. She waited expectantly as he lifted the lid of the gun case.

He removed the top cloth, instantly met with the combined odors of cleaning fluid and gun oil.

"Well?" she asked at last.

He whistled low as he inspected the dueling pistols. They were in mint condition, well-oiled and ready for action. No doubt they were worth a fortune.

Doris carefully picked one up, caressing the long barrel with one fake fingernail. "Aren't they gorgeous?"

He shifted slightly to block her view of the drapes. "Impressive."

She breathed lightly on the barrel, then rubbed the spot with her sleeve. "The story is that they belonged to an old southern family from Virginia. During the Reconstruction period, the eldest daughter of the family killed a swindler who charmed his way into their home and then tried to attack her."

She looked up at him. "Isn't it funny how history repeats itself?"

"Uh...I'm not sure what you mean." Noah edged back on the daybed. "By the way, is that thing loaded?"

She smiled, revealing a row of large, capped

teeth. "Since I'm the one holding the gun, I'll ask the questions. Let's start with what you're really doing here."

So much for his first, not to mention last, acting stint. "I already told you. I'm an insurance salesman. Your husband…"

"My husband has never paid one red cent for any kind of insurance. Niles doesn't believe in it. Besides, any extra money we had always went into his inventions."

Noah stood up. "Then I should quit wasting your time."

Doris cocked the pistol and pointed it straight at his chest. "Don't leave yet. Maybe you have something else I might be interested in."

Just the words he didn't want to hear. He stared down the wide barrel of the antique pistol, considering his options. "Something else?"

"That's right." She smiled as she rose slowly to her feet. "Take off your clothes."

4

SABRINA'S HEART skipped a beat at Doris's words. She stood frozen behind the drapes, afraid to move, afraid not to move. Noah had been right. This was a stupid plan.

"I think I'll leave my clothes on," he replied, sounding remarkably calm considering the request. "It's a little chilly in here."

Doris snorted. "It's the middle of August and I don't have air-conditioning."

"I'm cold-blooded."

"Cut the excuses. Take off your clothes so we can get down to business."

Sabrina heard the sound of Noah clearing his throat. "Exactly what kind of business?"

"I want information."

"I have trouble thinking clearly when I'm naked."

"Yeah, you and every other man on the planet. Now tell me something I don't know—like the real reason you're in my house. But first, take off your pants."

Sabrina closed her eyes, trying to think of some way out of this mess. If only she hadn't dragged

Noah into it. If only she'd never sent that stupid letter. If only she'd never attempted to read her own coffee grounds.

"Listen, Doris…"

"I've had enough of your stalling tactics," Doris interjected. "If you don't start stripping by the time I count to three, I'm gonna start shooting. One. Two…"

Sabrina heard the whir of a zipper, then a few seconds later, the muffled sound of clothes hitting the floor. She didn't want to imagine what was on the other side of those drapes. Well, actually she did, but this was hardly the time or the place.

"That's far enough," Doris ordered. "I'll let you leave your boxer shorts on."

"Gee, thanks," he said dryly.

"You're welcome. Speaking of boxer shorts, I see you're a Mighty Mouse fan."

"They were a gift from an old girlfriend," he said coolly.

Doris chuckled. "I hope that wasn't a subliminal comment on the size of your…sexual prowess."

"Can we get on with it?" he snapped. "What exactly do you want to know?" Noah didn't sound calm anymore. In fact, if Sabrina was any judge of temperament, he sounded like he was ready to wring somebody's neck. Most probably hers.

"Why don't we start with your name?"

"I already told you my name. Norm Calhoun."

"I remember that you flashed that card so fast the name on it was a blur. I'm sure you won't mind if I take a little look-see for myself. Now you just stand nice and still. This pistol has a hair trigger. Any sudden movements and I won't be responsible for my actions.''

Sabrina could hear the rustle of clothes and got a sinking feeling in the pit of her stomach. As if making him strip wasn't enough, Doris was now obviously rifling through his shirt and pants.

"Nice billfold. Ah, and here's a driver's license. Nice picture, too. Says here you're *Noah Callahan.*''

Sabrina winced. *Busted.* She'd told Doris his name two weeks ago when she'd tried unsuccessfully to explain that she had no interest in Niles.

"I've never cared for my real name," he said, still valiantly trying to salvage the situation. "Don't you think Calhoun has more pizzazz?''

"Well, well, well," Doris said. "Here's one of those business cards. Noah Callahan. Insurance Investigator. No wonder you were such a lousy salesman.''

"I'm trying to branch out.''

"Spare me, Callahan. Lies make me trigger-happy.''

Sabrina had never felt so helpless in her life. But what could she do? Revealing herself would only make Doris more furious. On the other hand, she couldn't just cower behind the curtains while Noah fought her battle. She squeezed her eyelids shut. *Think, Sabrina, think.*

"Relax, Doris. You're overreacting.''

"And you're hiding something. Or is it someone?"

A cold chill ran over Sabrina's body. She held her breath and pressed her spine against the windowpane.

"I don't know what you mean," he replied.

"I think you do. I think this charade was an attempt to distract me. In fact, I'll bet my collection of hand grenades that Sabrina Lovett is searching this house as we speak."

Relief washed over her. So Doris hadn't found her. Yet.

"Sabrina who?"

"Don't play dumb, Callahan. The woman claims she wants you instead of my husband. But frankly, now that I've seen you in the flesh, I'm not sure why. If you've seen one beefcake, you've seen them all." She shook her head, her gaze raking over him. "I just don't get it."

"Can I have my clothes back now?"

"I think I'll keep them while I search the rest of the house for that man-eating Sabrina."

"What about me?"

"Well, I've got your clothes, your wallet and your car keys. So unless you feel like streaking through the neighborhood, you can stay right here. I should warn you that I've got some very uptight neighbors. You won't get two blocks before the cops pick you up for indecent exposure."

A scant moment later, Sabrina heard the sound of the door opening, then closing, shortly followed by the turn of a key in the lock. She slowly released her pent-up breath. Noah was safe.

He was also a little upset.

A tanned, lean hand ripped open the drapes and Noah Callahan stood before her. An almost naked Noah Callahan. Her mouth actually went dry at the sight of him. If he ever got tired of the insurance business, he could have a long, lucrative career as a model for *Playgirl.*

She swallowed hard and tried not to stare. ''Nice boxer shorts.''

''They were a present. Mighty Mouse had nothing to do with my...sexual prowess. My prowess is just fine, thank you very much. In fact, it's more than fine.''

She held up both hands. ''Hey, I believe you. Now keep your voice down so Doris doesn't hear you.''

''Doris isn't the problem.'' He stabbed his index finger toward her. ''*You're* the problem. Ever since I met you, my life has been turned upside down.''

She frowned. ''We only met today.''

''Really? It seems longer than that. More like an eternity.''

His words only made her feel guiltier. ''Look, I know this is all my fault.''

''Damn straight.''

''And I promise to make it up to you.''

He looked skeptical. ''How?''

Good question. ''Well, the first thing I'll do is get us out of here.''

"And take the chance of meeting Doris and her prized pistol outside that door? No thank you."

"We'll go out the window." Then she looked at Noah again, distracted by all that bare skin. Not to mention the muscles rippling across his taut stomach.

For the first time, the full impact of her coffee-ground reading hit her. If Noah Callahan really was her perfect match, she'd soon be touching that body. Caressing those broad shoulders. Breathing in the scent of his skin. Kissing that firm, truculent mouth.

Her knees turned to jelly at the thought, she took a deep breath, pushing the images from her mind. Now was not the time to get pulled into a sexual fantasy. Even if that fantasy was standing right in front of her.

She turned to the daybed, removing the quilted coverlet on top, then stripped off the yellow gingham sheet underneath.

"Here," she said, wrapping it around him toga-style. "This will help."

"You're right," he said wryly. "This is much better. I'm sure no one will even give me as much as a second glance."

"It's this or Mighty Mouse. Take your pick."

"Fine," he bit out. "If we come across a toga party, I'll be ready."

She grinned. "I love a man who looks on the bright side."

Panic flared in his blue eyes. "What do you mean by love?"

She shook her head as she turned to the window. "Keep your shorts on, Callahan. It's just a figure of speech. Madam Sophia told me you were skittish about love and marriage."

"Skittish? Try allergic."

She rolled her eyes as she turned to crank open the window. "Does that mean I can't even say the word *love* around you?"

"Just be careful how you use it."

Sabrina popped out the screen. "Grab that chair over there."

Noah held up the sheet with one hand as he pulled the chair into position under the window. "Ladies first."

She flashed a smile at him as she stepped up onto the chair. "Thank you."

"Don't mention it. But if Doris starts shooting, you're on your own."

So much for chivalry. Sabrina swung one leg out the window, then jumped into the marigold bed on the other side. "At least we're on ground level."

"Are you always this optimistic?" he asked, as he followed her out the window.

"Yes."

"I really hate that." He adjusted his gingham toga, then glanced toward the front door. "Ready to make a run for it?"

"Where exactly are we running to?"

"My car. On the count of three. One, two...."

Sabrina took off, hearing Noah's muttered oaths behind her. She sprinted for the Mustang, her heart pounding in her chest, knowing that any moment Doris could see them and open fire. At last, she reached the passenger door, yanked it open, then dove inside, scrambling into the driver's seat to make room for Noah.

A split second later, Noah jumped in behind her. "We were supposed to go on three."

Sabrina struggled to catch her breath. "Yeah, but your legs are longer. I was afraid you'd get here first and leave without me."

He stared at her. "You think I'd actually leave you here at the mercy of Doris?"

"Doris has no mercy, or didn't you notice?"

"I noticed. She also has no taste in interior decorating." He adjusted that sheet over his hips. "But I still can't believe you think I'd leave you behind. Didn't I miss my own brothers' weddings to go after your cat?"

"You thought it was a baby."

"Which proves my point. Babies make me very nervous, yet I didn't even hesitate."

"I had to threaten you with breath spray!" She bent under the steering wheel and pulled several different colored wires out from underneath the dash.

He didn't say anything, just stared at her as she spliced two wires together. "What do you think you're doing?"

She didn't say anything for a moment, her concentration focused on the wires in her hand. "I'm hot-wiring your car. Doris has your keys, remember?''

"Hot-wiring my car?'' he echoed. "Where in the world did you learn to do that?''

"Istanbul.'' She'd learned a lot of things in Istanbul, but Noah seemed upset enough already. She'd wait until after their wedding to tell him the rest of the story. If he knew the truth, there might not be a wedding.

"I'm very impressed,'' he said as the engine turned over. "Now, let's get out of here!''

She shifted into drive, then peeled away from the curb. "Do you think she saw us?''

He glanced out the back window. "No. Her pickup truck is still parked in the driveway. But it won't take her too long to figure it out.''

"Then what?''

"Then Dangerous Doris comes after us.'' He raked one hand through his hair. "She has my clothes, my wallet and my keys—including the key to my apartment. She also has my driver's license, which means she'll know where to find me. And since she suspects I'm involved with you, I have no doubt she'll be paying me a visit.''

"Do you really believe she's dangerous?''

"I believed it enough to take off my clothes.''

Sabrina's hands flexed on the steering wheel. "Then I'm glad I convinced Madam Sophia to go to that reunion.''

Noah glanced at her. "Aunt Sophie doesn't know about Doris?''

Sabrina shook her head. "All she knows is that I blew my first coffee-ground reading. But this entire situation is getting out of hand. I've been staying at Madame Sophia's house…and Doris has been there."

He stiffened. "You never told me that."

"Nothing happened. Doris just left me a couple of messages taped to the front door. Well, threats, actually. That's why I took Beauty with me to the wedding."

"That's it," he clipped. "We're going to the police."

"It won't do any good. I don't have any proof that Doris is the one who left those notes. And she always seems to be one step ahead of me. She's probably filing breaking-and-entering charges as we speak."

"Speaking of breaking and entering, how did you get into her house? And now that I think of it, that hobby room of hers was locked, too."

She hesitated. "I sort of have this talent with paper clips."

He glanced over at her. "What kind of talent?"

She focused her gaze on the street. "I know how to jimmy locks with a paper clip. I used one to open the sliding glass door to her kitchen and also to open that hobby room of hers. I figured there was a good chance Beauty might be behind a locked door."

"But you didn't find her."

Her throat tightened. "She wasn't anywhere on

the main level and I didn't get a chance to look in the basement. Do you suppose Doris...did something to her?''

"You're an optimist, remember?" Noah said gently. "I'm sure Beauty is fine. And we'll find her soon. I promise."

Her gaze flicked to him, then back to the road. "We?"

"I'm involved now whether I like it or not. Doris isn't going to give up, and I don't have that many clothes." He glanced down at the sheet. "Do me a favor and take a left at the next intersection. I want to stop by my apartment."

She pulled up to the stoplight. "Then what?"

He sighed. "Good question."

SABRINA KNELT in front of Noah's apartment door, twisting one end of a paper clip into the keyhole. Her tongue touched the corner of her mouth and her brow furrowed in concentration.

Noah stood behind her, still wrapped in his sheet. He couldn't help but notice the way her auburn hair, swept back in a ponytail, curled at the ends. Her straight back led to nicely rounded hips encased in a pair of snug blue jeans. In his opinion, a man wouldn't ever get tired of looking at Sabrina Lovett.

A click sounded and she grinned up at him. "We're in."

Noah glanced at his watch as she followed her inside. "Twenty seconds. It only took you twenty seconds to break into my apartment."

"You're the one who didn't want to ask the building manager for a key."

"That's because the manager happens to be a good friend of my brother Jake. That's how I found this place. Unfortunately, the manager also has a big mouth and he'd never let me in my door without hearing the full story."

"So?"

He closed the door behind him and locked it. "So, I'd rather walk barefoot through hot tar than let my brothers find out what just happened to me."

He turned to see Sabrina staring at him and his body tightened at her perusal. A normal reaction to having a beautiful woman in his apartment, he told himself. If it was any other woman, he'd be opening a bottle of wine right about now. Setting up the CD player with soft, seductive music. And finding a much better use for this sheet.

Her gaze rose to meet his and something stirred deep inside of him. Her green eyes didn't waver, just looked into him as if she could see through to his soul. Almost without thought, he took a step closer to her. Then another.

She stood watching him, waiting, the air between them crackling with expectation. Fortunately, his common sense kicked in before it was too late, bringing him to a halt.

This wasn't just any beautiful woman. This was Sabrina Lovett. The woman who hijacked his car and picked locks and made enemies of NRA members. The woman who thought she was his perfect match.

He'd only known her a day, and it was already clear that she was the wrong woman for him. Wrong with a capital W. Even if she did have incredible eyes and a body that could keep him up all night.

"Aren't you going to answer it?"

He blinked, then realized his telephone was ringing. "Oh...I'll let the machine pick up."

When it did, the voice of the caller wiped all thoughts of Sabrina's luscious body out of his mind.

"Hello, this is Doris Dooley. I'm sorry you had to leave so suddenly, because I have an insurance question for you. If I took out a life-insurance policy on another person...say you, for example, is there a double-indemnity clause if you die a sudden, violent death?"

Her husky chuckle carried over the line. "I'm just curious. Stop by any time. You know where I live. And I know where you live...so I may stop in for a surprise visit one of these days. Bye-bye."

The beep sounded shortly after she hung up. Noah walked over and popped the minicassette out of the machine.

"I can't believe it!" Sabrina glared at the answering machine, her hands curled into fists and her eyes furious. "She just threatened to kill you!"

He tossed the cassette into a drawer, and replaced it with a new one. "Doris obviously gets a big thrill out of intimidating people. It gives her a sense of power. That doesn't mean she's going to follow through.''

Sabrina began pacing back and forth over the light blue carpet. "But what if she does? What if she's completely lost it?''

He moved toward her, then stopped, reminding himself not to get too close. "Doris knows exactly what she's doing. Did you hear that message? She knew better than to threaten me outright, so she turned it into a game. Not one word would stand up in court.''

"A game," she murmured, her brow crinkled. "You're right. She wants to play games.''

The sheet slipped and he tugged it back into place. "I need to go change. I'll be right back.''

He escaped into his bedroom, closing the door behind him before he stripped off the sheet. Once he'd donned a pair of Levi's and a blue polo shirt, he didn't feel quite so rattled. He could handle both his attraction to Sabrina and this problem with Doris Dooley. All he had to do was keep a clear head and a healthy distance from Sabrina.

But could he?

Doris knew where Sabrina lived, and she'd already taken her cat. What would she do next? And could he live with himself if anything happened to Sabrina? Especially after his promise to Aunt Sophie.

The answer was as clear as it was disturbing. Until this mess was resolved, he couldn't let Sabrina

Lovett out of his sight. With a sigh of resignation, he reached inside his closet for his duffel bag.

He carried it to his dresser, opening the top drawer and pulling out a handful of socks and underwear. His hand hovered over the box of condoms. His brothers might think him irresponsible, but when it came to sex Noah was never unprepared. Still, sex with Sabrina wasn't in his future.

His body wanted to argue with him, but he remained firm, leaving the condom box untouched. When he had finished packing, he headed out the bedroom door.

"I've got a plan," Sabrina exclaimed the moment he walked back into the living room. She sat on the sofa, one long leg tucked underneath her. Then she looked at the duffel bag in his hand. "Going somewhere?"

He dropped the bag on the floor by the door. "I'm moving in with you."

Her mouth opened, then closed again. At last she said, "This is rather sudden, isn't it? I mean, I know we're meant to be together, but..."

"Relax, Sabrina. This will be a purely platonic cohabitation. In fact, I want to make that clear from the start. The only reason I'll be staying with you is for protection."

"So you're scared of Doris coming after you?"

"For *your* protection," he growled. "Aunt Sophie would never forgive me if something happened to you. Now, what's this about a plan?"

She brightened. "Remember when you said

Doris was playing a game with us? Well, in most games, the best defense is a good offense. And I think it's time we went on the offensive."

He folded his arms across his chest. "You don't think breaking into the woman's house was offensive enough?"

"This is even better." She leaned forward. "What if we found Niles?"

"Then all our problems would be over. No more ransom. No more missing cat. No more Doris."

"Exactly. So, suppose Niles called his wife from Norway?"

Now he was confused. "What would Niles be doing in Norway?"

"Visiting the birthplace of his hero, Johan Vaaler, the inventor of the paper clip. Let's say he made a pilgrimage there, but now he's ready to come home and patch things up."

"Sounds great. But what makes you think Niles will call his wife?"

"He won't." She grinned. "You will."

He didn't need to hear any more. "It won't work."

"Of course it will. You just need to think positive."

"What I think is that this is your dumbest idea yet. And that's saying a lot."

She tipped up her chin. "There is no such thing as a dumb idea. There's just poor execution. Only this time you're the one who will be executing it."

He winced. "I wish you wouldn't use that word."

"What word? I thought the only taboo words were 'love' and 'marriage.'"

"You can add 'execution' to the list. They're all in the same family."

She rolled her eyes. "Have you ever thought of talking to a counselor? Because this marriage phobia of yours is a little extreme."

"I dated a counselor once. She told me some marriage horror stories that would make a polygamist impotent. Want to hear some?"

She frowned. "I think you're trying to change the subject."

"Is it working?"

"No."

"Well, neither will your plan. In the first place, I'm sure I sound nothing like Niles Dooley."

"I know. But I already figured out how to camouflage your voice."

"And in the second place," he continued, not waiting for her explanation, "Doris is bound to get suspicious when Niles doesn't show up."

"That's why you, pretending to be Niles, will tell her you'll be home in exactly one week. That will give us seven days to find the real Niles."

"And in the meantime, Doris will be so happy he's coming home that she'll forget all about us."

A smile lit her eyes. "Exactly. I told you it was perfect."

He hesitated, mulling over her plan in his mind.

It sounded as if it could work, but there had to be a flaw in it somewhere. "I don't know. I think it might be even more dangerous to get her hopes up."

Sabrina rose to her feet. "Don't go soft on me now, Noah. This is the woman who confiscated your clothes."

"I know, but…"

"The woman who held you at gunpoint."

"True, but…"

She took a step closer to him. "The woman who made fun of your Mighty Mouse underwear."

His jaw clenched. "You're right. She has to pay."

5

"THAT'S STRANGE," Sabrina said, as Noah pulled his car into Sophie's driveway. "All the lights are on."

He looked up at the big, two-story house, a light blazing in every window. "She was so excited about her trip, she probably just forgot to turn them off."

"You're probably right," she replied, as they both walked toward the back door. "I don't know about you, but I'm starving."

He caught the scent of her perfume in the breeze, a light delicate floral that teased his nostrils. "Why didn't you say so? We could have stopped to get a bite to eat."

She shook her head as she fumbled in her purse for her house keys. "Not necessary. There's a big bucket of leftover fried chicken in the fridge."

"Are you willing to share?"

"Anything but the wings. They're my favorite."

"Sounds good to me. I'm strictly a breast man." Then he realized he was staring at her chest. He cleared his throat and moved toward the door, trying the knob. It turned easily in his hand and the door swung open.

Sabrina stared at the door, dropping her keys back in her purse. "Now that's really strange."

His surprise turned to wariness. "Does Aunt Sophie ever leave her doors unlocked?"

"Never." She looked up at him. "Do you suppose…"

"Doris," he finished, saying the name she'd left unspoken.

"She wouldn't dare come here."

Noah raised one eyebrow. "If there's one thing I've learned tonight, it's to not underestimate Doris Dooley. Well, that, and to buy some new underwear."

"Let's look on the bright side. Maybe she just wants her sheet back."

"You wait here," Noah ordered, moving toward the door, "while I check out the house."

"No." She grabbed his arm. "I'm coming with you. We'll have a better chance if it's two against one."

"Forget it. I'm not putting you in that kind of danger."

"It's not your choice to make," she retorted. "I'm a grown woman. I can go wherever I want."

He swore softly under his breath. Today he'd also learned not to underestimate Sabrina Lovett. "All right, but stay behind me."

"There's no place I'd rather be."

He opened the door, wincing at the telltale creak.

The first thing he noticed was the mess. Dirty dishes littered the countertops. A box of soda crackers stood open on the kitchen table, surrounded by empty pop cans.

The hairs on the back of his neck rose. Something was very wrong. Sophie always took great pride in keeping her house spotless, thanks to the help of her good friend and housekeeper, Hannah.

He glanced at Sabrina, then nodded toward the living room, where the television blared. At least the noise had probably masked their entrance, giving them the advantage of surprise.

"Looks like Doris has made herself at home," she whispered.

A shadow fell across the kitchen threshold and Sabrina squeaked a warning. Noah tensed, pushing her back behind him.

The next moment, Ramon walked through the open doorway. He took one look at them, then staggered against the wall, dropping the half-eaten chicken drumstick in his hand as he grabbed his chest. "Jeez, you scared the crap out of me."

Noah's shoulders relaxed. "What the hell are you doing here?"

Ramon scowled. "I was about to ask you the same question." Then he looked beyond Noah's shoulder and a self-conscious blush crept up his neck. "Hi, Sabrina."

She moved beside Noah. "Hi, Ramon. We weren't expecting you."

"Surprise," he said, bending down to retrieve his

chicken leg from the kitchen floor. Then he walked over to the stainless steel sink and rinsed it off under the tap. "Madam Sophia told me I could stay here. My new brother-in-law just kicked me out of my house."

"It's Trace's house now," Noah reminded him. "He bought it so your sister could pay for your counseling, remember? Besides, he said you could stay there until after their honeymoon."

"Hey, I don't stay where I'm not wanted. Besides, they're having all the rooms repainted and the fumes plug up my sinuses."

"Well, you can't stay here with us."

Ramon looked confused. "Us?"

"I'm moving in with Sabrina." He tossed his duffel bag on the floor right in front of Ramon.

Ramon stared at the bag, his eyes widening in horror. "You're living together? Already? You just met today!"

Noah shrugged. "Women just can't resist us philanthropists."

Ramon set his chicken leg on the counter, then turned and walked out of the kitchen without another word.

Sabrina stared after him. "Do you think there's something wrong with him?"

"Do you want a list?"

They followed Ramon into the living room, where he sat on the green velvet divan with his head hanging down between his knees.

"Look, Ramon, I was just kidding," Noah explained, realizing Ramon's presence would be better than a cold shower to keep him away from Sabrina. "You're welcome to stay here with us."

He glanced up at them, his face pale. "I can't...catch my...breath."

Sabrina hurried to his side while Noah returned to the kitchen in search of a paper bag. He found one, along with a crispy, golden, fried-chicken breast and a cold beer. When he walked back into the living room, Ramon was lying on the sofa with his head in Sabrina's lap.

"He can't breathe," she said, her green eyes clouded with concern. She briskly fanned one hand over his pale face.

"He's all right. He's just hyperventilating." Noah handed her the paper bag, then took a seat in the recliner. "Trace said it happens all the time."

She held the small bag over Ramon's mouth until his breathing returned to normal. "Feeling better now?"

Ramon pushed the bag away, then stared up into her eyes. "You saved my life."

She tenderly swept the hair off his forehead. "Noah's the one who found the paper bag."

Ramon scowled. "You mean he's still here?"

Noah swallowed a mouthful of chicken. "Hey, don't thank me."

"Okay, I won't." Ramon gazed up at Sabrina. "Can I get you something to eat?"

She looked longingly at Noah's plate. "That

chicken looks delicious. But you don't have to go to any trouble. I can get it myself.''

Ramon leapt off the sofa. "No trouble at all. I'll be right back.''

Noah licked his fingers, then settled back in the chair with his beer. "I almost wish it *had* been Doris.''

"We'll call her at midnight," Sabrina whispered. "Agreed?''

"Don't you think that's a little late?''

"I'm afraid it might not be late enough. There's only a seven-hour time difference between St. Louis and Aurskog.''

"Aurskog?''

"The little town in Norway where Vaaler was born.''

Before Noah could tell her he had no intention of staying up past midnight, Ramon walked back into the room.

"Here we are," he said, setting a tray in front of her. "Enjoy.''

She stared in dismay at her plate. "What is this?''

"Radicchio and spinach leaves. No dressing. Very low-calorie. I tossed the rest of that bucket of chicken in the trash. That way you won't be tempted.''

Noah bit back a smile. At the moment, she looked ready to toss the salad greens right in Ramon's face. "Gee, thanks.''

"Oh, and before I forget," Ramon continued, "you've got to get rid of those jeans. They really make you look hippy.'' He turned to Noah. ''Don't you agree?''

Talk about a loaded question. Especially since he didn't agree at all. The way she fit into those jeans had been driving him to distraction all night. But he certainly didn't want to say anything to encourage her. ''Considering what I had on less than an hour ago, I'm hardly in any position to be a fashion critic.''

''Very diplomatic of you, Callahan,'' she said, a smile curving her mouth.

He couldn't help but smile back at her. He'd never met anyone quite like Sabrina before, although he couldn't quite figure out how she was different from other women. Other than the fact that she knew how to hot-wire a car and jimmy a lock with a paper clip. Hardly the typical traits of the girl-next-door type.

Sabrina Lovett made him more than a little curious. Although, he knew instinctively that a man could lose his head around her. Or his clothes. Which under different circumstances, might not be so bad.

Unfortunately, he couldn't take that kind of chance.

Noah clenched his jaw, firming his resolve at the same time. He simply couldn't let her get to him. Not when Sabrina believed he was husband material. Specifically, *her* husband material. And the last thing he wanted to do was lead her on.

Ramon scowled, looking back and forth between

the two of them. "Is there something going on here that I should know about?"

"Not a thing, Ramon," Noah replied, tipping up his beer. "Not a thing."

LONG PAST MIDNIGHT, Sabrina took a deep breath, then knocked lightly on Noah's bedroom door. Her toes curled on the hardwood floor as she waited for him to reply. When he didn't, she knocked again, only harder this time.

She tried to ignore the pounding of her heart. The stress of the car chase, the break-in, the pistol, and meeting her perfect match were obviously all beginning to catch up with her. And to think her parents had feared she'd have a boring life if she left the carnival.

At last she heard the sound of a groggy voice, though she couldn't decipher the words. She opened the door to his room and stuck her head inside. "May I come in?"

Noah blinked at the light shining in from the hallway, half sitting up in the bed. "Who is it?"

"Me. Sabrina."

He blinked again, then pulled the bedclothes up to his neck. "What do you want?"

She walked into the room, the hem of her green satin chemise swirling around her legs. "Are you ready, Noah?"

He stared at her, his Adam's apple bobbing in his throat. "Ready?"

She held up the cordless phone in her hand. "It's time to make the call."

"Oh." He relaxed against his pillows, then squinted at the clock on his bedside table. "It's almost two o'clock in the morning."

"Which means it's nine o'clock in Aurskog, Norway."

He rubbed one hand over his jaw, rough with dark whiskers. Then he regarded her with half-closed eyes. "I like your hair that way."

She laughed softly. "It's a mess. I just got out of bed."

"I know. That's what I like about it."

She moved closer to the bed. "Are you sure you're awake? You sound different."

When he folded his arms behind his head, the blanket slipped down to reveal the top half of his chest. "I'm only half-awake and I'm hoping like hell this is a dream. Of course, if it were a dream, you wouldn't be standing there."

She took a step closer to him, her voice a husky whisper. "What would I be doing?"

He closed his eyes. "Oh, Sabrina, I can think of a thousand things."

So could she. Especially with him lying there in the half shadows, his voice rough and low. It sent a primitive shiver through her. She'd heard the term "animal attraction" before, but she'd never really understood it until now.

But she wanted more than lust between them. She wanted to prove that he was her perfect match. To him, to Madame Sophia, and most importantly, to herself.

"Is one of those things dialing the telephone?" she asked playfully, breaking the intensely sensual moment between them.

He opened his eyes, a wry smile tipping up one corner out of his mouth. "No, but it's probably the safest one."

She sat primly on the edge of his bed, then handed him the telephone. "Do you know what you're going to say?"

"I haven't the faintest idea. I'm not thinking too clearly at the moment."

"That doesn't sound good."

"Tell me about it," he muttered. Then he sat farther up in the bed, placing a pillow behind his back. "Okay, I'm ready. Do I sound anything like Niles?"

She shook her head. "Not really. His voice is a little higher."

Noah cleared his throat, then spoke in a falsetto. "Like this?"

"Now go a little lower."

He grimaced. "I'm going to hurt myself before this is over."

He could hurt her, too, she suddenly realized. She'd come to like him quite well in the short time they'd known each other. And she didn't take to strangers easily.

"Pretend you're lifting a piano."

"Like this?" he said, straining his voice so it fell

somewhere between his naturally deep tone and a man suffering from a hernia.

She clapped her hands together. "That's perfect."

He rubbed his throat with his fingertips. "Okay, what's next?"

"I think you'll need a script."

He grabbed a notepad and pencil off the nightstand. "I'm ready when you are."

She nibbled on her thumbnail, wanting to choose just the right words. "Let's start with: 'Hello, Doris, this is Niles.'"

"Very creative," he quipped, jotting it down on the notepad.

"Then say: 'I've really missed you, honey.'"

"Do I have to?"

She arched a brow. "Isn't that what a loving husband would say?"

"You're asking the wrong man," he said, scribbling on the notepad. "But I'll take your word for it."

"I think the best thing to do is make this call short and to the point. The longer you're on the line, the more time she has to figure out you're not her husband."

"Good point. How about: 'See you in seven days'?"

"Not that short. Tell her you've done a lot of thinking and you want to come home and try again."

"'Come home and try again,'" he repeated as he wrote it down.

"And that you'll be there a week from today."

Noah looked up from the notepad. "Is it Saturday or Sunday in Norway?"

"Sunday. They're seven hours ahead of us."

He flipped the pencil in his hand and rubbed the eraser across the paper. "Then I'll be home next Sunday."

"Now we just have to think of the perfect romantic ending."

"I thought that *was* the ending. I'm supposed to keep it short and to the point, remember?"

"Aren't you even going to tell her goodbye?"

"'Goodbye,'" he said, printing the word out.

"'Goodbye, my darling,'" she amended.

"A real man doesn't talk like that."

"Niles called me darling several times during our one and only date."

"Which proves my point. It sounds like Niles could use a good punch in the mouth. I'm just glad you didn't fall for him."

Sabrina looked into his eyes. "He wasn't my perfect match."

Noah dropped his gaze to the telephone. "What's her number?"

She took the receiver out of his hands. "I'll dial it while you warm up."

He stretched his arms straight over his head, then leaned forward and drew his elbows back, flexing the muscles in his chest. He took two deep breaths, like a weight lifter about to go for the gold. "Okay," he said at last, "I think I'm ready."

"I meant warm up your voice," she said, her index finger poised over the buttons.

He cleared his throat. "Okay, now I'm ready."

"Now for the finishing touch." She turned to the clock radio on his bed stand, tuning it to static.

"What did you do that for?" he asked as she dialed the number, then handed him the phone. "Doris will hardly be able to hear me."

"That's the idea," she said over the static.

He motioned for her to be quiet, then spoke in an unnaturally high voice. "Hello, Doris. This is Niles. Your husband."

TOTAL SILENCE greeted Noah at the other end of the line. For a moment, he thought she'd hung up on him. "Doris, are you there?"

"I'm here." Her voice sounded gruff, and Noah had no doubt he'd just gotten her out of bed. Good. Maybe that would teach her to steal a man's clothes.

"I've really missed you, honey," he said, reading off of his notes. "I've done a lot of…" His voice trailed off as he tried to decipher the next word. He didn't have the best penmanship, especially at two o'clock in the morning.

"Thinking," Sabrina whispered beside him.

"Thinking," he blurted, "and I'd really like to come home and try again."

After a long pause, Doris asked, "Try what again?"

"Uh...the marriage thing. You know, for better or worse."

Sabrina grimaced and made a frantic crisscrossing motion over her chest with one finger.

"And your bra size doesn't matter to me anymore," he improvised, panic setting in. "I've learned...here in Norway...that there are more important things than big breasts."

Sabrina fell straight back onto his bed with a loud groan.

"'Bye, hon...uh, my darling. I'll see you in exactly one week." He punched the off button, then turned to her. She lay with both hands over her face.

"Well?"

Her body shook, her face still concealed from him.

He sighed. "That bad, huh?"

She drew her hands away, unable to conceal her laughter any longer. "That was worse than I ever imagined."

He scowled, then leaned over her, propping his chin in his hand. "Those aren't exactly the words a man wants to hear from the woman lying in his bed."

"Sorry, but it's the truth. Why did you have to mention her breasts?"

"I thought you were giving me a sign, like in baseball."

"Well, you read it completely wrong. I was trying to get you to say you loved her with all your heart."

"That wasn't in the script. Besides, how was I possibly supposed to know what this meant?" He mimicked her motion with his finger, accidentally grazing the lace bodice of her chemise.

She sucked in her breath and Noah's own breathing hitched at the contact. When she stared into his eyes, he suddenly realized how very close he was to her. Only scant millimeters away from her mouth. Before he could stop to think, he leaned forward, lightly brushing her lips with his own.

Her arms curled around his neck as he deepened the kiss, a low moan emanating from his throat. His hand found her waist, smoothing the supple fabric of her chemise as he molded her hip. She wasn't gaunt and bony, like so many women who had no idea what turned a man on. She was all woman. And she was all his.

The thought doused his ardor like a splash of cold water.

He broke the kiss, his body screaming in protest. She blinked up at him, looking so soft and sexy he could barely stand it.

"That was some good-night kiss," she said huskily. Then she sat up and rose off the bed, wobbling just a little. She steadied herself against the mattress. "Do you want me to tuck you in?"

"No, thanks. I'm a big boy."

"I can tell," she said with a small smile as she glided out the bedroom door.

He plopped back against the pillows, furious with himself. If he couldn't even last one day without kissing her, how was he ever going to last two weeks?

He got up and closed the door behind her, half wishing it had a lock. Not to keep her out, but to keep him in.

It was going to be a very long night.

THE NIGHT GOT even longer when he awoke to a bright blinding white light shining in his face a couple of hours later. He squinted, shielding his eyes with his hand and half rising off of his pillow.

The light wavered. "Are you awake?"

Ramon.

He swallowed a groan. "I am now. What the hell are you doing up at this hour?"

"Twenty dollars."

Noah sat up in bed. "You're not making any sense. Are you sleepwalking? Or did you forget to take your medicine?"

"My counselor said I don't have to take medicine anymore. I'm making wonderful progress." He shone the flashlight directly in Noah's eyes. "You look tired."

"Turn that damn thing off! Of course I'm tired." He glanced at the illuminated dial of the clock radio on the nightstand. "It's four o'clock in the morning!"

Ramon switched off the flashlight, then flipped on the overhead light. "Man, and I thought Trace was cranky. I just wanted to make sure we could talk in private."

Noah winced at the brightness. "What do you want?"

"Twenty bucks."

"I'm not giving you money."

"No, I mean I want to give *you* twenty bucks."

"For what?" Noah rubbed his eyes, trying to make sense of this convoluted conversation. It was hard enough to comprehend Ramon's ramblings when he was fully conscious.

"For leaving. In fact, now would be a perfect time."

"You're paying me to leave?"

"The sooner, the better. In fact, I'll throw in five bucks as an incentive if you're out of here in the next five minutes."

"Why?"

"Because I'm a naturally generous guy. Just ask anybody." Ramon hesitated. "Well, on second thought, don't ask my cousin Viper. He's still upset about leaving that winning raffle ticket at my place. Don't ask Carl at work, either. I'm almost positive that was my tip on the coffee bar. The kid who delivers the newspaper wouldn't be a good reference, either. But I think almost anyone else would agree."

Noah closed his eyes, wondering if this was a nightmare. "Ramon, I am not taking your money."

"You mean you'll leave for free?"

"No. I'm not leaving. Period." He lay back down and drew the blanket over his shoulder. "Good night."

Ramon began pacing the room. "Thirty bucks."

"I'm going to sleep now."

"Thirty-one. That's my highest offer."

Noah cracked one eye. "Why are you so anxious for me to leave?"

"Because you're cramping my style, Callahan. There's a gorgeous woman living in this house and I'd like a chance to romance her in private."

"Romance her?" Noah laughed out loud. "You told her she should consider liposuction!"

Ramon scowled at him. "It's a perfectly safe procedure."

Noah laughed. "Sabrina is not fat. She's not even close to fat. She's got a killer body. Long legs. Great hips. Round, lush..." His voice trailed off, and he pushed the blanket off his chest, feeling uncomfortably warm.

"Thirty-one dollars and fifty cents," Ramon offered, then he folded his arms across his chest. "You know, it's not like I consider you a real threat. Everybody knows your relationships with women don't last as long as the life span of a gnat."

The contention irritated him, even if it was true. "So what's the problem?"

"You're a distraction. I saw the way Sabrina was staring at you tonight. Like she'd never seen a few muscles before."

"Ramon, it's late. I'm tired and you look like you're about to start hyperventilating again."

"Thirty-two dollars. That's my final offer. Take it or leave it."

"I'll leave it." Noah yawned. "Could you turn off the light on your way out?"

Ramon pressed his lips together, then headed for the door. "I hope you don't regret it, Callahan." He flipped the switch, plunging the room into darkness. "I really hope you don't regret it."

vestigations.

6

THE NEXT MORNING, Noah opened up Café Romeo
at 6:00 a.m. sharp, informed the employees he'd be
managing the coffeehouse for Madame Sophia for
the next two weeks, then shut himself in his aunt's
tiny office and promptly fell asleep at the desk.

At 7:00 a.m. a knock sounded at the door. "Hey,
Callahan," a male voice called. "You in there?"

Noah lifted his head off the desk. "Keep it down
out there. Some of us are trying to sleep."

The door opened and Ty Burke, a stocky African-
American cop only a couple of years older than
Noah, walked inside. "I hear you've started pushing
my favorite legal drug."

A year ago, Ty had headed up a complex criminal
investigation that Noah had worked from the insurance angle. The two had become fast friends, sharing a common interest in sports cars, beautiful
women and baseball.

"What are you doing here so early?"

"Some of us have to work—even on Sunday."
Burke held up a small foam cup. "I stop here every
morning for my caffeine fix. There's nothing like a

cup of espresso and a couple of chocolate biscotti to start the day.''

"What, no donuts?"

"That's an ugly stereotype." He sat down in a chair next to the desk. "Cops are much classier than people think. Certainly classier than insurance investigators.''

"Shouldn't you be out fighting crime?"

"Man, you are cranky this morning.''

"I didn't get much sleep last night.''

Burke grinned. "I should have known. Since when don't you spend Saturday night with a beautiful woman in your bed?"

In truth, it had been a hell of a long time. Longer than Noah wanted to admit. That probably explained his strong attraction to Sabrina. Abstinence obviously didn't agree with him.

Although, technically he had had a beautiful woman in his bed last night. She just hadn't stayed there. "Just living up to my reputation. Or so the ladies tell me.''

Burke snorted. "Man, you are so full of shit. I'm just waiting for the day some woman brings you to your knees.''

"Spoken like a married man. How is Margo, anyway?"

Burke beamed. "Beautiful, sexy, and six weeks pregnant.''

Noah blinked, surprised one of his old bachelor buddies had transformed so quickly, and apparently easily, into a proud husband and father-to-be. "Hey, that's great! You must be really excited."

Burke nodded. "And scared shitless. But I've felt that way ever since I met Margo, so I'm starting to get used to it."

"Speaking of scary women," Noah said slowly, "have you met Sabrina?"

Burke knitted his brow. "Sabrina?"

"She's my Aunt Sophie's new apprentice. She started working here about a month ago."

Burke leaned forward in his chair. "You mean the redhead? Tall, built, beautiful?"

"That's the one."

Burke nodded his approval. "She is quite the dish."

Inexplicably, Noah felt a burst of masculine pride. "She's been having some trouble with a woman named Doris Dooley."

"She's not the only one. I hear you've been making house calls."

Noah blinked at the sudden shift of subject. Though it shouldn't have surprised him, since he knew it was the way Burke worked. He'd just never been on the receiving end before. "I take it you've heard from Doris."

Burke pulled a small memo pad out of his shirt pocket. "Doris Dooley came into the station last night. Apparently, she was quite upset."

"She wasn't the only one," he muttered under his breath.

"She claims you entered her home under false pretenses."

"And?"

Burke studied him for a moment. "And took your clothes off."

"What!"

"And stole a sheet."

Noah clenched his jaw. "She's twisting this all out of proportion."

Burke arched a brow. "So you're saying it didn't happen?"

He wished he could. Unfortunately, everything she claimed was true. She'd just conveniently omitted a few pertinent details.

"Doris invited me into her house to discuss insurance," he began.

"Since when do you go door-to-door?"

He could tell the truth—or he could protect Sabrina. "I'm branching out."

Burke snorted. "Give me a break, Callahan. I'm trying to help you here. Doris hasn't pressed any charges yet, but she's seriously considering it. I also heard she's thinking about filing sexual-harassment charges against your insurance company."

"Damn." Noah looked at Burke. "Would you believe me if I told you she held me at gunpoint, made me strip, then confiscated my clothes?"

Burke looked at him skeptically as he sat back in the chair, tapping his pen against the memo pad. "So what does Sabrina have to do with all of this?"

"Doris has been harassing her. Yesterday she

stole her cat. I was just trying to help her get it back.''

"Rescuing damsels in distress? That doesn't sound like your style. You're more of the kiss-and-run type.''

The assessment made him bristle. "Gee, thanks.''

"Hey, it's nothing personal. I just call 'em like I see 'em.''

Noah fiddled with the paper clip on top of the desk. "Well, I'm not planning to kiss Sabrina,'' he lied. "But I am sticking close to her, at least for the next two weeks. This Doris is a wacko.''

Burke rose to his feet. "Maybe. But thanks to the Constitution, even the wackos have rights. If she decides to file charges against you, I'm not sure I can stop her. You might want to consult a good attorney.''

Noah closed his eyes with a frustrated sigh. "Twenty-four hours ago, my life was perfectly normal. Then I meet Sabrina Lovett and all hell breaks loose.''

Burke laughed as he moved toward the door. "Spoken like a man falling in love.''

He was out the door before Noah could contradict him. Falling in love? After only one day? No way. Then he thought of his brothers. Had the same thing happened to Jake and Trace?

He picked up a pen and studied the receipts in front of him, trying to shake off a sense of doom. A man couldn't fall in love with a woman against his will.

No matter what the coffee grounds said.

SABRINA SAT curled up on a dilapidated armchair in the cramped storeroom at Café Romeo, reading a textbook that Madame Sophia had lent her. It was entitled *The Definitive Guide to Reading Coffee Grounds and Tea Leaves*. Now that the morning rush was over, this was the perfect opportunity to take a long break and study up on her craft.

"'Good technique is vital for an accurate reading,'" she read aloud. The words blurred as her mind drifted to the night before. Noah Callahan had excellent technique. She closed her eyes, reliving that kiss, her body tingling just as it had done then. He was good. He was very, very good.

She opened her eyes and cleared her throat, forcing her attention back on the page. "'Technique can be taught, but a true artist needs something more. Talent.'"

She frowned. Did she have talent? Lately, it seemed she only had a talent for trouble. Years ago, she'd discovered an entirely different kind of talent. One that required a certain amount of charm, the nerve of a high-stakes gambler, and an ability to think on her feet.

Noah could have used the latter last night on the telephone. She bit back a reluctant smile at the thought of his performance. They'd be lucky if Doris hadn't already figured out their ploy and decided to take revenge. Then her smile faded.

Would Beauty suffer for it?

She swallowed hard as all the worries she'd

shoved to the back of her mind came rushing back. Was her cat hungry? Thirsty? Afraid? The only thing that gave her solace was the fact that Beauty was a scrapper. She'd managed to survive a long time on the streets before Sabrina had found her and tamed her.

Her hand tightened on the book. She'd find her again. Her search had started this morning when she'd called every animal shelter in St. Louis. But none of the cats matched her description of Beauty. Still, she'd left her name and phone number, just in case Beauty showed up. She'd also called the newspaper to put a notice in the lost-and-found section, offering a reward. It wasn't five thousand dollars, but it was all the money Sabrina had in her meager savings account.

She took a deep breath, forcing her concentration back on the book in her lap. "'Talent can't be taught or bought,'" she read aloud. "'It is an inborn gift that only a rare few possess. Attempts by an amateur to force a reading could result in disaster.'"

She reached up to turn the page. *Disaster* pretty much summed up the events of the last twenty-four hours. Was it her fault? Things had turned bad after she'd mistakenly predicted Niles Dooley as her perfect match. They'd gotten much worse since she'd met Noah. Which meant…

Which meant Noah Callahan might not be her perfect match. Her heart plummeted at the possibility. Before she'd met him, she'd wanted Noah to be the one in order to prove herself as Madame Sophia's replacement. Now…now she wanted him to be her perfect match for entirely different reasons.

She turned her attention back to the textbook, determined to think positive. That was when she saw it. A small, sealed envelope stuck in the crease of the book. She picked it up and turned it over in her hand, recognizing Madame Sophia's unique handwriting in pink ink on the front.

Sabrina,

After your unfortunate experience with that nasty Niles Dooley, I took the liberty of reading your coffee grounds for you. When you're ready to try again, just open this envelope. The name of your perfect match is inside.

Love,
Sophie

Sabrina stared at the envelope. She hadn't told Madame Sophia that she'd done a second reading. Or that she believed Noah Callahan was her perfect match.

Now she could find out for sure.

She turned the envelope over to break the seal, then hesitated. Once she opened it, she'd know if she really had a future at Café Romeo. Even more importantly, a future with Noah.

The door to the storeroom opened and she hastily

stuck the envelope back into the book, then slammed it shut.

"I thought I'd never find you." Noah put down the shopping bag he had in his hand, his handsome face set in a scowl.

She set the book aside. "Is something wrong?"

He walked into the storeroom. "Yes, something's wrong. You can't just disappear like that. I was worried sick about you."

Her heart did a ridiculous somersault at his words. "I told Carl I'd be in here in case anyone needed me."

"Carl's shift ended fifteen minutes ago." He took a step closer to her. "I want you to promise never to disappear like that again."

"I didn't disappear." She stood up, feeling at a distinct disadvantage when he towered over her. "Did you want me for something?"

He gave her a lazy smile. "Now that's a loaded question."

Her gaze fell to his mouth and her lips tingled in response. It was his fault for looking so irresistible in black denim jeans, a blue T-shirt and black sports jacket.

"I need a picture of your cat," he said at last.

She looked up from his mouth. "Beauty? Why?"

"I'm going to put an ad in the newspaper and offer a reward. I thought a picture would be the best way to identify her."

Now it was her turn to smile. "Thanks, but it's

already taken care of. I placed an ad in the classifieds about an hour ago.''

''Then I guess it's true what they say—great minds really do think alike.''

If his mind was in the same place as hers, he wouldn't be standing there right now. Or wearing clothes. Sabrina abruptly sat down again, overwhelmed by a sudden surge of desire. She'd been attracted to men before, but the intensity of her reaction to Noah surprised her. Maybe the fact that he was her perfect match explained it. She glanced at the book next to her.

There was one way to find out.

Noah grabbed an old bar stool from the corner. ''There's another reason I wanted to find you.''

She looked up at him. ''Oh?''

He pulled the stool closer to her chair, then straddled it. ''I want to apologize for last night.''

She smiled. ''Don't worry. You did your best. I've probably just had a lot more practice at that sort of thing.''

He arched a brow. ''Have you?''

Sabrina bit her tongue, wishing she'd kept her mouth shut. The last thing she wanted to do was get into a detailed discussion of her past. That would just give him one more reason not to fall in love with her.

She waved the subject away with her hand. ''Forget it, Noah. These things happen.''

He nodded thoughtfully. ''You're right. It was

late and we were both tired. I assure you it will never happen again.''

She stared at him, thoroughly confused.

"We'll just forget it ever happened," he continued. "After all, it was only a kiss."

Heat burned up her cheeks. She'd read him all wrong. He wasn't apologizing to her for screwing up that phone call to Doris. He was apologizing for kissing her!

Even worse, he'd just promised it would never happen again.

"Is something wrong?" he asked, studying her. "You look flushed."

"No. Of course not." She flapped her hand in front of her face. "It's just a little warm in here."

He nodded. "I'll adjust the air conditioner."

She stood up, tucking the book firmly under her arm. "Well, if that's all, I really need to get back to work."

"Just one more thing."

She moved toward the door, not looking at him. "Yes?"

"I bought you something." He walked toward her, then picked up the shopping bag he'd dropped by the door.

"Here," he said, shoving it into her hands. "I really hope you like it."

"Noah, you shouldn't have…" she began, but he was already out the door.

She held up the shopping bag, noting the familiar name of the boutique located just around the corner from Café Romeo on the front. Then she opened it and pulled out her present.

It was a bathrobe. A long-sleeved, floor-length green terry-cloth robe. With a zipper from hem to neck. It was the ugliest robe she'd ever seen, even if the color did match her nightgown.

And she couldn't have been happier about it.

Noah might be resistant to her charms, but he obviously wasn't immune, otherwise he wouldn't go to so much trouble to cover them up. She hugged the robe to her, hope taking the place of despair.

If everything went according to plan the next few days, she'd find Niles, get Beauty back and teach Noah a very valuable lesson.

Never say never.

THAT NIGHT Sabrina made lasagna for supper, splurged on a bottle of full-bodied Chianti, and wore her sexiest dress, a black strapless number that made breathing problematic. She only forgot one thing.

Ramon.

He walked through the back door just as she pulled the lasagna pan out of the oven. Then he took one look at her and froze in his tracks. "Wow."

"Hello, Ramon," she said, setting the hot pan on a trivet in the center of the table. Disappointment knifed through her, but she tried hard not to show it. Ramon might be a little flaky, but he was also sensitive and a good friend. "I thought you had to work tonight."

"I did, but Callahan gave me the night off." He leaned over and inhaled the lasagna. "Smells great. I'll bet you didn't know this is Noah's favorite dish."

He'd lose that bet. She'd done her research on Noah Callahan before she'd even met him. Once she'd discerned that he was her perfect match, she'd stealthily grilled his aunt, and even his brother Jake, who managed the accounts at Café Romeo, about every facet of his life.

She knew he liked lasagna, old black-and-white private-eye flicks, and leggy blondes. Not necessarily in that order. She'd been hoping to discover a few of his other likes and dislikes over an intimate, candlelight dinner.

Ramon pulled out a chair and sat down, snapping open the white linen napkin she'd spent so much time artfully folding. Then he tucked the napkin into the front of his shirt. "When do we eat?"

"It's ready now," she said, resigning herself to dinner for three. She walked over to the refrigerator to retrieve the salad. "Would you please tell Noah it's time to eat?"

Ramon leaned toward the doorway and shouted, "Hey, Callahan, it's time to eat."

"Thanks," she said dryly, setting the salad on the table.

She turned just as Noah walked into the kitchen. He stopped abruptly and stared. His eyes took the slow route from her head to her feet and back again. "What's all this?"

"I just wanted to thank you for your gift. So I thought I'd make supper tonight."

Ramon reached for a slice of garlic bread. "Gift? What gift?"

Sabrina looked at Noah and noted that he was still staring. She took that as a good sign. "He bought me a nice warm, terry-cloth robe."

Ramon wrinkled his nose. "Warm? In the middle of August?"

"It's the thought that counts," she said, setting another place at the table. "Go ahead and sit down, Noah, before it gets cold."

He stood rooted to the spot. "Does the robe fit?"

"It's perfect. I'll model it for you later." She poured three glasses of wine, then set the bottle back on the table.

He swallowed hard. "I'd really like to see you put it on now."

Ramon nodded, waving his fork in the air. "You know, that's not a bad idea. It's already warm in here from the oven. If you put on a big robe, it will be just like sitting in a sauna. That's a great way to shed a few of those pesky extra pounds." He half rose out of his chair. "I'll go get it for you."

She pushed down hard on his shoulder. "I'm not wearing the robe."

"Are you sure? That dress looks pretty tight."

"Eat, Ramon," she ordered, wondering if she'd overdone it with the dress. Vamping really wasn't her style. At least, not anymore.

She turned around to see Noah holding her chair out for her. "Thank you."

"You look...amazing." His fingers brushed against her bare shoulder as she sat down. His touch electrified her and she realized Ramon was right—the kitchen had turned into a sauna.

Noah sat down across the table from her. "Everything looks delicious."

A blush crept up her neck when she realized he wasn't looking at the food. He was still staring at her. She picked up her fork. "I hope you like it."

He followed suit. "It's almost irresistible."

Almost. Sabrina reached for her wine, studying Noah through her lashes. He ate with an enthusiasm that surprised her. Intrigued her. As she sipped her wine, she wondered what it would be like to be on the receiving end of all that intensity.

Ramon forked up a bite of lasagna, gooey with melted mozzarella. "I wonder what Chloe and Trace are doing right now."

Noah caught her gaze and held it. For a long moment, it was almost as if they were alone in the room. His hungry expression left no doubt about what he'd like to be doing right now. Then he turned his attention back to his plate and she wondered if she'd just imagined it.

"I wonder if Chloe's happy," Ramon pondered, picking up his wineglass.

Noah reached for a slice of garlic bread. "They probably don't have any regrets yet."

"Yet?" Sabrina echoed.

He shrugged. "Let's face it. Trace and Chloe really don't know each other all that well. They met, fell in love, and got married all within the span of a few short weeks."

Ramon nodded. "Your brother is kind of a jerk—once you get to know him. But Chloe still seems to like him."

"She's crazy about him," Sabrina countered. "And he's even crazier about her. Anyone could see that at the reception."

"That's because he's blinded by love," Noah said. "Just like Jake. There's no way they could know if they married the right women."

"How can you be so sure they married the *wrong* ones?"

He shrugged. "I just wish they'd taken their time. Shopped around a little instead of rushing into marriage."

She laughed. "Jake's almost thirty, and Trace isn't too far behind him. You call that rushing into marriage?"

Noah took a sip of his wine. "I think they could have taken a little more time to check out their prospective brides."

She smiled. "My parents only knew each other for two weeks when my father proposed. They'll be celebrating their thirtieth wedding anniversary next month."

"Then they're the exception, not the rule. My father married my mother after only knowing her for ten months. She left eight years later."

Her gaze softened. "I'm sorry."

He shrugged. "It happens. Aunt Sophie always said he picked the wrong woman. So what happens when Jake discovers that Nina has some little habit that drives him crazy? Or when Trace finds another D'Onofrio family skeleton in the closet?"

"Hey," Ramon protested, "I resent that."

"I'm just saying that love can't always survive secrets. And there's no way two people can learn each other's secrets in the space of a few weeks. It takes years."

"Years?" Sabrina's grip tightened on the stem of her wineglass. She had a few secrets of her own. Secrets she hadn't planned to share with anyone— including her future husband. "Isn't that a little extreme?"

"Not as extreme as marriage to a virtual stranger."

She rolled her eyes. "Your reasoning is totally impractical—for a woman who wants children, anyway. She can't wait years if her biological clock is ticking."

Ramon perked up. "D'Onofrio men are very virile. We can handle any clock around. Just in case you're interested."

Noah glowered at him. "How generous of you."

Sabrina suppressed a smile. "Thanks for the offer, Ramon. I'm only twenty-four, so it's hardly an emergency situation yet." She paused a beat, impulsively deciding to spill one of her secrets. "But I do want six kids."

Noah choked on his lasagna. Ramon reached over and pounded him on the back until he recovered. Noah stared at her disbelief. "Six kids?"

"Three girls and three boys would be nice, but I'm flexible."

"I think there's another word for it." He picked up his wineglass. "*Six kids.* You'd have enough for your very own volleyball team."

"I love volleyball."

"I'm a baseball fan myself," Noah countered. "But what about your husband? Won't he have any say in the matter?"

"I suppose so, since it would be hard to make six babies without him." She knew she was goading him, but she couldn't help it. He was so cute when he was flustered. "I'd need a man with a lot of stamina."

Ramon settled back in his chair. "I've been lifting weights."

"He'll need more than stamina," Noah said, tossing his napkin on top of his empty plate. "He'll need his head examined."

She bristled. "Are you saying a man would have to be crazy to want to marry me?"

"Of course not. I'm simply saying…" His voice trailed off as his gaze fell to her mouth.

"Yes?" she prodded.

His gaze met hers and his voice dropped to a low, husky whisper. "You're definitely driving me crazy."

That was when Sabrina decided her dinner party was a smashing success.

7

Time was running out.

Five days after their fake telephone call to Doris Dooley, Noah and Sabrina were no closer to finding Niles. Assuming he'd left the city, they'd checked the airport, bus station, train station and all the rental-car agencies. But unless the man had used an alias, there was no record of him anywhere. According to the DMV, the Dooleys only owned one vehicle and that was the black pickup truck Doris always drove.

On Wednesday afternoon, Noah sat in the office at Café Romeo, going over his checklist once again. There just weren't that many places left to look. Especially since they didn't have one single clue to lead them in the right direction.

And that wasn't the only problem.

He didn't know how much longer he could hold out. Spending day and night with Sabrina Lovett had taken its toll. He couldn't eat. Couldn't sleep. Couldn't stop thinking about her.

Worst of all, he couldn't remember all the reasons why he shouldn't fall for her. She was a beautiful, intelligent, fascinating woman. But was she the right woman? That was the question. How the hell was he supposed to know the answer? Especially in less than two weeks.

He'd always sworn to himself he wouldn't make the same mistake as his father. He wouldn't pick the wrong woman. He'd just never stopped to figure out how to tell the difference.

Noah swore softly under his breath, massaging his temple with his fingertips. He looked at the wall calendar. The date he was scheduled to leave for Cleveland was marked with a big red circle. All he had to do was tough it out a little longer. That and continue taking a lot of cold showers.

The door opened and Ramon struck his head inside. "One of the toilets in the men's room is plugged up."

"Again?"

Ramon shrugged. "Maybe you didn't use the plunger right the last time."

He'd used the plunger three times in the last three hours. And on a different toilet each time. If he didn't know better, he'd think someone was deliberately stuffing them with toilet paper just to cause him trouble.

"You'd better hurry," Ramon said with a smirk. "There's a line forming."

Noah leaned back in his chair, staring down the waiter. "Why don't you take care of it this time?"

Ramon stood in the doorway, folding his arms across his narrow chest. "Madame Sophia hired me as a waiter, not a plumber. I suppose next you'll want me to take the kitchen sink apart.''

The back of his neck prickled. ''What's wrong with the kitchen sink?''

''Someone dropped a couple of forks down the garbage disposal. It's really making a racket.''

Noah struggled to hold on to his temper. He knew if he started yelling, Ramon would threaten to call Aunt Sophie again. The last thing he wanted was his aunt thinking he couldn't handle a few minor problems. Or even a major problem. Like Ramon.

''It's not going to work,'' he warned.

The waiter blinked innocently at him. ''What's not going to work?''

''All these little games you've been playing. Like plugging the toilets and the garbage disposal here at Café Romeo. And hiding the television remote control at Aunt Sophie's house. Don't you think that's just a little childish?''

Ramon shifted. ''You're the one playing games. Only you're playing them with Sabrina. It's obvious she's crazy about you. And you just keep leading her on!''

Noah's jaw clenched. ''I am not leading her on.''

Ramon rolled his eyes. ''Oh, please! You came down to breakfast without a shirt on this morning. How am I supposed to compete with that?''

He sat up. ''You're the one who took my shirts out of the laundry room and hid them in the broom closet.''

"I already told you, I thought they were cleaning rags."

"You're wasting your time, Ramon. Sabrina and I are just..." His voice trailed off as he tried to think of an appropriate word to describe their relationship. He wouldn't exactly call them friends, even though he did enjoy spending time with her. Enjoyed it way too much for his own peace of mind.

Ramon took another step into the room. "Just what?"

"Just acquaintances who happen to be living in the same house—temporarily."

Ramon snorted. "Right. Like you're not trying every trick in the book to get her into your bed. I've warned her about you, Callahan, but I don't think it's done a hell of a lot of good."

He knew he shouldn't ask, but he couldn't help himself. "What do you mean?"

"*What do I mean?* How about the way she's always staring at you when you're not looking? Or the way she hangs on your every word? It makes me want to puke."

"I think you're exaggerating," Noah replied, trying to ignore the warm glow deep inside of him.

"That's what she said when I told her all the bad stuff about you."

He scowled. "What bad stuff?"

"Like the fact that you're a runner."

"What the hell does that mean?"

"Figure it out for yourself, Callahan. All the women you've dated have whiplash from you slammin' on the brakes the minute they want to get serious. Then your aunt reads your coffee grounds and what do you do? Put in for a transfer to another state. It's all very clear.''

''Well, I'm glad it's clear to one of us.''

''It's a defensive mechanism. I learned all about it during my stay at the Oracle Clinic.''

''Spare me the drive-through psychology.''

Ramon smiled. ''The problem with you, Callahan, is that you always run away when the going gets rough.''

Noah surged to his feet. ''Okay, that's it.''

Ramon backed up a step. ''Hey, I was just trying to help.''

''Don't worry about me, Ramon, worry about yourself.'' He lowered his voice and took a step closer to him. ''Because if the toilets and sinks keep plugging up, or any other catastrophe happens around here, I'm coming after you. Then we'll see who's running away.''

Ramon's lower lip trembled ominously. ''You wouldn't dare beat me up.''

''Give me one good reason why not!'' Noah snapped, knowing Ramon was right. Not because he was afraid of the scrawny waiter, but because he'd never pick on someone weaker than himself.

''I'll give you two good reasons—Trace and Madame Sophia.'' He tipped up his chin. ''Trace is my brother-in-law now, so he has to protect me, whether he likes it or not. And we both know Madame Sophia would be furious if you laid so much as a finger on me.''

Noah didn't say anything for a long moment, waiting for his temper to cool. ''Trace I can handle. But you're right about Aunt Sophie. So let's call a truce.''

Ramon looked skeptical. ''A truce?''

He nodded. ''In another week, I'll be long gone. Until then, I don't want you to do or say anything to make me mad. Got it?''

Ramon clenched his jaw, not saying a word.

Noah took another menacing step toward him.

Ramon backed up against the wall, holding his hands up in front of him. ''Okay, okay. I've got it.''

''Good.''

Ramon slowly lowered his hands. ''So…let me ask you a hypothetical question. Suppose someone asked me to give you a message, but I sort of forgot about it. Would that make you mad?''

''Definitely.''

''Okay.'' Ramon turned toward the door. ''Bye.''

''Ramon?''

He hesitated, one hand wrapped around the door frame. ''What?''

''Do you have a message for me?''

Ramon glanced over his shoulder. ''Not if it will make you mad.''

''I'll only get mad if you walk out that door without giving it to me.''

Ramon's left eye twitched. ''Sabrina called.''

His pulse picked up. "Called? From where? Isn't she here?"

"If she was here, why would she be calling?"

Good question. The last time he'd seen her was this morning, when she'd caught a ride to Café Romeo with him. He'd been hidden away in the office most of the day—when he wasn't unplugging toilets—trying to figure how to track down Niles.

"What did she say?"

Ramon edged farther out the door. "Are you sure you're not mad?"

"Positive," he said between clenched teeth.

"Well, she wants you to meet her."

He silently counted to ten. "Where and when?"

"Ducky's Bar on Benton Street," Ramon replied, one foot out the door. "Two hours ago." Then he fled before Noah could make a move. Which was a good thing, because he'd probably have gone for the guy's throat.

Ducky's Bar? Ramon must have gotten the message wrong. What would Sabrina be doing in that place? It was owned by one of Chloe D'Onofrio Callahan's disreputable relatives and had gained a reputation for catering to an eclectic crowd of small-time hoods and local theater buffs.

He glanced out the window. The midafternoon sun shone through, illuminating the dust motes on the venetian blinds. Surely she wouldn't wait two hours for him to show up. Then another thought occurred to him. What if someone else had shown up? What if Doris had followed her there?

Noah rose slowly to his feet, his stomach knotting from a combination of frustration and fear. He'd told her not to go anywhere without him. Naturally, she hadn't listened. She never wore that damn robe, either. When he found her, he definitely planned to set her straight about a few things. But first things first.

He reached for the plunger.

SABRINA LEANED OVER the pool table and took aim at the cue ball. Country music twanged out of the jukebox and even though the bar was practically empty, a haze of smoke hung around the pool light just above her. She cued up, shot, and missed.

Her opponent grinned. "Oops."

She looked up at him. "Can I have a do-over?"

Viper D'Onofrio, the bouncer at Ducky's Bar and a man in serious need of a shave, shook his head. "No do-overs in pool, babe."

She wished she could do over this entire day. No, make that the whole last week. Her cat was still missing and they weren't any closer to finding Niles. To make matters worse, Noah hadn't even come close to kissing her again.

She'd tried everything to entice him, but the man must be made of ice. She, on the other hand, had almost melted into the floor when she'd met him coming out of the shower last night, a towel slung low on his hips.

Of course, having Ramon panting at her heels like an eager puppy hadn't helped. She'd tried every way she knew to gently discourage him, but the guy just wouldn't give up. This morning at breakfast he'd spelled out the words I Love You with link sausages.

That was why she'd been hoping for some private time with Noah over lunch. Until he'd stood her up. Then Viper had refused to give her the information she needed until she'd agreed to let him buy her a beer and teach her the game of pool.

He'd been a tenacious, hands-on instructor, but a few well-aimed jabs with her pool cue had taught him to keep a respectful distance. Now if she could only teach him to keep his mouth shut.

"A pool stick is like a woman," he said, slowly sliding one blunt-tipped finger down the length of his cue. "If you touch her just right, she'll do anything you want."

Sabrina tried not to gag on her beer. She set down the bottle on a nearby table. "It's your shot."

Viper leaned over the table, then shot three balls in quick succession, making every one. He grinned, his gaze roaming over the territory below her neck. "I can do it fast or I can do it slow. Either way I'm damn good."

His grin faded when he missed an easy bank shot of the last ball on the table.

Sabrina bit back a smile. "Ooh, you almost had that one."

He stared hard at the tip of his cue, as if baffled by its behavior. "Looks like I need some chalk."

She handed him the cube of blue chalk, then studied the table. "Only one ball left."

He chalked up his cue. "That's right. If you sink the eight ball, then you win the game." His tone told her there was no chance of that happening.

She took her time chalking her cue, then leaned over the table to take aim.

Viper moved around the edge of the table until he was directly across from her, his gaze fixed on her cleavage. "You need to bend over just a little more, babe."

That did it. Time to teach Viper a lesson he'd never forget. At least this way her day wouldn't be a total loss.

She bent down until the tips of her breasts almost touched the table. "Is that better?"

He licked his lips. "Oh, honey, that's much better."

She took her aim, drew back her cue stick, then hesitated.

"What's wrong?"

She looked up at Viper. "What do I get if I make this shot?"

He gave her a slow smile. "Babe, I'll give you anything you want."

She pretended to think about it. "How about ten bucks?"

He laughed. "Hey, I don't want to take your money."

She chewed her lower lip. "But I really think I can make this one."

He shrugged his shoulders. "Okay, but it's tougher than it looks."

She pointed at the table with her cue stick. "Ten dollars says I can sink it in that hole over there."

He gave her an indulgent smile. "It's called the corner pocket."

"That's right. I keep forgetting." She took careful aim once more, then executed her shot. The eight ball bounced against the cushion three times, then rolled away from the pocket.

"Too bad," Viper said cheerfully. "It came mighty close."

She feigned a frown. "No do-overs?"

"No way." He grinned and held out his hand. "You owe me ten bucks."

She retrieved her purse from the table and pulled out a ten. "Well, if you won't let me shoot over, at least give me a chance to win my money back. Let's play another game, double or nothing."

He chuckled. "Hey, if you want to make another donation to the Viper Foundation, I'm not going to argue with you. Rack 'em up."

NOAH STRODE into Ducky's Bar. It took a moment for his eyes to adjust to the dim interior. In contrast to the hot, bright August afternoon, it was dark and cool inside. An elderly man sat at the bar nursing a frosty mug of beer. The bartender stood across from his customer, engrossed in a crossword puzzle. The whir of the ceiling fans blended with the honkytonk music emanating from the jukebox.

The only other activity in the place was at the pool table in the far corner. He heard a familiar laugh and his pulse quickened. Sabrina. He could hear her but he couldn't see her, due to the large man at the pool table blocking his view.

Relief at finding her battled with irritation. Didn't she know he had better things to do than chase after her? Didn't she know that Ducky's Bar was no place for a woman alone? He stalked toward the pool table, ready to inform her of a few facts of life.

Then he saw her and stopped dead in his tracks. She wore a sassy red halter dress that hugged her slender waist, flared out at her hips, and revealed much more of her cleavage than was necessary. Especially to the leering cretin playing pool with her.

"This is it," she said, unaware of Noah approaching behind her. "Eight ball in the side pocket."

Her burly opponent wiped his brow. "You're really a fast learner."

She looked up and gave him a brilliant smile. "That's because you're such a good teacher, Viper. I especially liked your lesson on how to *stroke* it just right."

Viper let the beer can slip from his grasp at the same moment she drew back her cue stick. The can clattered loudly on the tile floor, foamy beer spilling out of the top.

"Whoops." He gave her a sheepish smile. "Sorry."

She backed away from the table and chalked her cue. "No problem."

"Don't forget," Viper admonished, as she lined up for the shot once more. "There's eighty bucks riding on this shot. Not to pressure you or anything."

She glanced up at him. "Eighty? I think you mean a hundred, don't you?"

He winced. "Oh, yeah, I guess you're right. A hundred."

Noah watched in fascination as she focused her total concentration on the pool table. Then she took her shot, neatly pocketing the eight ball.

Viper sagged against the table. "Damn."

She replaced her stick on the rack, then walked over to him, holding out her hand. "It's been a pleasure playing with you."

Viper grumbled under his breath as he drew out his wallet, then grudgingly counted out five twenty-dollar bills. Tossing his stick on the table, he grabbed his beer and headed for the bar.

Sabrina tapped the bills together, then turned around, her face paling the instant she saw him. "Noah! What are you doing here?"

"You invited me, remember?" He looked pointedly at the money in her hands. "The question is, where the hell did you learn to play pool like that?"

She shrugged her shoulders, not quite meeting his gaze. "I just got lucky."

He nodded to the bills in her hand. "And made a tidy chunk of change."

"I'm going to add it to the reward money for Beauty." She opened her purse and stuffed the money into it.

Viper walked up to them, another beer in his

hand and a fierce scowl on his face. "This guy bothering you, Sabrina?"

"No. I'm fine, Viper. Really."

Viper turned to Noah and stuck out his jaw. "You got any ID?"

"You're joking, right?"

Viper took another step closer to him. "Do I look like I'm joking?"

Sabrina quickly stepped between them. "I'll vouch for him, Viper. This is Noah Callahan. He's Trace's brother."

Noah arched a brow. "You know Trace?"

Viper crossed his arms across his massive chest. "He just married my cousin. I'm Viper D'Onofrio. We missed you at the wedding."

"Something came up," Noah muttered, wondering if Trace had actually met cousin Viper. This was the reason a man shouldn't rush into marriage. Who knew what kind of unsavory relatives might pop out of the woodwork? As if having Ramon for a brother-in-law wasn't bad enough.

"'Something came up'?" Viper echoed. "Man, that's lame. Weren't you supposed to be the best man?"

"It's a long story," Noah clipped out.

The bartender leaned across the bar and shouted, "Hey, Viper, phone for you."

After he left, Noah escorted Sabrina to the nearest table. "Now I want to know exactly what you're doing here." He sat down across from her. "Other than getting lucky at pool."

"Since we only have a few days left to find Niles, I thought this would be a good place to start."

He looked around the empty bar. "I don't see him here."

She glared at him. "I know that. The problem is he's not anywhere. So I started thinking."

"Uh-oh."

"Very funny." She arched a brow. "Do you want me to go on or not?"

"Please," he said, as his knee lightly pressed against hers under the table. He pretended not to notice the contact, even though it sent tiny shock waves through his leg. She didn't move. Neither did he.

"Well, I started thinking about your phobia about picking the wrong woman."

He scowled. "Phobia? I wouldn't go that far. Besides, I thought we were talking about Niles—a man who definitely picked the wrong woman."

"A mistake he was apparently trying to rectify when he signed up to have his coffee grounds read at Café Romeo. After our dinner at the Vienna House, he asked me to have a drink with him at Ducky's. So I thought I'd take a chance he was a regular here."

"And?"

She beamed. "And I was right."

His heart beat erratically in the glow of her smile. Just another sign this woman wouldn't be good for him.

She leaned toward him. "According to Viper, Niles was in here with a different woman almost every week."

He whistled low. "Fooling around on Doris? Sounds like the worm likes to live dangerously. Frankly, I'm surprised she let him out of the house that often. She had to be suspicious."

Sabrina shook her head. "He had an alibi. Niles volunteered at the community playhouse. He painted scenery, built props, even performed a non-speaking role once or twice. Some of the stagehands are regulars at Ducky's. That's how Niles found the place. They invited him to join them for a beer one night after a show."

"How does Viper know all this?"

A smile played on her lips. "Oh, he remembers Niles very well. It seems alcohol doesn't agree with him and he returned his beer and asked for a full refund."

"So?"

"So he'd already chugged the beer. He returned it by upchucking it all over Viper. Niles was so grateful to Ducky when she stepped in to save him from certain annihilation that he kept coming back. Until three weeks ago."

"Does Viper have any clue where to find him?"

She shook her head. "No, but he did give me the name of the guy Niles hung around with the most. Even better, he gave me an address."

"So where do we go from here?" he asked, noting the excited glitter in her eye.

"The city morgue."

8

THE NEXT DAY, Noah stood with Sabrina outside the city morgue. She turned to him, her green eyes gleaming with excitement. "I've got a really good feeling about this."

He couldn't help but smile at her enthusiasm. "You said the same thing about that mental hospital, remember? But we didn't find Niles there, either."

"You're the one who said any man crazy enough to marry Doris Dooley belongs in a mental hospital. I was just following through on your hunch."

"Actually, I said any man crazy enough to *marry* belongs in a mental hospital." He followed her up the long flight of concrete steps that led to the entrance, definitely enjoying the view from behind. But then, he enjoyed viewing Sabrina Lovett from every angle.

Surprisingly, he also enjoyed spending time with her. His previous relationships with women had always been based on physical attraction alone, since he'd never been interested in much more than a weekend fling.

But Sabrina was different.

Because of his self-inflicted vow of abstinence, he'd done things with her that he'd never done with other women. Like staying up past midnight playing Scrabble, with dirty words counting double. Or enjoying an old-movie marathon, complete with hot buttered popcorn and chocolate malts. Just last night, they'd snuck into the kitchen of Café Romeo and indulged in the chocolate-chip cookie dough chilling in the refrigerator.

Tonight, he'd need to find another distraction. Maybe he'd teach her how to play poker. He'd initiated these "safe" pursuits to keep his mind off certain other activities. He'd certainly never expected to have so much fun in the process.

Sabrina paused by the double doors in front of the morgue, the sun making fiery streaks glint in her hair. The breeze swirled her blue broom skirt around her legs and a tiny locket nestled in the V-neck of her white blouse. A slow smile curved her mouth. "Ready?"

Something shifted inside of him. Something…*unusual.* He tried to shake it off as he held the door open for her. He told himself he was probably coming down with the flu as he followed her inside.

A heavy, disinfectant odor permeated the air. He wrinkled his nose. "Maybe I should wait right here."

"Chicken?" she teased, taking a step closer to him.

"Of course not." He glanced uneasily down the

long sterile hallway. "I just think we should consider our strategy. This is a delicate situation."

She laughed. "You *are* chicken."

"Look, all we know about this guy is that his name is Lou Murillo and that he and Niles used to hang out together."

"Maybe we should have called first."

He shook his head. "The best way to get information from people is to catch them off guard. Trust me."

She looked steadily into his eyes. "I do."

Her words should have scared him. The expression on her face should have sent him into a panic. Instead, he experienced a slight inward shift again, like someone trying to find his sea legs on a gently rocking boat.

"Good," he said, trying to keep his focus. "Then I think it's best if *you* wait here."

She frowned. "Why?"

"Because Lou might be more willing to open up to me, you know, man-to-man. He'll be too nervous if you're there." Hell, she made *him* nervous, and he'd been around beautiful women all his adult life.

"Am I that intimidating?"

"That's not exactly the word I'd use to describe you." He reached out one hand to brush the hair gently off her temple.

Her green eyes softened at his touch. "Tell me."

"If I do, will you wait in the hallway while I interview Lou?"

Her eyes narrowed. "You don't play fair."

"Remember that when we play poker tonight. So what's it going to be?"

She regarded him thoughtfully. "If you really think it's best, I'll wait out here. I'd rather be the one grilling Lou, but all that really matters to me is getting Beauty back."

He winked at her, then turned down the hallway. "Wish me luck."

"Hey, wait a minute," she called after him, "what's the word?"

Noah turned around, walking backward now so he could see her. "What word?"

She made an impatient gesture with her hands. "The word you'd use to describe me."

"Oh, that word."

"Well?"

"I'd say you're…perfect."

Her mouth fell open and he grinned as he made a quick escape around the corner. Then he cleared his throat and sobered his expression, telling himself he shouldn't be this cheerful in a morgue.

He walked down another long, narrow hallway, following the posted signs and acutely aware of the loud echo of his shoes on the concrete floor. Another set of double doors led to a small reception area, where he was met by a cool blast from an air-conditioner vent in the ceiling and an even cooler blonde at the reception desk. She wore a killer red dress with lipstick to match.

Finally, a woman with the right dimensions to take his mind off Sabrina. Only the longer he looked at her, the more he realized she didn't entice him at all.

A surge of alarm ran through him. Something was wrong. Something was very wrong. He liked cool blondes. In fact, they'd always been at the top of his list. He took a deep breath and stared into her curious blue eyes. Nothing. Nada. Zilch.

"May I help you?" Her voice was low and throaty.

And it didn't affect him a bit. He took another deep breath, telling himself not to panic. This was a fluke. An aberration. It didn't mean he was falling for Sabrina. And it certainly didn't mean he'd never find another woman attractive.

She arched a thin, blond brow. "Sir?"

He cleared his throat, desperately trying to summon up an impromptu fantasy about the blonde. But the only woman in his fantasies had auburn hair and green eyes and an incredibly luscious mouth. This was bad. This was very bad.

"Should I call a doctor?"

"No," he said, collecting himself. A doctor would only make matters worse when he discovered the sultry blonde hadn't raised Noah's pulse even a fraction of a beat. "I'm perfectly fine."

It was a lie. He wasn't fine. If he was fine, he'd be flirting with this woman. Admiring her figure. Paying her compliments and angling for a date. But he didn't have the energy or the desire to do anything of those things.

It was pathetic.

Especially since he'd been intensely aware of Sabrina all week. The way her hair smelled like apples. The way her forehead crinkled whenever she was deep in thought. The way she licked the butter off her fingers when they shared a big bowl of popcorn. Even worse, he dreamed about her. Hot, murky dreams that prominently featured her long legs and her unforgettable face and everything in between.

He tugged at his collar, wondering when the air conditioner had shut off. Then he looked at the receptionist, not surprised to find her still staring at him. "I'm looking for a man."

She opened the file folder on her desk. "Dead or alive?"

"Preferably alive. His name is Lou Murillo."

She stiffened, then slowly closed the file in front of her and stood up. "Follow me, please."

As he trailed after her down another long hallway, his despair deepened. The slow swing of her hips had absolutely no effect on him. He might as well throw his little black book away. Or maybe he should auction it off—earn enough money for a getaway to a tropical paradise where he could forget all about Sabrina.

The receptionist led him into a small, windowless break room. An old refrigerator hummed in one corner, next to a small table littered with candy wrappers. He watched as she stared at the empty wastebasket for a long, silent moment, then turned to face him. "Why do you want to see Lou?"

"It's personal."

She smiled coyly at him. "You can tell me."

"Sorry." He forced a smile, tired of wasting time. Especially since Sabrina was cooling her heels in the hallway.

She laughed. "You don't understand. *I* am Lou Murillo."

This time his smile was genuine. "As in Louise Murillo?"

"No. As in Louis Anthony Murillo. I'm a female impersonator. In other words, a man."

His jaw sagged. *A man.* The woman standing in front of him with the Marilyn Monroe measurements was really a man.

Lou's smile widened. "I really had you fooled, didn't I?"

"Completely." Then realization sunk in. He hadn't been attracted to the blond bombshell receptionist because the blond bombshell was really a man. Relief flooded him. He sank down into a empty chair, relishing the fact that he hadn't been the least bit attracted to Lou. He'd known there had to be a logical explanation for his lack of interest.

And it was so simple. She was a man.

Noah sagged back against the chair. "I can't tell you how happy I am to hear that."

Lou sat down across from him. "I like your attitude. Most men aren't too thrilled when I tell them. Especially if they've been trying to look down my blouse."

"Hey, that's their problem."

"So what brings you here...I'm sorry, I didn't catch your name."

"Noah. Noah Callahan." He held out his hand, mildly surprised when Lou responded with a firm, hearty shake. "I'm an insurance investigator, but this isn't about business."

"Damn," Lou muttered, tugging hard on a blond curl. "Sorry, this stupid wig slips sometimes. Now, how can I help you?"

"I'm looking for man by the name of Niles Dooley."

Lou blinked. "Niles? Why?"

"He seems to be missing."

"Seems to be?"

"He disappeared three weeks ago and no one has seen or heard from him since. His wife believes he ran off and left her."

"I've never met his wife," Lou said, crossing one long leg over the other. "Niles and I spent most of our time together hitting the bars. He was always on the prowl."

"What about you? Or did you go as a..."

"A woman?" Lou smiled. "No. I didn't start dressing as a woman on a regular basis until I needed a job. Despite the fact that I excelled in all areas at secretarial school, most companies want a pretty face at the reception desk."

Noah wasn't certain why that was necessary at a morgue, but they'd veered far enough off topic already. "So Niles liked the ladies?"

Lou shrugged. "He certainly liked their money.

But he didn't get lucky too often. Especially with his wife. At least, that's what he claimed.''

"So you're not surprised he left her?"

"I'm surprised he married her in the first place. He certainly didn't act like a married man. Although, he didn't like working either, so I guess he needed someone to support him."

Noah sat back in his chair. "How long have you known Niles?"

"Since *Seven Brides For Seven Brothers*." Lou grinned. "That's a musical that ran at the theater a couple of years ago. Niles was the prop man and I played one of the brothers."

Noah arched a brow. "You look more like the bride type to me."

"Thanks. I hadn't perfected the female routine yet. It's harder than it looks."

"I can imagine," Noah said dryly.

"Niles actually helped me quite a bit. He has a good eye for color and helped me pick out the right wigs and clothes and makeup."

"Too bad he has such bad taste in wives."

Lou frowned. "Yeah. I'm worried about him. I can't believe he'd just leave town without telling me."

"Do you have any idea where I might find him?"

"None. In fact, the more I think about it, the stranger it seems. If he did leave, he sure wouldn't get very far. He told me once that Doris controlled all their money. She used to give him an allowance. Twenty dollars a week. Can you believe it?"

Noah pondered that for a moment. "He couldn't get very far on twenty bucks a week, even if he'd been saving for a while."

"Tell me about it," Lou said. "And I doubt he saved anything, because a few times he had to borrow money from me. He always paid me back, though."

Noah rubbed his jaw, thoroughly frustrated. "If you do hear from him, will you give me a call?" He handed Lou his business card.

"Sure thing," Lou said, pocketing the card. "But if you want my opinion, maybe you shouldn't be looking for Niles. Maybe you should be looking for Niles's body."

THAT EVENING, Sabrina decided to come clean. Noah had thrown her for a loop at the morgue when he'd accused her of being perfect. She wasn't perfect. Not by a long shot.

And he needed to know the truth. At first, she'd wanted to conceal it from him so he'd fall in love with her. Now she realized she didn't want Noah's love under false pretenses. She wanted him to fall in love with the real Sabrina Lovett. Not with the woman she'd pretended to be.

Only, she couldn't seem to find the words to tell him about her past. He, on the other hand, couldn't seem to stop talking. First, about the female impersonator he'd found in the morgue, then about his brothers, his job, his hobbies and his friends. She'd learned a lot about Noah in the last few hours.

And it only made her want him more.

"It's your bet." Noah sat at Sophie's kitchen table, slowly fanning open the playing cards in his hand.

A sultry breeze sifted through the open windows and a chorus of crickets welcomed the full moon. Sabrina stared at her cards as the ceiling fan whirred above her.

"Is something wrong?" He leaned forward. "You've hardly said a word since we left the morgue."

She lowered her cards and cleared her throat. "I'm fine."

"You're disappointed," he countered. "Because we're no closer to Niles than before. That's it, isn't it?"

She licked her lips, feeling guilty because her mind hadn't been on Niles at all. Or even on Beauty. Just more proof that she was a horrible person.

"Don't give up," he said, "there's still one day left. In fact, this can be over tomorrow. I'll loan you the ransom money."

She blinked at him. *"Five thousand dollars?"*

"It's no hardship. I've built up my savings over the years." He looked sheepish. "I probably should have offered the money to you in the first place. If anything happens to your cat…"

She swallowed hard. "I can't take your money."

"I want to help you, Sabrina. These last few days have been…" His voice trailed off, then he said softly, "It's just that I've never met a woman like you before."

That was an understatement. She squared her shoulders. This was the moment to tell him everything. To lay her cards on the table—figuratively and literally.

She could start at the beginning. Tell him how she'd started falling for him when she was just a child. How Noah had filled her girlish dreams and assuaged her loneliness. How her plans to someday travel to St. Louis and meet him had fallen apart when she was sixteen. That's when her mother's performances as a contortionist had been curtailed by arthritis. Her mother needed expensive medication and with her father barely able to keep the carnival afloat financially, Sabrina needed to find some way to help her family.

That's when her life had taken an entirely different turn.

She cleared her throat. "You don't really know me, Noah."

He smiled. That bone-melting smile that was so reminiscent of the seven-year-old boy in the picture.

"I know you're one stubborn woman," he said. "And smart. Beautiful. Sexy." His gaze softened on her. "And I know I can't resist you anymore."

Her heart flipped over in her chest. She dropped her gaze to her cards and took a deep, steadying breath. "Is it my bet?"

He studied her for a moment, then leaned back in his chair. "I just raised you two toothpicks."

"Oh." She stared at her cards, not really seeing them. Noah wanted her. Finally. So why didn't she do something about it? Throw herself into his arms, for instance. The answer was simple.

She was a fake.

"The secret of this game is the bluff," he said, misinterpreting her silence. "You don't want to give away the strength or weakness of your hand to your opponent. That way I won't know if you're risking ten toothpicks on a royal flush or a pair of deuces."

She glanced down at the table. "I only have one toothpick left."

He grinned. "Then you'll have to bet something else."

"You already know I don't have any money."

"Hmm," he mused, staring up at the ceiling, "what else could you bet?" Then a mischievous twinkle lit his blue eyes. "I know. Ever play strip poker?"

Sabrina opened her mouth, then closed it again. If she wasn't brave enough to tell him the truth, maybe she could show him. "You're on."

An hour later, Sabrina had lost two earrings and a shoe. Noah had lost his shoes, his socks, his watch, his shirt and his belt. Now he was down to his pants, and he didn't look happy about it.

"This isn't as much fun as I thought it would be."

Her gaze centered on his broad, bare chest. "I'm having a great time."

He shook his head. "I've heard of beginner's luck, but this is ridiculous."

"It's your bet," she reminded him.

He looked at his hand, then rubbed one finger over his square chin. "Your luck has just run out, Sabrina. I'll see your shoe and raise my pants."

She smiled. "Now there's an intriguing picture. I'll call your bet."

He frowned. "Are you sure you want to do that?"

"Positive."

He tossed his cards on the table. "A pair of fours."

"Good one." She fanned her cards out in front of him. "Only not good enough. I have aces over sixes." Then she leaned back in her chair. "Take your pants off, Callahan."

"Where have I heard that before?" he said as he rose to his feet.

Sabrina's mouth went dry as his hands went to the waistband of his jeans. She should stop him now, tell him he'd never stood a chance in the first place. Unfortunately, she'd never been good at resisting temptation.

She cupped her chin in her hand. "Will I see Mighty Mouse again?"

He unzipped his jeans. "Something much better. And hotter."

"Be still, my heart." Only she wasn't joking. Her heart was beating an erratic tattoo in her chest and she couldn't quite catch her breath.

Noah shoved his jeans to his ankles, then stepped out of them. No Mighty Mouse this time. Instead he wore a pair of light blue boxer shorts imprinted with race cars.

She'd done it. She'd stripped him naked. Well, almost naked. Now it was her turn.

"Now it's your turn," he said, echoing her thoughts as he moved toward her.

She rose unsteadily to her feet. "Noah, I…"

He caught her and kissed her before she could say another word. His strong arms wrapped around her, pulling her close enough to feel the warmth of his body. Her fingers splayed over his bare back as his mouth devoured her own.

She closed her eyes, growing dizzy with the kiss and the lack of air and the knowledge that Noah wanted her. Really wanted her. His fingers threaded through her hair, then cupped her face as he abandoned her mouth to scatter kisses over her nose and forehead and chin.

"I've wanted to do this forever," he breathed against her neck. "At least it seems like forever."

"I know," she murmured, leaning bonelessly against him. "I know."

He pulled back just far enough to trace the curve of her cheek. "You're perfect."

She stiffened, then backed out of his arms. "You're wrong, Noah. I'm not perfect. I'm far from perfect."

He tilted his head. "In what way?"

She took a deep breath, the pain of the truth cutting into her like a knife. "Well, for starters, I know how to bluff. In fact, I've been doing it all week."

His brows drew together in confusion. "Doing what?"

"Bluffing. About everything." She gave a small shrug. "Well, almost everything."

The coolness she felt in the room wasn't coming from the open windows. Noah stared at her for a long, uncomfortable moment. "Such as?"

She forced herself to meet his gaze. "I have no idea how to read coffee grounds. Madame Sophia has explained it numerous times, but they just look like sludge in the bottom of the cup to me. That's why I screwed up the first time. Seeing something that wasn't really there."

"And the second time?"

She swallowed. "Wishful thinking. I wanted it to be you. And by then, I knew I didn't have any real talent for it. I think I just saw what I wanted to see."

He frowned. "I don't understand. You didn't even know me."

"No, but I knew all about you from Madame Sophia's letters. I think I started falling in love with you years ago, or at least, with my fantasy of you."

He arched a brow. "I take it I didn't live up to the fantasy."

Her gaze traveled over his barely clad body. "Oh, Noah, you far exceed any fantasy I've ever had."

He moved closer to her, his taut expression relaxing. "So what's the problem? I've had a few fantasies myself. Who cares about the stupid coffee grounds? The important thing is how we feel about each other now."

She tipped up her chin. "How do you feel about the fact that I used to hustle pool for a living?"

He blinked. "What?"

"And poker. Did you know you have a 'tell'? Whenever you're bluffing, you rub your chin. I've become quite good at spotting tells over the years, although pool was where I made the most money."

"Like at Ducky's?"

She nodded. "Viper made a perfect pigeon. Cocky and overconfident. Easy pickings."

"Just like me," he murmured, more to himself than to her.

She motioned helplessly toward the table. "Tonight was just for fun."

"Fun," he echoed flatly. Then he glanced down at his boxer shorts. "Guess I turned out to be easy pickings, too."

She could feel him slipping away from her. "Please let me explain."

"I think I've already heard more than enough. Let me keep a few illusions."

"Don't you even want to know why I started hustling? Or why I stopped?"

"It doesn't matter."

Before she could explain, the kitchen door swung open. Ramon walked in, took one look at Noah standing there in his boxer shorts, then stopped short. "Gee, I hope I'm not interrupting anything."

A muscle flickered in Noah's jaw, but he didn't take his eyes off Sabrina. "Actually, your timing couldn't be better."

"I hope you still feel that way when I tell you about the explosion."

Noah whirled around. "What explosion?"

"At Café Romeo. But don't worry, the fire department got the flames under control pretty fast."

"Fire department?" Noah grabbed his pants off the floor, hastily stepping into them. "Why the hell didn't you call me?"

Ramon stuck out his chin. "You left me specific instructions not to bother you tonight. I wasn't even supposed to be working, remember? But you insisted."

"Save the excuses, Ramon," he said, pulling his T-shirt over his head. "Just tell me what happened. Was anyone hurt?"

"No. It was almost closing time when the fire started."

"What the hell happened?" Noah asked between clenched teeth.

Sabrina clutched the chair, desperately hoping Café Romeo hadn't burned to the ground. "Please tell us, Ramon."

He shrugged. "The fireman said it was probably a wiring defect in that new cappuccino machine. The cord burst into flames, so I immediately called 911."

"That's it?" Noah glared at him. "Just the cord?"

"And a stack of coffee filters. There might have been some napkins scorched, too. It was a very traumatic event in my life. It's all kind of blurry."

Noah sighed as he slipped his bare feet into his running shoes, leaving his socks on the floor. "I'd better run down there and take a look."

"Do I have to come with you?" Ramon asked.

"Yes." Then Noah turned to her. "I have to go."

"I know."

He hesitated on his way out the door. "Will you be all right here?"

Her throat tightened. "Don't worry about me. I know how to take care of myself."

9

"YOU REALLY BLEW IT this time," Sabrina muttered to herself as she drove through the quiet suburban streets of St. Louis. The muted roar of the Nova's muffler accompanied her self-recriminations. She'd blown it with Noah. Big-time. Part of her wanted to spend the next three months in bed, surrounded by boxes of tissue and chocolates. Another part of her was glad she'd finally come clean. She might not be perfect, but she'd learned from her mistakes. And she truly was trying to change.

That was the main reason she'd come to St. Louis. Hustling might have helped support her vagabond parents and paid her way through college, but it was hardly a way of life. At least, not the kind of life she'd always dreamed about.

She wanted the white picket fence and the swing set in the backyard. A tree house for her kids to play in with their friends. She wanted a job that kept her fulfilled and challenged, one that used the skills she'd perfected in business school. Most of all, she wanted a husband who looked forward to coming

home to her every night. A father for her children.
A lover who fulfilled all her fantasies.

A soul mate to share the rest of her life with.

Sabrina turned into another subdivision, lights
glowing in the windows of the snug houses. She'd
wanted to live in a place like this so badly when
she was growing up. Other children might have en-
vied her life on the road, but in all her twenty-four
years Sabrina had never had a home to call her own.

As the car rounded a corner, its headlights illuminated another house. A salmon-pink house. Doris
Dooley's house. She pulled slowly along the curb,
then shifted into park, letting the Nova idle. She
hadn't consciously decided to come here when
she'd gotten into her car tonight. But now that she
was here...

She cut the engine, then got out of the car. No
lights shone in the front windows of the Dooley
house. And the black pickup truck wasn't in the
driveway. Which meant Doris must be working.

Giving Sabrina the perfect opportunity to finish
her search.

Her pulse picked up as she walked purposefully
toward the backyard. This had gone on long
enough. She needed to find Beauty, or at least find
some evidence of where Doris had hidden her.

She climbed over the fence, then fished a paper
clip out of her pocket. Noah might no longer think
she was perfect, but she couldn't mold herself into
some cookie-cutter design of the perfect woman.
Not that such a creature even existed.

Her past life was a part of her. And it wasn't all bad. She'd learned how to hot-wire cars from a friend in Istanbul. In Paris, she'd haunted the art museums, absorbing the history and the culture of ages past. In Madrid, she'd kissed her first boy. A handsome charmer by the name of Rafael. He'd even asked her to marry him.

Only she'd long ago set her heart on someone else.

But if Noah couldn't accept her for herself, then maybe he wasn't her perfect match, after all. Maybe she was better off without him. Even if her heart literally ached at the thought.

She knelt down in front of the sliding glass door, slipping the unbent paper clip into the keyhole. A few deft twists, and the lock clicked. She slid the door open a crack and peered into the kitchen, the oven light illuminating enough of the room to assure her it was empty.

She stepped silently inside, closing the door behind her. The house was completely quiet and dark. Moving stealthily past the sink and refrigerator, she pulled open another door that led to a steep wooden staircase.

With one last look over her shoulder, she started down the steps that led to the basement.

"HEY, CALLAHAN, sounds like you had a little excitement here tonight."

Noah looked up from the coffee bar to see Ty

Burke framed in the doorway of Café Romeo. "How'd you find out about it?"

"I heard it on the scanner and thought I'd stop by after my shift ended and check out the damage. You know I can't live without my espresso and biscotti."

"Your breakfast is safe." He held up a fried cord. "The cappuccino machine bit the dust. Faulty wiring."

Burke leaned over the coffee bar. "Looks like you might want to file a claim with the insurance company."

"Thanks for the advice," Noah said dryly.

Ramon walked through the swinging kitchen doors, his eyes going wide when he saw the detective. He held up his hands. "Hey, I'm innocent. I didn't do anything."

"Relax, Ramon," Burke replied. "I'm not here to arrest you."

"Oh." Ramon lowered his hands. "Sorry. It's sort of an automatic reflex for a D'Onofrio."

Noah turned to him. "Why don't you go into the office and write up your account of the incident. We'll need it when we file the claim."

"Will do," Ramon said, then headed toward the back of the coffeehouse. "I know just how I'm going to start my story—'It was the best of cappuccino machines, it was the worst of cappuccino machines....'"

Noah waited until he was out of earshot. "I suppose I should mention that I came down here tonight because I thought the fire might have been started intentionally.''

Burke arched a brow. ''By whom?''

Noah shrugged. ''Ramon came to mind, but despite his...idiosyncrasies, I don't believe he's a violent person. Not intentionally, anyway,'' he added, remembering the power-saw incident involving Ramon and his brother Trace.

''Who else then?''

''Doris Dooley.''

Burke looked steadily at him. ''You know, after the last time we talked, I decided to do a little research on your friend Doris.''

''Find anything interesting?''

''As a matter of fact, I did. She's filed five harassment complaints in the last year.''

Noah blinked. ''Five?''

''That's right. And all of them against women. Single women.''

''Can you give me any names?''

He shook his head. ''Sorry, confidential. But I was curious myself, so I made some contacts. I reached three of the women. They were reluctant to talk about it at first, but gradually I learned their stories. One had met Niles Dooley through a video-dating service, the other two through the personal ads in the newspaper.''

Noah whistled low. ''Same M.O. he used on Sabrina. Sounds like Niles really got around.''

''That's right. He'd present himself as a single man looking for love. Only Doris always found out about it. Then she made sure the women paid for 'stealing' her husband. And I mean *paid,* in the literal sense.''

This sounded all too familiar. ''Extortion?''

Burke shrugged. ''None of the women would say the word, but it was pretty clear what Doris's game was when I put all their stories together. She'd simply harass and intimidate them until they paid to shut her up.''

''So go arrest her. That's illegal, isn't it?''

''Definitely. But I don't have any solid evidence. Not one of the women will come forward. They all want to put it behind them. Frankly, I think they fear retaliation from Doris.''

''With good reason,'' Noah muttered. ''What about Sabrina? She can provide proof. Doris is holding her cat for ransom.''

''First, answer me a few questions.'' Burke folded his arms across his chest. ''Did you enter the Dooley house under false pretenses? Did you take your pants off in front of Doris? How was Sabrina involved?''

Noah opened his mouth, then closed it again. He wasn't about to squeal on Sabrina for breaking and entering. No matter how much she'd screwed up his life. He was still reeling from her revelations this evening. He hated secrets. Hated lies even more. But she hadn't technically lied to him. He'd just never bothered to ask her about her past.

Great, he was rationalizing now. That was a bad sign.

"I'm still waiting," Burke prodded.

"I'm taking the fifth."

"I thought so." Burke leveled his perceptive gaze on him. "Look, I realize Doris has probably made your lives hell, but until I have solid proof, I can't do anything about it. Otherwise, it's just your word against hers, and you two aren't exactly squeaky-clean, either."

"What kind of proof do you need?"

A wry smile tipped up his mouth. "A written confession would be nice."

"Fat chance. But you might want to contact a guy by the name of Lou Murillo who works at the city morgue. He's an old friend of Niles's. Lou suspects foul play in his disappearance."

"What about you?"

"I suspect Niles finally hooked up with a rich woman who's willing to support him and is long gone."

Burke pulled out his notepad. "Spell Lou's last name for me."

"M-u-r-i-l-l-o. He's got blond hair, blue eyes and great legs."

Burke looked at him askance. "Is there something I should know?"

"Lou Murillo is a female impersonator. So don't get too hot and bothered when you see her. I mean him."

Burke flipped his notepad shut. "Speaking of hot, try to keep Sabrina out of trouble. It sounds like you've both crossed the line a time or two already."

Noah nodded, then looked up at his friend. "How soon did you know you loved Margo?"

Burke's brows rose up to his hairline. "Where did *that* come from?"

"It's just a simple question."

"Well, let's see, the first time I met Margo..."

"I was with you," Noah interjected, "so you can skip the preliminaries. In fact, I'm the one who introduced you, remember?"

Burke laughed. "I remember she turned you down flat when you tried out one of your lame pickup lines on her at that sports bar."

"I was just trying to make you look good."

"You succeeded. To this day, she still thanks me for rescuing her."

Noah scowled. "Very funny. Seriously, though, when did you know?"

Burke slid onto a bar stool. "Seriously? It would have to be the night she got sick in my car."

Noah blanched. "Not your Maserati."

"The very one. We'd been out to a new restaurant downtown. On the way home I found out Mediterranean food doesn't agree with her."

"Your black Maserati with the turbo engine?" Noah asked, just for clarification.

Burke nodded. "That's when I knew for sure."

"Knew what?"

His brown eyes softened. "That I'd fallen in love with her."

Noah looked around the empty coffeehouse, then

back at the detective. "Am I missing something here?"

"Don't you get it, Callahan? I was more worried about Margo than my car."

"But you love that car."

"Exactly. Only I love Margo more. A hell of a lot more." He glanced at his watch, then rose off the bar stool. "Speaking of which, I should have been home twenty minutes ago."

Noah locked the front door after him, then retrieved Ramon from the office.

"I'm up to seven pages on my story already," Ramon boasted as they walked out the back entrance. "And I haven't even gotten to the good part yet."

Noah half listened to Ramon's ramblings as he drove back to Sophie's place, pulling up in front of the garage where Sabrina usually kept her Nova. It was after midnight and most of the lights were out in the house.

Ramon yawned as they walked up to the back door. "Sabrina must be in bed already."

Noah didn't know whether to be disappointed or relieved. On the one hand, he wanted time to think over everything she'd told him. On the other hand, he itched to see her again.

But when he walked inside, he found the main level deserted. He started for the staircase, then abruptly changed his mind.

It was late and he was exhausted. Probably not the best time to make any snap decisions. Tomorrow morning would be soon enough to tell Sabrina exactly how he felt.

SABRINA CREPT SLOWLY down the Dooleys' basement stairway, feeling her way along the wooden railing in the darkness. When she reached the landing, she moved her hand along the wall, searching for a light switch. She encountered dust and several cobwebs before she finally found it.

She flipped the switch and a bare lightbulb, hanging from the ceiling, illuminated the dank, cluttered basement. Crates and boxes lined the old plaster walls, and a pink feather boa hung haphazardly out of one of them. An old makeup mirror stood in one corner, next to a naked, headless mannequin. Sections of scenery and stage props lay scattered across the floor.

It looked like Niles had done more than volunteer at the theater. He'd actually brought bits and pieces of it home with him. The dank, dusty air invaded her nostrils, making her sneeze.

Then she heard a plaintive meow.

"Beauty?" She hurried across the basement, tripping over a broken piano stool. She hit the rough cement floor, scraping her knees. But the angle allowed her to see Beauty. She was caged in a large pet carrier buried under a stack of rolled-up rugs.

Sabrina rushed to open the latch on the door, then Beauty flew into her arms. Tears stung her eyes as she hugged her cat close, hearing that familiar purr emanating from Beauty's furry chest.

"How are you?" Sabrina whispered, stroking Beauty's head and scratching behind her ears. Beauty closed her eyes in ecstasy.

Her hand snagged on a collar that hadn't been there before. A narrow rhinestone collar interspersed with silver filigree links. Sabrina bent down to look in the cage. "Did she take good care of you, baby?"

A small dish full of anchovies sat near the front of the carrier, as well as a bowl of clean water. The box was surprisingly clean, leading Sabrina to believe her beloved pet hadn't been trapped in there the entire time.

Rising up once again, she cradled Beauty in her arms. "We're getting out of here."

Beauty meowed in acquiescence, nestling her head against Sabrina's collarbone.

Her throat tightened as she moved toward the stairs. She'd suppressed her fears for so long that now they threatened to burst forth. She'd lost Beauty, then found her again. And tonight she'd lost Noah—possibly forever.

"Be very quiet now," Sabrina instructed Beauty as she climbed carefully up the steep stairs. She winced at each creak, which seemed louder now than before.

Reaching the landing at last, she pushed open the narrow door and stepped into the kitchen. A man stood at the sink, his attention drawn to the squeaking door.

He screamed. So did she. Beauty emitted an affronted howl as Sabrina pressed the cat close to her chest.

Niles Dooley placed both hands on the counter-top, taking deep, uneven breaths. "You scared me to death!"

Sabrina's heart nearly burst out of her chest. She loosened her grip on Beauty as a thousand questions raced through her mind. She decided to start with the most obvious one. "What are you doing here?"

He was barefoot, wearing a white undershirt and a pair of ragged denim cutoffs. "I live here."

She took a step toward him. "But you've been missing for weeks!"

He turned to her, faint smudges, almost like faded bruises, under his eyes. "I came home last night. To tell you the truth, my money ran out, so I didn't have much choice in the matter."

"Does Doris know?"

He gave a brisk nod. "We talked. Or maybe I should say, she yelled and I listened." He glanced over his shoulder. "Look, Sabrina, my wife could come home at any minute. You'd better leave before she finds you here."

"Your wife took my cat," Sabrina informed him. "And held her for ransom."

He nodded. "I know. Look, I'm sorry about all the trouble. If it makes you feel any better, Doris really took a liking to your cat. She even bought it a new collar and a bunch of cat toys this morning."

"No, it doesn't make me feel any better. It makes

me believe she had no intention of giving Beauty back!''

"Well, she is a little possessive..."

"Your wife is a menace. And she's got a room full of illegal weapons!''

He tensed. "I think I hear her pickup. You have to get out of here!''

She tipped up her chin. "I'm taking Beauty with me.''

"Fine. Just go." He pushed her toward the sliding door. "And don't come back. Ever!''

The next moment, Sabrina found herself in the Dooleys' backyard. Holding Beauty snugly in her arms, she walked along the house until she reached the fence. Then she craned her head around the corner to see if Doris's pickup truck was in the driveway. But it was empty.

She breathed a silent sigh of relief, then looked down at Beauty. "False alarm.''

She dropped Beauty onto the other side of the fence, then jumped over herself, though much less gracefully. Picking the cat back up in her arms, she hurried to her car. Once safely inside and a good mile from the Dooley house, she glanced down at Beauty, who sat patiently in the passenger seat, waiting for something new and exciting to happen.

"I'm so tempted to just keep on driving," she said, flipping on the windshield wipers to counteract the light mist. "But the more I think about it, the more certain I am that Noah Callahan is a jerk. I mean, the least he could have done was let me explain.''

Beauty expressed her agreement by remaining silent.

''All right, I admit it. I've made a few mistakes in my past. He isn't exactly perfect, either. Did I tell you I found his little black book?''

Beauty looked up at her.

''Yes, the man really owns one. It's got more names in it than the city phone directory. Do I really want a man with that kind of history?''

Beauty began licking her paw.

''I mean, I know people can change. And Noah definitely has potential. Not to mention the fact that he's a fantastic kisser. Even better than Rafael.''

Beauty looked impressed. Or bored. It was hard to tell.

''So maybe I shouldn't give up on him so easily. What I should do is go back there and *make* him listen to me. Especially since this will be my last chance.''

She reached over and stroked Beauty's neck, relishing the simple joy of petting her cat. ''Now that Niles is back, Doris won't be terrorizing us anymore. And once Madame Sophia returns from her vacation, Noah will be on his way to Cleveland.''

Beauty curled up on the car seat and closed her eyes.

Sabrina turned onto the street where Sophie lived, then reached over with one hand to brush the soft fur on Beauty's stomach with her fingertips. ''I think you'd like him, Beauty. He's smart and funny. Even chivalrous. Do you know he actually changed the tire on my car after I hijacked him? Let's face it, I'm not going to find a man like that every day.

"Wait a minute. I've got an idea." Sabrina parked along the curb since Noah's red Mustang blocked the entrance to the garage. "I'll open the envelope Sophia gave me. Then I'll know once and for all if Noah Callahan really is my perfect match."

THE NEXT MORNING Noah walked into the kitchen and found the last person he expected to see sitting at the table. "Trace? What the hell are you doing here?"

Trace picked up his glass of orange juice. "Checking up on you, little brother. Why didn't you call me?"

Noah grabbed a glass out of the cupboard, then pulled out a chair and sat down. "Why would I call you?"

"Oh, I don't know. Maybe because Café Romeo almost burned to the ground."

"That's a slight exaggeration," Noah said dryly. He reached for the carton of orange juice, then filled his glass to the brim. "How did you find out about it?"

"Chloe and I have a police scanner in our honeymoon suite."

Noah paused, his glass halfway to his mouth. "You're not serious."

Trace nodded. "Our honeymoon suite also happens to be the D'Onofrio family hideout, so the scanner is a permanent fixture.''

"Why am I not surprised?"

"So tell me about the fire."

"There's not much to tell. Faulty wiring, a little smoke, minimal damage. The customers won't even notice.''

Trace looked surprised. "You can open today?''

"Of course. Do you think I'd just be sitting here if there was serious damage? I'd be out getting estimates, filing claims and hiring contractors.''

Trace held up one hand. "Take it easy. Jeez, you always were cranky in the mornings. I feel sorry for Sabrina." He leaned back his chair. "So have you set the wedding date yet?"

Noah stared at him. "What are you talking about?''

"The wedding. You know, flowers, tuxedoes, hives. Ring a bell?"

"What makes you think I'm getting married?"

"Two words—coffee grounds. Madame Sophia read yours, just like she read mine and Jake's. Besides, you can't fool me, little brother. I saw Sabrina's Nova parked outside.''

"So?''

"So, you certainly move fast. What's it been, a week, and you're already living together?''

Noah downed the rest of his juice. "It's not what you think.''

Trace snorted. "Right. Next I suppose you'll be telling me you haven't slept with her yet.''

He clenched his jaw. "I'm not telling you anything, because it's none of your damn business."

Ramon stumbled into the kitchen, then blinked at
Trace. "Did Chloe dump you already?"

"Not a chance, Ramon," Trace said, helping
himself to more juice. "I just stopped by to check
up on things."

Ramon turned to Noah. "What have you done
with Sabrina?"

"What do you mean? I haven't seen her yet this
morning."

"Neither have I. She's not in her bed."

Noah glowered at him. "What were you doing
in her bedroom?"

"I wanted to give her a present." He tossed a
gaudily wrapped package on the table. "It's that
new *Disco Diet & Exercise* videotape they were ad-
vertising on television. I wanted it to be a surprise."

Noah combed his fingers through his unruly hair.
"I'm sure she'll be thrilled."

"She won't be thrilled if I can't give it to her.
She's gone."

Noah pushed out his chair. "Gone? That's impossible. Her car's parked right outside."

"She's not upstairs," Ramon countered. "Or
anywhere else in the house. I've already looked.
Did you say something to scare her off?"

"Of course not. I didn't say anything." It suddenly hit him that she might have misinterpreted his
silence. Naturally, he'd been surprised by her revelation. And his pride might have been a little

bruised when she'd bested him at poker. Not to mention the fact that he'd been standing there in his boxer shorts while she was still fully dressed.

Still, she couldn't get very far without her car. His gut twisted as another thought occurred to him. A possibility he didn't even want to consider. "Ramon, did you see Sabrina last night after we got back from Café Romeo?"

He shook his head. "Since it was so late, I assumed she was asleep. Her bedroom door was shut."

Without another word, he bolted out of his chair and headed for the staircase. He could hear Ramon and Trace following behind him. Taking the steps two at a time, he rounded the newel post at the top and knocked sharply on her bedroom door.

"I already told you," Ramon said from behind him. "She's not there."

Noah swung open the door and walked into the room. Ramon was right—it was empty. He went over to the neatly made bed and pulled down the covers. The sheets were cold to the touch.

But that wasn't his only clue that she hadn't slept here. The freshly laundered sheets were smooth, with not one wrinkle or crease. The crisp white pillowcase didn't have one strand of auburn hair on it. All of which made him suspect the worst—Sabrina had left the house last night.

And had never come back.

10

LESS THAN AN HOUR later, Noah stormed into Ty Burke's tiny office. "She's gone."

Ty looked up from his desk. "I was just about to call you."

"Sabrina is missing," Noah reiterated. His heart hadn't stopped pounding since he'd left the house. Guilt tore at him when he thought about Sabrina being in danger while he'd slept peacefully in his bed. "I think Doris is involved. Hell, I can't think of any other explanation."

"Calm down."

Noah raked one hand through his hair. "Don't tell me to calm down! Sabrina is missing. I think she's been missing for the last twelve hours. What if..." He stopped, unable to put his worst fears into words.

"She's not missing."

Noah stared stupidly at him. "What?"

"I said she's not missing. Sabrina is here. She was arrested last night."

He stared at Burke in disbelief. "Arrested?"

"For possession of stolen property, as well as

breaking and entering. Both serious offenses, by the way.''

Noah sagged down into a chair. ''There must be some mistake. Sabrina would never do anything like that.'' Or would she? Until last night, he never would have suspected she could hustle pool, either. Or literally beat the pants off of him in poker. What other secrets was Sabrina Lovett hiding?

Then he mentally shook himself. This was crazy. Only one explanation made sense. He leveled his gaze on Burke. ''Doris Dooley is behind this, isn't she?''

Burke flipped open the file on his desk. ''Mrs. Dooley reported the incident at 11:47 last night. A cruiser picked up Miss Lovett outside of your aunt's home approximately fifteen minutes later.''

Only ten minutes after he'd returned from Café Romeo. ''And?''

''And Sabrina admitted breaking into the Dooley home. She also had stolen merchandise from that home in her possession.''

''What stolen merchandise?''

''She had a cat with her.''

''Beauty? Good for her. That cat happens to belong to Sabrina. Doris is the one who kidnapped her.''

''Don't you mean catnapped?''

''This is not funny,'' he said between clenched teeth.

Burke sighed. ''You're right. Besides, the cat isn't the problem. In fact, one of the arresting officers offered to take her temporarily. It's the diamond bracelet the cat was wearing as a collar that is the basis of the charge.''

''Let me see Sabrina,'' he said, rising out of the chair. ''Then we can straighten this whole mess out.''

''Hold it, Noah.'' Burke held up one hand. ''You can't see her.''

''Why the hell not?''

''Because she specifically requested it. Don't worry, she's got a lawyer.''

''She doesn't need a lawyer. Don't you get it, Ty? This is all a setup. You can't hold Sabrina on the basis of these ridiculous charges.''

''She's got a bail hearing in two hours.'' Burke sat forward in his chair. ''If you want her out of here, I suggest you bring your checkbook. Look, Callahan, I'm on your side. But my hands are tied. She's already admitted to breaking into the Dooley house.''

''There's got to be something more I can do.''

Burke shook his head. ''It's too late. The only thing that will stop the process now is if Doris Dooley drops the charges. And after all we've learned about her, what do you think the chances are of that?''

Noah headed toward the door. ''Maybe better than you think.''

DETECTIVE TY BURKE escorted Sabrina to a special holding room. When they reached the door, he turned to her. "I'll give you ten minutes. I'm already bending the rules by allowing this visit."

"Thank you, Detective," she said, as he opened the door for her.

"Darling!" Ramon jumped to his feet and rushed toward her. He took her hands in his, then stepped back a pace, his horrified gaze raking over her. "You look awful."

"I'm fine," she reassured him. "Really. But you'd better sit down. You look a little pale."

Ramon took her advice, pulling out a chair for her first. "I couldn't believe it when I heard you were in jail. I mean, why didn't you call us last night and tell us what happened?"

"I wanted to handle this myself." The events of last night still seemed more like a nightmare than reality. The flashing red lights in her rearview mirror. The officer reading her the Miranda rights. The exhausting questions.

"Noah was pretty mad about it."

"I can imagine," she said dryly. At least she'd been spared the humiliation of Noah witnessing her arrest.

"I'm much more understanding." Ramon scooted his chair closer to her. "My ex-fiancée is incarcerated at the Women's Correctional Center in Vandalia. She was Mom's cell mate. That's how we met."

She blinked at him in surprise. "I had no idea you'd been engaged once. Why did you break up?"

He sighed. "My fiancée shot me. It's kind of a long story."

She glanced at her watch. "I've got seven minutes to hear it."

He shook his head. "I don't want to waste time with small talk. We've got something much more important to discuss."

"We do?"

"Your bail money. I know this bail bondsman who provides services for all the D'Onofrios. He even gives us a special rate."

"I really appreciate it, but…"

"Just listen," he interjected. "In return, all you have to do is marry me."

She blinked. "What?"

He gazed at her with his soulful eyes. "We could have a really long engagement, so you could get used to the idea. I'll write you every day and show up on visiting days."

"Oh, Ramon. That's very sweet. But that wouldn't be fair to you."

"I'm used to jailhouse romances."

"That's not what I mean," she said gently. "It's just that I don't love you."

"Maybe you could grow to love me."

She smiled. "Maybe. But I'm already in love with someone else."

His face fell. "Callahan."

"I'm afraid so."

He sighed. "I had a feeling there was something

going on between you two when I saw him in his boxer shorts.''

Someone knocked on the door, and Detective Burke stuck his head inside. ''Time's up.''

Ramon turned to her. ''I'll still call the bondsman. And I'll make him give you the special rate, too.''

After Ramon left, Detective Burke turned to her. ''You may not need bail money.''

She looked up at him. ''What do you mean?''

''Well, I probably shouldn't be telling you this, but Noah was here earlier. In fact, he almost punched me when I said he couldn't see you.''

Despite her situation, a tiny flicker of hope lit inside of her. ''He did?''

Burke nodded, then grinned. ''The boy's got it bad.''

She frowned in confusion. ''Are we talking about the same Noah Callahan? The one who likes fast cars and perfect women?''

''That's the one.''

She swallowed hard. ''I've changed my mind, Detective. I would like to see him.''

''Too late. He left.''

''Oh.'' Disappointment shot through her. ''Can I have one more phone call? Or could you call him for me?''

He hesitated. ''I could, but I don't think I'd reach him at home or at Café Romeo. From the way he talked, I'd say he's headed for Doris Dooley's house.''

She shot out of her chair. "You've got to stop him. Please, before she frames him, too."

Burke arched a brow. "You were framed?"

"It's a long story. If you leave now, you might still be able to catch him."

"Noah Callahan knows how to take care of himself. You, however, seem to attract trouble like a magnet." He pulled a chair toward him, then straddled the back. "Now, I'm not going anywhere until you tell me everything, Ms. Lovett. Why don't you start at the beginning?"

DORIS DOOLEY opened the front door of her house and smiled. She wore baggy black jeans and an oversize red Cardinals sweatshirt that matched the polish on her toenails. "Well, if isn't Mr. Calhoun."

"Good morning, Doris," Noah said politely. "May I come in?"

"Of course." She stepped back a pace and motioned him inside. "I thought you'd never get here."

"I didn't know you were expecting me," he replied as he walked into her living room.

"Somehow I just got the feeling you'd show up this morning. In fact, I was banking on it, if you know what I mean."

"I think I do." He looked around the small, sparse living room, noting the dirty ashtray on the coffee table, next to an issue of *Variety* and a cordless telephone.

Then Noah turned to face her. "I'm here about Sabrina."

"Big surprise."

"I want you to drop the charges."

"Another big surprise." Doris tugged a blond curl behind her ear.

Something about the gesture struck him as oddly familiar.

She smiled at him. "Care to offer me a little incentive, Mr. Calhoun?"

Noah pulled a cashier's check out of his shirt pocket. "Here are five thousand reasons to make the call."

Doris reached for the check, but Noah slipped it back into his pocket. "You have to earn it first."

Doris fluttered her eyelashes, thick with heavy black mascara. "What exactly did you have in mind?"

That's when it clicked. Realization washed over him like a tidal wave, almost knocking him to his knees. But before he could act on his hunch, he had to clear Sabrina's name.

He picked up the cordless phone. "Call Detective Tyrone Burke of the St. Louis Police. Tell him you made a big mistake and that you're dropping all charges against Sabrina Lovett."

"Is that all?"

"That's enough. If you try and reinstate the charges later, the police won't waste their time. And a prosecutor wouldn't touch the case. Not when the chief witness can't make up her mind."

Doris snorted. "As far as I'm concerned, the sooner that Lovett woman is out of my life, the better."

Noah dialed the number, swearing softly under his breath when the operator told him that Detective Burke was unavailable. Settling for a junior detective, he handed the phone to Doris, who performed her part to perfection.

Then she hung up the phone. "My money, please?"

He snapped his fingers. "Oh, wait a minute. I want you to do one more thing."

Her overplucked brows drew together. "What?"

"Take off your pants."

Doris blanched. "Forget it, Callahan."

"You can do it here or down at the police station. Take your pick."

She pondered the choice for a moment, then made a mad dash for the hallway. He followed after her, slamming up against the locked door of her hobby room.

"Damn," he muttered, knowing exactly how well Doris could defend herself if he gave her time to unlock that weapon cabinet. He backed up, then crashed against the door, using his shoulder as a battering ram. Once. Twice. Three times. His shoulder was throbbing when he finally burst through and made a dive for Doris's ankles as she stood in front of the cabinet.

"Let go of me, you jerk!" Her legs flailed wildly as she hoarsely shouted obscenities. Then she aimed a vicious kick right in Noah's face, catching him on the nose.

He heard the sound of bone cracking as pain ripped through his face. He lost his precarious grip on her ankles and she shot up and out the door. His eyes watered and blood flowed from his nose as he struggled to his feet and raced after her. She had almost made it out the front door when another man blocked her path.

Detective Ty Burke, with Sabrina right behind him.

"Going somewhere?" Ty asked, as Doris backed slowly into the living room.

She pointed a shaky finger at Noah, her voice unnaturally high. "That man forced his way in here and attacked me. I'm a married woman and he...and he..."

Burke scowled as he looked at Noah. "Is this true?"

"Yes." Noah gingerly held a handkerchief up to his bleeding, broken nose. "Everything except the 'married woman' part. Doris isn't married to Niles. It's not possible."

Sabrina rushed to his side, looking thoroughly baffled, worried and beautiful. "Oh, Noah, are you all right?"

"I'm fine," he said softly, savoring the look of love on her face.

Burke walked over to Doris, who stood huddled against the wall. "So this is Doris Dooley."

"Not exactly," Noah replied. "Ty, I'd like you to meet Niles Dooley."

SABRINA STARED at her nemesis in bewilderment. "Doris is Niles?"

"Actually, Niles is Doris." He closed his eyes against the pain in his face. "Niles invented a wife, then took on the role himself."

Burke whistled low. "Amazing."

"It explains why Niles presumably disappeared without a trace," Noah added.

Sabrina nodded slowly. "He was here all the time. That's why I found him in the kitchen last night. And those smudges under his eyes were from all that mascara Doris always wore."

"He's been pulling this scam for almost a year." Noah tilted his head up slightly, still holding the handkerchief to his nose. "Dating desperate women, then acting like the enraged wife until they coughed up enough money to stop the harassment."

"Desperate?" Sabrina echoed, frowning at him. "I was never desperate."

"Of course not," Niles snapped, his anger bringing him out of character. "At least not desperate enough to date someone like me. They always think of some lame excuse." He motioned to Sabrina. "Hers was a real doozy. Some drivel about finding her perfect match in a cup of soggy coffee grounds."

Burke stepped forward. "I want to warn you that

after this point, anything you say can be used against you in a court of law. Do you understand?''

"Of course I understand. I'm not a moron. I'm certainly not as dumb as these two.'' He flung one hand toward Noah and Sabrina. "You wouldn't believe all the trouble they went to because of that stupid cat. Making prank phone calls and breaking into my house. That's why I rigged the cat with my grandma's old bracelet. Just a little insurance to make certain I got my money one way or the other.''

"Your insurance backfired,'' Noah replied. "Next time let us professionals handle it.''

Niles ripped off his wig and hurled it to the floor. "If you had just paid me the money, this could have been over a long time ago.''

"What?'' Noah quipped, his nose throbbing. "And miss all the fun?''

"Gotta hand it to you, Callahan,'' Ty said. "Damn good detective work. I would have wasted a lot of time looking for the extortionist Doris Dooley, when Doris doesn't even exist.''

Sabrina folded her arms across her chest. "Niles obviously planned it that way. He made it look like he was the innocent victim while his 'wife' did all the dirty work. Then, after the payoff, Doris would conveniently disappear until Niles was certain the blackmail victim wouldn't go to the police.''

"Almost the perfect crime,'' Burke mused.

Sabrina turned to Noah. "I still don't understand how you figured it all out.''

"Hey, you're not the only one who can recognize a 'tell.'" He slowly removed the handkerchief. His nose had stopped bleeding, but it was beginning to swell. "When I interviewed Lou Murillo, he tugged on his hair, complaining that his wig sometimes slipped a little. Today I saw Doris do the same thing."

"It's not unusual for a woman to wear a wig," Burke countered.

"Yes, but when you add in the heavy makeup and the fact that Niles had completely disappeared it starts to make sense." Noah picked up the copy of *Variety* off the coffee table. "Especially for a wannabe actor."

"Lucky guess," Niles muttered under his breath.

Burke handcuffed him, read him his Miranda rights, then escorted him out the door.

Sabrina looked up at Noah. "You're hurt."

He took a step closer to her. "I think I need a kiss to make it better."

She smiled, slipping her hands around his waist, then reached up to place a tentative kiss on one corner of his mouth. "I'm afraid I'll hurt you more."

He pulled her close, his arms tightening around her. "You'll only hurt me if you walk out of my life. I don't want to lose you, Sabrina. I love you too much."

"I'm not going anywhere," she whispered, planting tiny kisses along his jaw. "You're the one headed to Cleveland."

"Not anymore. I'm staying right here—with you." He kissed her, then pulled back abruptly. "Oh, and one more thing. About the six kids."

She tensed. "You don't want six?"

"No. I want seven. Then we'll have enough for a baseball team—counting you and me."

Giddy laughter bubbled up in her throat. She'd wanted him in her life so badly, for so long, she was almost afraid to believe it. "Is the pain making you delirious?"

"No, but your kisses seem to have that effect on me. I've been off balance ever since we met. There's only one possible explanation. At first, I refused to believe it. Then I was afraid to believe it. Now..." He pulled her close for another kiss, this one deeper and hotter than before.

"Now?" she prodded, slightly breathless when the kiss finally ended.

"Now I know you must be my perfect match."

Her breath caught in her throat. "There's one way to find out."

"What do you mean?" he asked as she stepped out of his arms.

Sabrina reached for her purse, which grateful Detective Burke had retrieved from the property desk for her. "Madame Sophia left me an envelope with the name of my perfect match inside. I haven't opened it yet, but now may be just the right time."

She pulled the small envelope out of her purse, then handed it to him. "You do the honors."

He smiled, then ripped the envelope in half.

"Noah!" she exclaimed, half outraged, half laughing.

He tore it again and again, until it was just tiny white shreds in his big hands. "Maybe I'm your perfect match or maybe I'm not."

She placed her hands on her hips in mock outrage. "Now we'll never know. Unless we ask Madame Sophia."

"Don't bother." He pulled her close and kissed her. "Like I said last night, it doesn't matter. Because I've already fallen in love with you."

"Well, you're in luck," she whispered, her voice tight with emotion. "Because I happen to love you, too. Very much. But I'm not perfect. There are still a lot of things that you don't know about me."

"Maybe so. But I know the most important thing about you." He enfolded her in his arms and she knew she'd finally found the place where she belonged.

"Tell me."

He threw the shredded paper up in the air and it rained down on them like confetti. Then he looked into her eyes. "Sabrina Lovett, you may not be the perfect woman, but you're the perfect woman for me."

Epilogue

Three months later

HIVES. Dozens of them, covering Noah from neck to waist. Standing only half-dressed in front of the long mirror in the chapel dressing room, he stared in dismay at his reflection.

"This is awful," he breathed, holding both sides of his stiff, white dress shirt open for a closer look. The shirt was rented, along with the tuxedo. Only the boxer shorts and socks were his own.

"I agree." Jake adjusted his bow tie. "You're about to become a married man. You have to get better taste in boxer shorts."

Noah glanced down at the white boxer shorts imprinted with bright red lipstick kisses. "These are my favorite pair. Sabrina...decorated them for me."

Trace glanced at Jake. "Don't ask."

"Well, soon she won't have time to decorate your boxer shorts," Jake said as he buttoned his tuxedo jacket. "I've asked her to take over the business management of Café Romeo. I'm already managing three other places and I want more time to spend with my wife."

"Thanks, Jake," Noah said, reaching out to shake his hand. "Sabrina already told me she plans to accept your offer. That's the best wedding present you could have given her."

"My pleasure."

Noah turned back to the mirror and frowned at his reflection once more. "I can't go on my honeymoon like this. It was hard enough to get Sabrina to agree to marry me this soon. If she suspects I'm having subconscious second thoughts, she'll make me wait even longer!"

"Put some of that calamine lotion on it," Trace suggested as he adjusted his dove-gray cummerbund.

Noah set his jaw. "I refuse to wear pink to my wedding."

A knock sounded on the door, then Ramon walked in wearing a tuxedo and a big grin. "Everybody decent?"

"Be nice," Trace muttered to his brothers. "He's my brother-in-law."

"Wow, you look awful," Ramon said, circling Noah. "I hope you're not contagious."

Noah began buttoning his shirt. "Just itchy."

Ramon settled onto a chair. "Sabrina looks terrific. I just saw her. Did I tell you she asked me to give her away?"

"About fifty times," Jake said under his breath. Then he looked at Noah. "I can't believe her parents aren't coming to your wedding."

Noah shrugged. "They're in Slovenia or Transylvania. One of those scary-sounding countries. Sabrina wasn't sure how to reach them and she didn't think they'd be able to leave the carnival for that long anyway. We'll track them down after the honeymoon.''

"Three weeks in Istanbul." Jake smiled. "Sounds intriguing."

Noah pulled on his tuxedo pants. "It was Sabrina's idea. She wants to show me some of her favorite places."

Trace grinned. "Now that really sounds intriguing."

Ramon perked up. "Are we going to talk about sex now?"

"No," chorused all three men in unison.

Ramon sighed. "I really need some advice."

Trace walked over to him. "Didn't you read that book I gave you?"

"No, I just looked at the pictures. But the thing is, I just saw a beautiful blond bombshell sitting out there in the chapel."

"So what's the problem?" Trace asked. "Just go up to her, introduce yourself, and ask her out. Only make sure you show her who's in charge right away. Otherwise, she'll run right over you."

Jake looked at Trace's back. "Yep, I can see Chloe's heel marks all up and down your spine."

"Very funny," Trace said. "At least I haven't been reduced to wearing an apron yet."

Noah looked at Jake, a former heavyweight boxer. "An apron?"

"With lace," Trace added.

Jake folded his arms across his powerful chest. "Nina's teaching me to cook. She thinks I have a lot of potential in the kitchen."

Trace grinned. "How about the bedroom?"

Ramon brightened. "Are we going to talk about sex now?"

All three men turned to him in unison. "No!"

Noah shrugged into his tuxedo jacket, trying to ignore the ferocious itch underneath his shirt. Even worse, now it had spread slightly beneath the waistband of his dress pants.

Jake turned to Ramon. "If you want my advice, become her friend first, then make your move."

Noah swiped a comb through his hair one last time. "You guys are nuts. All he has to do is have Aunt Sophie read his coffee grounds. Then he'll be guaranteed a happily-ever-after." He froze. "Wait a minute. Describe the blonde."

Ramon breathed a wistful sigh. "Tall, built, maybe a little husky around the shoulders. But I like 'em big. She's got on this awesome red dress."

"Uh…Ramon," Noah said, not quite sure where to start. "I don't think she's the right woman for you."

He stuck out his lower lip. "Look, you already took Sabrina away from me. The blonde is mine. You can't have all the women."

"The blonde isn't a woman. She's a man."

Dead silence pervaded the small room, broken only when Aunt Sophie walked in, the jingle of her bangle bracelets preceding her arrival. "It's almost time!" Then she took one look at them and clasped one hand to her chest. "You're all gorgeous."

"So are you, Aunt Sophie." Noah leaned down to kiss her cheek. She wrapped her arms around him and gave him a big hug.

"Aunt Sophie," he said, still wrapped in her embrace.

"Yes, Noah, dear?"

"Could you scratch that spot right below my left shoulder blade?"

She pulled back. "What's wrong?"

He grimaced, then pulled down the collar of his shirt to reveal the ugly blotches. "Hives."

She reached out and fingered his shirt. "Well, no wonder. This shirt is full of starch. When you were little, laundry starch always gave you hives."

"It did?"

She pulled off his tuxedo jacket. "Get that shirt off, Noah Callahan. You can wear the one you had on when you got here. I doubt anyone will even notice."

He stripped out of the stiff dress shirt and exchanged it for his familiar white Oxford. "I feel better already."

Ramon stood up, obviously distraught. "What do you mean, she's a man?"

Noah clapped him on the shoulder. "Don't feel bad, Ramon. I made the same mistake. Lou Murillo is a female impersonator. And a hell of a nice guy. He unknowingly taught Niles all the cosmetic and wardrobe tricks it took to make his scam so successful. Lou's also the one who provided enough additional evidence against Dooley to put him away for a good long time.''

''Maybe you shouldn't try to pick a woman on your own, Ramon,'' Trace suggested. ''It's too dangerous.''

''He's absolutely right,'' Sophie said, wrapping her arm around Ramon's waist. ''Don't worry. As soon as this wedding is over, I'll make you a cup of my special Jamaican almond blend.''

All three Callahan men looked at each other. And grinned.

Sophie headed toward the door, pulling Ramon along with her. Then she glanced over her shoulder at her nephews. ''Oh, I forgot to tell you. I learned a new method for reading coffee grounds in New Orleans.''

''What can you predict now,'' Noah asked wryly. ''Blizzards?''

''No.'' Sophie beamed. ''Babies.''

Play the

"LAS VEGAS"

GAME

GET 3 FREE GIFTS!

FREE GIFTS!

FREE GIFTS!

FREE GIFTS!

TURN THE PAGE TO PLAY! Details inside!

Play the
"LAS VEGAS" Game
and get
3 FREE GIFTS!

FREE GIFTS!

FREE GIFTS!

1. Pull back all 3 tabs on the card at right. Then check the claim chart to see what we have for you — 2 FREE BOOKS and a gift — ALL YOURS! AL FREE!

2. Send back this card and you'll receive brand-new Harlequin Duets™ novels. These books have a cover price of $5.99 each in the U.S. and $6.99 each in Canada, but they are yours to keep absolutely free.

3. There's no catch. You're under no obligation to buy anything. We char; nothing — ZERO — for your first shipment. And you don't have to ma any minimum number of purchases — not even one!

4. The fact is thousands of readers enjoy receiving books by mail from the Harlequin Reader Service®. They like the convenience of home delivery.. they like getting the best new novels BEFORE they're available in stores.. and they love our discount prices!

5. We hope that after receiving your free books you'll want to remain a subscriber. But the choice is yours — to continue or cancel, any time a all! So why not take us up on our invitation, with no risk of any kind. You'll be glad you did!

Visit us online at
www.eHarlequin.com

FREE!
No Obligation to Buy!
No Purchase Necessary!

Play the

"LAS VEGAS" Game

YES! I have pulled back the 3 tabs. Please send me all the free Harlequin Duets™ books and the gift for which I qualify. I understand that I am under no obligation to purchase any books, as explained on the back and opposite page.

311 HDL C23R   **111 HDL C23J**

NAME   (PLEASE PRINT CLEARLY)

ADDRESS

APT.#   CITY

STATE/PROV.   ZIP/POSTAL CODE

GET 2 FREE BOOKS & A FREE MYSTERY GIFT!

GET 2 FREE BOOKS!

GET 1 FREE BOOK!

TRY AGAIN!

◄ **DETACH AND MAIL TODAY** ▼

The Harlequin Reader Service®—Here's how it works:

Accepting your 2 free books and gift places you under no obligation to buy anything. You may keep the books and gift and return the shipping statement marked "cancel." If you do not cancel, about a month later we'll send you 2 additional novels and bill you just $5.14 each in the U.S., or $6.14 each in Canada, plus 50¢ delivery per book and applicable taxes if any.* That's the complete price and — compared to cover prices of $5.99 each in the U.S. and $6.99 each in Canada — it's quite a bargain! You may cancel at any time, but if you choose to continue, every month we'll send you 2 more books, which you may either purchase at the discount price or return to us and cancel your subscription.

*Terms and prices subject to change without notice. Sales tax applicable in N.Y. Canadian residents will be charged applicable provincial taxes and GST.

GWEN
PEMBERTON

Counterfeit
Daddy

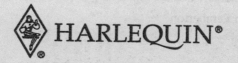

TORONTO • NEW YORK • LONDON
AMSTERDAM • PARIS • SYDNEY • HAMBURG
STOCKHOLM • ATHENS • TOKYO • MILAN • MADRID
PRAGUE • WARSAW • BUDAPEST • AUCKLAND

Dear Reader,

My husband travels a lot. Being alone with our two sons for weeks at a time has given me an inkling of what single parenting is like. "Not easy," I informed my hubby when he asked in all innocence, "How hard can it be?"

When I left home for a five-day conference, he found out firsthand just how interesting it can be. I left him with a refrigerator full of microwavable meals and the washing machine loaded with wet clothes to be tossed in the dryer. I briefed him on the kids' routines, food preferences, and armed him with phone numbers. "You'll do fine," I assured him. Nonetheless I called every evening to check.

"Everything's great," he always answered.

I returned to find the microwavable meals untouched, the laundry molding in the washing machine and the house full of new toys. "We ate out and Daddy took us shopping every day. It was great," the boys said.

"See, you were right," my hubby added. "I did fine."

And so did Chet, the hero in *Counterfeit Daddy*. I hope you enjoy reading how our hero survived his parenting adventures while he was falling hopelessly in love.

Gwen Pemberton

Books by Gwen Pemberton
HARLEQUIN LOVE & LAUGHTER
30—WOOING WANDA
49—REGARDING RITA

To my loving husband.

Prologue

CHET JAMES didn't like rejection, but it was something he was getting used to...unfortunately. This one didn't even come on proper stationery, just a meager message printed on a note sheet. With one hand he crumpled the letter and tossed it into the trash can, then readjusted the phone between his ear and shoulder.

"A form letter of all things. No *Dear Mr. James*...no signature," Ann said.

As usual, his older sister was taking the news worse than he was, which put him in the odd position of having to be upbeat when he really wanted to spit nails.

"Not your basic form letter, this one had a hand-written note," Chet said.

"Oh, well that's—wait a second—" He heard her put down the receiver and yell, "Sean. Turn off that video game." Then she was back. "Well, that's something. What does it say?"

She had to ask. "'Lacks spark, lacks originality,'" he read, then kicked himself for not lying.

"As if any of those magazines are original. You can tell time by them. Spring—it's body building along with divorce and how to pick up women. Summer—it's hot adventure spots for the vacationing he-man, divorce and how to pick up women. Fall—wardrobe, investment, divorce and how to pick up women and winter—''

"Divorce and how to pick up women," Chet added.

"Okay. If they want divorce, write about yours. You had a real doozy."

"That's one thing I don't need to rehash, not even for money." Which stopped flowing the minute his articles stopped selling. Soon his bank account would qualify for the endangered registry.

"You know you can always—Sean, I said turn that *off*."

"Look, I'll call you later." After his hearing returned.

"No...no. I can talk. What was I saying? Oh, yeah, you can always go back to teaching and research. Not at Tech, of course, some other university."

Chet swallowed. "I'm through with academia," he said.

"Well, I can't blame you, but—Brittany, you are not going anywhere in that outfit. Fig leaves cover up more."

"But, Mom." Chet could hear his thirteen-year-old niece's voice, distant but clear, her suffering drawn out in the old you-don't-understand-me whine.

"I said no. Upstairs and change," Ann yelled, then sighed into the phone. "Kids. I know what I'd read, any and every article about coping as a single parent. Too bad you can't do that for one of those men's magazines."

"Wouldn't get past the macho police."

"Ah, Chet…"

"Hey." He knew that meltdown sound in her voice. He couldn't let her fret. Besides, ever since they were teens, he'd been the one looking after her. "Not to worry. You know me—Mr. Resourceful. I'll work this out."

She sighed. "Well, I'll see you tomorrow. You are coming for dinner, right?"

"My new motto, Will Write For Food."

"In that case, I'll serve broccoli."

"Sadist." Right before he disconnected, he heard her yell to Kevin, the youngest of the brood.

Ann needing advice on child rearing seemed like a joke. His niece and nephews could prove a handful at times, still, they were charming youngsters. Ann had things under control. She made sure the kids never pushed the limits too far.

Simply by using her as a model, he could write a great article on single parenting. There were probably enough bachelor dads out there who'd be interested.

His breath caught. A rush of heat followed. He was on to something. He dashed to his office and turned on his computer. He drummed the desk, waiting for it to boot up.

Yeah, he thought. Why not? It was original. It had spark. And it beat the hell out of all that how-to-pick-up-women drivel.

Chet took a deep breath then typed "Living and Learning, A Single Dad's Experiences in Child Rearing."

P.J. West smoothed down her black miniskirt, slipped into the matching jacket, then marched for her office door and froze.

"Now what?" Flasher's tenor came from across the room. Exaggerated weariness colored his voice.

She turned to face her young friend and colleague. He was perched on the edge of her desk, his long legs crossed at the ankles like a fashion princess.

"How do I look? I mean, *really*, how do I look?" she asked.

"Fine," he said.

"I need more than fine. Come on, you're the photographer. You're the one with the critical eye. Tell me...and I want brutal honesty now...how do I look?"

Flasher tipped his head to one side and stroked his chin. "Okay, as a photographer and critic...you still look fine."

P.J. moaned. Being summoned by the new chief editor called for something with a lot more pizzazz than *fine*. She had to project cool professionalism, tempered assertiveness and a this-magazine-would-be-lost-without-me attitude all laced with the right amount of fashion flair. *Fine* simply didn't cut it.

"It's my hair, isn't it?" P.J. patted her head, checking for errant strands.

"Your hair is perfect, as always."

"My makeup?"

"Perfect, too."

"You sure?" She rushed back to her desk, anyway, and yanked a small mirror from her bottom drawer.

"All right," Flasher said. "If you insist upon nitpicking yourself to death, I might as well help. There is one thing."

"What, what?"

Flasher held up his hands and wiggled his fingers.

"Nails, darling."

She inspected her chewed-down stubs. "What do you suggest?"

"Stop biting them sounds like a good plan."

"Hypnosis. Maybe I should try hypnosis." Or one of those twelve-step programs, but one she could complete in three steps max.

"Does anyone other than me know about this flustered-little-girl side of you?" Flasher asked.

"Her name is Patty Jean and I keep her locked away from public view. I'm the only woman editor ever to work for *Modern Man Magazine* and survive. To everyone here, I'm P.J. West, Ms. Tough as Nails." She pointed her finger at Flasher then noticed her stubs. "Make that steel...Tough as Steel. So if my cover gets blown, I'll know it was either you or my potted geranium."

Flasher made a zipped-lip gesture. "I don't know what you're so worried about. He's not about to fire you."

If only she were as sure as her friend. The new boss had only arrived at their Chicago headquarters two weeks ago. Like all bad news, his reputation had arrived months ahead of him. Deleting budgets and staff with cold-blooded efficiency had earned him the nickname The Grim Reaper. His first week on the job he'd fired the senior editor and had yet to name a replacement.

Then again, Flasher may be right. Thanks to her, *Modern Man* had the hottest column in the business. "Living and Learning, A Single Dad's Experiences in Child Rearing" had given the readers something to digest besides the usual sex and fashion.

So why was she so nervous? She chewed on what was left of a nail and stared at the door. Thank goodness she was safe inside her six-by-six box of an office. She could fall apart without fear of damaging her tough-cookie persona.

"Ouch," she said, jerking her finger from her mouth.

"You were right. Hypnosis is the answer. Look into my eyes," Flasher said, his voice transformed into a decent Boris Karloff imitation.

Smiling, she waved him away, but her friend stood, rounded the desk and grabbed hold of her shoulders. She looked into his eyes and saw his honey-let's-have-a-serious-talk glint staring her down.

"Who's the best editor this magazine has ever had?" he asked.

"Me, but only the two of us are in on the secret."

"And who single-handedly increased circulation by fifty percent?"

"Fifty? I wish."

"Don't interrupt. And who's the kindest soul I know hiding in steel panty hose?"

He reached into her bottom drawer and retrieved her emergency makeup kit. With an expert's ease, he dabbed powder on her nose, chin and forehead. Only Flasher would she trust to such a task. She stood still while he first outlined her mouth then reapplied her lipstick.

"Look, you're the best thing this magazine has ever had. You're fresh, honest and full of ideas. That senior editor job is yours."

"Mine." She thought she'd said it with more than enough conviction, but Flasher's raised eyebrow told different.

"Doll, you haven't put up with those macho monsters you've worked with these past six years for nothing. You deserve that promotion, now go for it."

P.J. felt the tension seep out of her. She took a deep breath and filled her lungs with newfound confidence.

"Go for it. Right," she said, and gave a sharp nod.

That would have impressed her father. *P.J. West, Senior Editor.* And why not? That was her goal. She could see it now, sitting at the head of the table at staff meetings she had called. Making decisions, influencing the tone of the magazine and bit by bit sensitizing the male population to the female perspective.

P.J. felt her smile break into what she suspected was a full self-congratulatory grin.

"You're wonderful," she told Flasher. "I wish every man was like you."

"What? Brawny, gorgeous and gay?"

She gave him a mock left to his chin. "Sweet, caring and loyal."

"Can't have everything."

Didn't she know it. Well, she was going to make good on one of the two goals of her life. The other goal—a dream actually—of finding a decent, honest man, she'd all but given up on. Hadn't she kissed enough toads to know it was quitting time?

She may have introduced a few changes at the magazine, but any results from her campaign to sensitize the male population would come too late to help her in her search for Mr. Right.

Mr. Right. Fat chance.

The only two men who possessed any of the qualities she was looking for in a life-mate were Flasher and her author, Chet Greene. And that said it all. One was definitely not a possibility and the other one... She'd only read his submissions and spoken to him over the phone once. Still she would never forget that deep voice with a hint of the South. So warm and seductive.

Snap out of it, girl. Why, she'd never even met the man. So where was the possibility in that?

There wasn't any.

Concentrate on reality, she told herself. Concentrate on the career. She closed her eyes and saw a bright balloon floating upward. Dream Number One. Now, that was a reality.

This time when she marched to her door, she strode out with no hesitation.

THREE MINUTES LATER she knocked and opened her boss's door. With hands curled to hide her nails, she flashed a confident smile, crossed the threshold, and froze.

Five of her male colleagues sat around the conference table. The Reaper was nowhere in sight.

"Hey, hey. The gang's all here," one of the men said.

She hesitated, then pulled herself erect and breezed into the room. "Not that I don't enjoy seeing all of you, but I thought this was to be—"

"A private meeting," Jones finished. "Join the club of the misinformed."

"So where's Owens?" she asked, scanning the faces.

"Fired this morning. The Reaper didn't like his last two contributions."

"How to pick up women? You mean his last fifty contributions," Smith said and laughed.

It could easily have been any of them, but P.J. didn't detect a bit of sympathy in her colleagues' voices. Men. They stuck together...like a bunch of sharks. Pity the one among them who'd been wounded and smelled of blood. That poor sucker became fair game.

What would they do if they ever discovered her weakness? She clasped her hands together to keep from biting her nails.

"Just like that? No notice?" she said.

"You have nothing to worry about, West. I hear he likes women."

"Well, you fellows may not mind making it on your physical charms. I prefer being judged by my work not my curves."

"And nice curves they are."

"You're all animals...almost," P.J. said after the wolf whistles stopped. "Two more steps up the evolutionary ladder and you'd almost qualify."

"The way your new series took off, your job's safe. Who would have thought a wimpy advice column for daddies would make it?"

The door swung open and P.J. and her co-workers snapped to attention. The editor-in-chief marched forward.

"Good morning. I've reviewed the plans for our upcoming issues," he said, walking while he spoke and looking at no one. He sat, then glanced up and frowned, a facial gesture he could ill afford. His tough, overly tanned skin already made him look like an angry alligator with a face-lift. Even so, it was his eyes that held P.J.'s attention. They were as passionless as a shark's.

"I have some concerns," The Reaper said. "Let's start with 'Living and Learning' and this Chet Greene, the so-called fatherhood specialist."

P.J.'s muscles tightened. Was it her imagination

or did his voice sound icier than usual, like a scythe slicing the air above her head?

"I've a hunch the man's a fraud. I needn't tell you the damage such a thing would cause this magazine…and your career." The Reaper turned his flat stare on her.

P.J. envisioned her balloon floating overhead. The words Dream Number One stretched across its swell.

Pop.

She blinked. No way. Countless pins had already pierced her other dream. She wasn't about to let the same happen to this one. Not without a fight.

She leaned forward and splayed her hands on the table, cool professionalism and stubby nails forgotten.

"What do you mean, *fraud?*"

CHET WALKED UP the petunia-lined walk toward his sister's white frame Colonial. The perfect house on a charming tree-lined street in the good old Southern town of Richmond, Virginia. Just right for a divorced homemaker with the requisite three kids, two gerbils and a goldfish. Perfect for his sister, Ann, but entirely too domestic for him, Chet James, devout bachelor and lover of slipknots and other such nonbinding arrangements. That's why Chet had signed the house over to her after their aunt had willed it to him.

The setting, however, was perfect for his alter ego, Chet Greene single dad and author. Fortunately for both Chets, these visits to his sister's provided enough material for months' worth of articles.

He rapped on the polished oak door and peered through the translucent screen of sheer curtains that covered the glass insert. He could see the approaching form of his sister. When she opened the door, he caught a whiff of hot rolls and pot roast.

"Smells good," he said, kissing Ann's cheek.

"Everything smells good to someone who lives on pizza and popcorn."

"Pizza, popcorn and the occasional beer," he corrected.

"More than occasional by the looks of your waistline."

"Liar."

There was nothing wrong with his waistline or any other part of his body. He worked out, and not because he was vain. He knew that sitting in front of a computer every day for eight or nine hours could cause serious health problems for the thirty-something male who didn't exercise.

What he didn't do was eat properly, but Ann had made feeding him her new mission in life.

"Uncle Chet." Four-year-old Kevin ran into the room and barreled into his stomach. Chet hoisted the youngster up until the boy's grinning face met his own.

"Hey, monkey," Chet said, nuzzling his nephew.

"I'm no monkey, I'm a lion."

"Weren't you a monkey a few days ago?"

"Monkeys have to eat vegetables." He looked at his mother and made a face.

"Oh, I see. And what do lions eat?" Chet asked.

"Monkeys," Kevin said and roared.

"So where are your brother and sister? Don't tell me you ate them?"

"Uck. Nobody would eat them, but they may eat you. They're mad 'cause you put us in your magazine again."

"Did not," Chet said.

"Did, too," Kevin and Ann chorused.

"What were they doing reading *Modern Man*, anyway?"

"They found it at their father's house, and don't change the subject. You put them in your article again."

"Just a few of their experiences, and I even changed the details. Hey, I didn't use names."

"What you need is a wife and family of your own to write about," Ann said.

Chet shuddered. "Worse than vegetables. Besides, this arrangement's better."

"Coward. So you got burned once, join the club."

"You got burned," he said. "I got chopped into little pieces and fed to the lawyers."

Living with his ex-wife and then going through her version of a divorce had taught him all he ever needed to know about permanent relationships—avoid them.

That was the second major lesson he'd learned. Academia had taught him the first. He'd spent years heading up a high profile research project only to have his department head receive all the credit. And he'd been naive enough to think a formal protest would help.

Screaming foul had landed him with nothing— no commendations, no job, no savings. He'd learned quickly enough that a fat bank account was the only means of security.

That's how he measured his success these days. Everything else they could take away from you. Thanks to "Living and Learning," his account was getting fat around the middle.

The fatter it got, the more he could help out Ann and the kids. Her divorce settlement had left her poor. Not that her ex didn't pay child support. The man paid through the nose and never complained, but squeezing his small paycheck left him poor, also.

Another good reason to avoid that marriage-divorce trap.

His nephew's squirming brought Chet back to the present.

"Sean and Brittany are real mad," Kevin reminded him.

"And what about you, Mr. Lion? You mad?"

"Uh-hh." Kevin twisted his mouth as he considered.

"This calls for uncle magic. What should I conjure up? How about a new CD for Sean, a dress for Brittany, and a bag of gummies for you?" He tickled his nephew until the boy squealed.

"No bribes," Ann said, walking back into the kitchen with Chet following.

"Two bags," Kevin whispered in his ear.

"Deal," Chet said.

P.J. SAT AT HER DESK, searching through drawers, trying to find her antacids. She always kept a pack at work, one at home and one... She grabbed her purse. Yes, and one in her handbag. She popped two tablets and chewed.

How could The Reaper think that Chet Greene was a fraud? That some unknown housewife was actually writing the articles while Greene answered her phones and let her use his name? Ridiculous.

P.J. could tell the real thing when she read it. And Chet Greene was real, a widowed father trying to raise three children on his own. Reading his articles told her so. She could feel his uncertainty when he faced big problems, his relief when they were solved. She could feel his joy as well as his love for his family.

The man's emotions were laid bare and that more than anything was probably what bothered her boss. Bothered him? Heck, it scared the man. Scared him and the other macho specimens she worked with. But it didn't scare the readers. The fan mail and the sales proved that.

No, Chet Greene was the most authentic thing she'd run across in years. She would stake her reputation on it.

P.J. swallowed hard and popped two more tablets. She had staked her reputation on it. And her job.

"I'll prove he's no fraud," she'd announced. "I'll do an in-depth interview of the author and his children...in their own home. The readers will eat it up."

The Reaper surely had. She could almost see the dollar signs replacing the question marks as they flashed through his brain. Her proposal received an enthusiastic go-ahead, even as her job lay on the line. If the interview proved Chet Greene was indeed a fraud...

Well, she could kiss everything goodbye—her reputation, her job and her dream of becoming *Modern Man*'s first woman senior editor.

But she didn't have to worry about that. All she had to do was convince a very private man, one who used a pen name to shield his children and himself from the limelight, that he had to go public or lose a very lucrative income. Put that way, what family man would refuse?

P.J. checked her watch. Nine o'clock at night. Another late day at the office. Too late to call anyone living on the East Coast. She would ring him early the next morning.

CHET STRETCHED and raked his hands through his hair as he shuffled into the kitchen. Sunlight sliced through the half-open louvers and made him blink. At nine o'clock in the morning, the July sun hadn't yet reached its full potential, still it was strong enough to blind him.

With his eyes half closed, he walked to the counter and slapped down his notes. He would work on his next article while he ate, but right now he needed caffeine, that marvelous wake-me-up that took over where the alarm clock left off.

Chet spooned instant crystals into the cup of water he'd nuked to a boil. He took the milk from the fridge, opened the carton and sniffed.

"And I'll have it black," he said, not wanting to taste-test java with clotted curds.

After three sips, the hot liquid had jarred his system enough so he could open his eyes and even reflect upon yesterday's visit with Ann and the kids. Luckily, everything had turned out okay.

With the mention of a new Breaker Boys CD, eleven-year-old Sean had forgiven him for writing about the kid's recent grounding. Kevin didn't really care that he'd been featured as the Mad Streaker of the South, but the promise of two bags of gummies pleased him just the same.

Brittany proved tougher. How was he to have known that writing about her first period was a major taboo? He had promised two new outfits before he won the thirteen-year-old's smile.

Chet suspected the kids really didn't mind being the subjects of his parenting column. The bribe routine, as Ann called it, was no more than a harmless game. All kids liked presents, and he welcomed the excuse to spoil them. Besides, his so-called bribes were simply another way to help Ann with expenses.

Yep, dinner at Ann's had been fruitful, he thought, pulling from the fridge the leftovers his sister had insisted he take home. One visit had netted enough food for almost a week and enough material for at least three articles.

Chet was sitting at his counter, devouring his re-heated pot roast and going over his notes when the phone rang. He was so engrossed in both activities that he almost didn't answer, but after the tenth ring he gave in. He needed to be more vigilant about using his answering machine.

"Hello, Mr. Greene? How are you this morning?" a crisp voice sparkled through the line.

"Not interested," he said and hung up.

Telephone solicitors. Did they have built-in radar or something? They always managed to catch a person in the middle of a meal. He activated his answering device and returned to his notes and breakfast.

Just as he lifted his food-laden fork, the phone rang again. Chet jerked around toward the sound. Beef and carrots fell onto his freshly laundered jeans and onto his notes.

Fast as he could, he picked up the spilled bits of food and popped them into his mouth. He was wiping the stain from his notes when the same crisp voice came over the message machine.

"Mr. Greene, I'm not selling a thing, but I have an offer you can't refuse."

"Yeah, I bet," he said to the phone. In spite of the no-nonsense tone, he had to admit there was a sexy quality to this mystery woman's voice. There was a familiar note, as well.

"This is P.J. West, from *Modern Man*. I know you're there. Pick up."

"Damn," Chet said, and dropped his fork on top of his notes.

In his rush to the phone, he knocked over the counter stool and tripped in its legs. Kick as he might, he couldn't untangle himself.

P.J. West started rattling off her number and the extension. Chet scooted on his belly across the floor, the stool in tow.

All he could think of were her words about the *offer he couldn't refuse.* What could that be? An expanded format? A book deal? That was possible. That's why he'd targeted the magazine in the first place. The company that put out *Modern Man* also published books.

That would bulk up his bank account nicely.

"Hello?" He practically shouted into the phone. "Hello?" he said again.

The dial tone buzzed in his ear.

Defeat washed over him. He raised his face to the ceiling. "No," he screamed, then lowered his head. His forehead whacked against the floor. This time he really screamed as pain arrowed between his eyes.

He flipped onto his back and rubbed his injury. Good thing his readers couldn't see him—thirty-seven-year-old Chet James, a.k.a. Greene, lying on his kitchen floor with his legs caged by a stool. He lay there a bit longer, letting the pain blossom into a full-scale headache.

How stupid could he have been, brushing off his editor like that and then getting tripped by a chair? He may well have missed a book deal. Stupid, stupid, stupid, he bashed himself.

Then he remembered. The phone number.

Chet pushed the button and had the information memorized on the first playback.

She picked up after the first ring. No nonsense. He'd pegged her as such the first time he'd spoken with her several months ago. Since then, they'd only communicated by e-mail. His request, but she hadn't objected. Now hearing her voice a third time—twice today alone—he couldn't ignore its seductive quality and couldn't help wonder if his e-mail suggestion hadn't been a mistake.

"Mr. Greene," she said.

He was all ears. He was all slamming heart, too, but he was certain that had nothing to do with her sensual voice. Nope, the possibility of a book contract was the thing seducing him.

"I have exciting news for you," she continued.

I bet you do. Chet's smile was wide and growing wider.

"Our magazine is going to do a feature article on you."

"What?" he croaked.

"We're doing a special on you, Mr. Greene, or should I say, Mr. James?"

"Greene is fine, and no. You're not."

"I beg your pardon," she said. From the sharp edge in her voice, Chet suspected she wasn't the type to beg for anything, especially not his pardon.

"Look, I write articles, I have no intention of being the subject of someone else's story."

"I understand you don't like the limelight, Mr. Greene, but I'm afraid you'll have to make an exception this time."

Chet listened in stunned silence as she related the details of the meeting with her boss.

"What do you *mean* he thinks I'm a woman?" Chet said.

"He doesn't think you're a woman. He thinks a woman is ghostwriting your column. He needs to be convinced otherwise."

"Send me a plane ticket and I'll be in his office tomorrow convincing the hell out of him. I'll even write my next installment on his computer."

"That won't be necessary. I'm coming to Richmond."

"Here? Why?"

"I'm writing the article myself. It'll be a day in the life of *Modern Man*'s most popular contributor and his children."

The children. Sweat broke out on his forehead. His stomach muscles twisted. He tasted his pot roast, which was far from appetizing the second time around.

"How does this Friday sound?" she asked.

That was only three days away. "That's...that's impossible, and damned inconvenient."

"Then we have to arrange something convenient, and the sooner the better. Would next Friday work?"

Interview. No way. What had made him think her voice was alluring? Why, the woman had the resonance of a steel bell. She was probably just as cold in person. A witch. A steel witch in iron pants, spouting orders and telling him she had an offer he couldn't refuse. The hell he could. *And would.*

"Like I said, I have no intention of being the subject of anyone's story."

Chet listened to the long pause on the other end. Finally he heard her sigh, not an I-give-up sigh, but a dig-in-the-heels type of sound.

"Let me explain this another way," she said. "My boss thinks you're a fraud. If he's not convinced otherwise, this month's issue will be the last for 'Living and Learning.'"

Fraud? How dare her boss accuse him of being a fraud. Maybe he pretended to be a single dad, but he didn't plagiarize. That column was his, every last word, every last idea. He was no fraud. He was a...a...

Okay, in a sense he *was* a fraud. And if P.J. West came to Richmond, she'd agree. But if she didn't... Bye-bye column. Bye-bye security. And bye-bye income.

Where would that leave Ann and the kids? He'd planned on milking an income from the column for years, through braces and tuition. Heck, through Brittany's wedding even.

Not only that, his own security was at stake.

He had to do something. And he had to do it before next Friday.

2

CHET STOOD holding the cab door open while Ann kissed the kids goodbye for the fifth time. "If you don't hurry, you'll miss the plane," he reminded her.

One more round of kisses then she slid into the seat only to bolt right back out. "You have everything?" she asked. "The kids' schedules, the doctor's phone number?"

Chet nodded after each question.

"The dentist?" she said. "What about the dentist's number? Heaven forbid one of them chips a tooth. Oh, the hotel phone number?"

"Ann, I booked the hotel. I have the number."

She smiled and stroked his cheek. "Chet, this is so sweet of you. All that money for a three-day holiday."

"If you miss the plane, it'll be all that money for nothing. You need a little pampering. Now get going. It's seven-fifteen. Your flight leaves at eight-fifty." *And P.J. West arrives at nine-thirty.*

"I can't do this...leaving you here to watch the kids while I relax at a spa. It's not fair."

"Sure it is. Think of it as payment for all those dinners I've mooched off you."

"Mom, it's cool," Brittany said. The other two nodded.

Ann smiled, then bit her lip. "I'm sure there's something I'm forgetting."

"The plane," Chet and the kids shouted.

After Ann's cab disappeared around the corner, Chet exhaled with relief. Now on to Phase Two, transforming the house into a bachelor dad's abode before his editor arrived, but first he had to finagle the kids' cooperation.

"Okay, guys, let's go inside. Time for a family meeting."

They didn't move. The three of them seemed as rooted in the tree box as the fifty-year-old maples.

"We know. Time to hear about *the rules*," Sean said.

"No. The deal. I need a favor."

"Is this one of those, I'll-scratch-your-back sort of deals?" Brittany asked.

Chet remembered the last "let's make a deal"— Ann's surprise birthday party. Their silence had cost him three CDs, a new skateboard and a bag of gummy candy.

"My editor is coming to interview me, and I want—"

"Us to pretend we're your kids," Brittany said. She and Sean exchanged looks and smiled.

"This is going to cost me big-time, isn't it?"

Their grins broadened. "But it'll be worth it…Dad."

Chet frowned. They all knew his bribes were all in fun, but he was beginning to suspect Ann was right. Maybe the time had come for him to cool it on the gift giving. He would do just that...next week.

"Deal. So for the rest of the day, who am I?"

"Dad," Sean and Brittany said while their brother blinked and stared at his shoes.

"Kevin?"

"I miss Mommie," the little guy answered. As he whimpered, a lone tear forged a trail down his cheek.

Chet knelt to his nephew's level and gazed at the tyke's tear-filled eyes and trembling mouth. Not only did the boy's failed attempt at a stiff upper lip slice at Chet's heart, it shot a spear of panic through him.

What was he to do with a crying child? He hated tears, anyone's tears. A four-year-old's sobs would wrench Chet in two. Even worse, Kevin's outburst could prove contagious for the other kids.

"Hey, we can't have this," Chet said, wiping away tears with his thumb. "Lions don't cry."

"I'm not a lion. I'm a puppy."

"You're a crybaby," Sean said.

Before Chet could intervene, the name-calling turned into a singsong chant.

"Okay, end the game," Chet said.

Kevin was beyond paying attention. He charged, head down, fist swinging. With Chet as his shield, Sean dodged his little brother while Brittany egged both boys on with her laughter.

"Enough," Chet said, catching Sean by the arm just as Kevin wound up for another swing.

"Didn't I say—"

Thwop. One mini fist connected with Chet's crotch.

"Stop?" His last word came out in falsetto.

He released Sean, doubled over and hung there as though he were sitting on an invisible chair. Pain concentrated in one spot, then spread like an ink blot.

"Uh-oh," murmured the three instant allies.

Crouched and mouth agape, Chet watched as the kids fled into the house. Squeals and the sound of racing feet carried loudly enough to bring a few neighbors to their windows.

Thank goodness everyone on the block knew him. At least they wouldn't call 9-1-1, but he couldn't have any of them coming out to snoop.

One inch at a time, he pulled himself upright until he stood as close to erect as possible. He smiled and waved to the old biddy next door. The woman snorted and closed her curtains.

After a few deep breaths, he bow-legged it toward the house.

An hour and a half later Chet was headed for the basement with an oversize box of knickknacks he'd deemed too feminine for a male household. The passage was close and dark, with narrow steps constructed at a steep pitch. He'd only descended five of them when the doorbell rang.

He tried to turn around, but the carton wedged against the walls of the narrow stairwell.

The bell rang a second time. He heard Brittany running toward the foyer, yelling, "I'll get it."

No. They had all agreed that he would supervise the introductions. That first face-to-face encounter was critical. One slip...one wrong word...a slight hesitation and the game would be over. *He* was supposed to answer the door.

But where was he? Stuck in the stairwell, like some ant trapped in a tunnel by the oversize crumb he was carrying.

Chet heard the front door open, heard Brittany's perky *hello.* Then he heard that other voice, the one he knew only from phone conversations. Its smooth alto set his insides humming.

Captivated, he paused and listened. Her voice was so clear, he caught every word. She introduced herself, then her photographer, Flasher.

A new wave of panic doused him. His palms and forehead budded with sweat. What was a photographer doing here? He hadn't agreed to pictures.

Flasher. What kind of a name was that?

Suddenly he heard Sean's footsteps and voice. More introductions. He had to get up there and fast. But the only way he could go was down. Ten steps.

"Huh, nice house. Ultra country, but cozy," he heard Flasher say.

Trust a camera jockey to notice decor. Chet started the countdown. *Nine steps.*

"Yeah, Mom did it all by herself," Brittany said, then giggled.

"Damn," Chet muttered. Hadn't they also agreed no one would talk about *Mom* unless he was present? He took two steps at once and momentarily lost his balance. *Seven and counting.*

"So where's your father?" he heard his editor ask.

"Who?" Sean answered.

"Crap." Chet forgot the box, the tight space, and turned.

Crash.

"Are you hurt?" The voice, clear, smooth, alluring.

Chet looked up and got his first glimpse of P.J. West.

She was dressed in a long skirt and boxy jacket, both black and dramatic against her fair skin. Damn, she even wore kick-me-senseless platform shoes, black, of course.

Her blond hair was close-cropped on the sides but full on top and swept to the left. She stared at him with almond-shaped eyes he thought were blue, but in the dim light, he couldn't be sure.

He guessed she was trying for a certain look. Severe, perhaps? Indeed, the entire package screamed, *Look at me, I'm tough,* but he wasn't sold. Severe? No way. Striking? Most definitely. He noticed a softness in her face, a concern and caring no woman of steel would have.

P.J. West looked like a fake—like a virgin in full biker's regalia and wash-off tattoos. And she looked damn attractive. He felt a tightness in his stomach that traveled below his belt.

Now there's a project, he thought, letting his gaze slide over her. The woman was dressed to look about as yielding as a cube. That harsh color would have to go, he thought, and imagined himself pulling off all that black and kneading any sharp angles into a curvy mellowness. He stared at her lips painted candy-apple red and imagined parting them with kisses and coaxing out a few husky moans.

He pushed up on his elbow for a better view.

Flash. The photographer's strobe fired with the blinding intensity of a white explosion. Chet jerked backward, once again hitting his head on the dirt floor. He hardly noticed the pain.

P.J. STOOD at the top of the stairs looking down at what appeared to be a collection of legs and arms hugging a box.

"Why didn't you turn on both lights, *Dad?*" Brittany asked before flicking the switch.

With the space brightened, P.J. realized that the legs and arms weren't what she would call run-of-the-mill extremities. These limbs were well-muscled and solid. The man's stone-washed jeans were molded to his calves and thighs. His rolled up sleeves framed what could pass for lumberjack biceps.

Flash. P.J. blinked away the fantasies before they took hold.

"Are you all right?" she asked again and was rewarded by a grunt.

"Define all right," a voice groaned.

The voice came from behind the box. A head of thick brown hair came next and then a face poked from around the carton. His sheepish, lopsided smile, made him look as though he were apologizing, but his bad-boy twinkling eyes suggested he was still up to something.

"Cool," Sean said. "Were you airborne?"

"Nope. I did your basic backside slide."

P.J. winced.

"It could have been front side down," Flasher said.

"For the last few steps, it was," Chet replied.

"Oh." Flasher raised both eyebrows. "Mind if I get a few shots of your black 'n blues?"

P.J. was horrified. How could they all joke? The poor man could be in pain with bruises covering his back and his... She felt her face grow hot.

"Do you need help?" she asked and cleared away the catch in her voice.

"A few bandages for my pride, a sling for my ego. That ought to do."

With amazing agility, he disentangled himself, then bounded up the stairs and stopped in front of her. Though he stood one step below her, their faces lined up perfectly. A bit too perfectly. His nose seemed inches away. His body heat fanned over her. At least she hoped it was *his* warmth she felt and not her own.

He grinned.

She stared for a moment, feeling her composure melt as the warmth spread. This was not the time for her flustered Patty Jean persona to make an appearance. She needed distance, but that was impossible with three other people crowding her from behind.

If not physical distance, she would have to settle

for symbolic distance—formality. Using a reserved tone, she introduced her photographer and herself. However, when she extended her hand, she found herself hoping that Chet wouldn't notice her nails.

He didn't. He reached out and touched her, then swallowed her hand in his. He held on a bit longer than professionally correct. She should have pulled away, especially after he gave a little squeeze, but for some reason she couldn't. She merely stared into his eyes and stopped breathing.

Flash. The camera's blinding strobe snapped her back into the present. Thankfully it also put an end to the handshake.

Still she didn't breathe easier until Chet gestured all of them off the landing and into the kitchen. P.J. found herself in a large open room with two huge bay windows. Sunlight bounced off polished copper pots and pans that hung from the ceiling.

"Definitely country." Flasher spoke and snapped pictures at the same time.

"Can't you curb that trigger finger?" Chet said, then turned to P.J. "I never agreed to photos."

"I assumed you knew. Pictures make the interview. They add intimacy."

"If I wanted intimacy I wouldn't use a pen name. What I want is anonymity for myself and the kids." He couldn't have pictures of them or the house circulating around the country. At the mere thought of that, he almost swallowed his tonsils.

She puffed up to her full height. Her whole body looked rigid. She opened her mouth to speak, then paused.

"Very well, Mr. Greene. We'll compromise. No pictures of the children except side or back shots where the face is unidentifiable. Any photos of you will have the background in soft focus. Agreed?"

Both he and Flasher nodded. He'd find a way to destroy the film, but he would have to time his move just right. Otherwise, Flasher would simply do a reshoot.

"It's a shame not to showcase this house, though," P.J. went on. "It's lovely. I understand your late wife did the decorating herself. Brittany was telling—"

"So you've met everyone," Chet interrupted. "All except Kevin. I wonder where he is?"

"Hiding, probably," Brittany said, and looked around the room.

"Here, boy. Here, boy," Sean called.

P.J.'s focus darted from one speaker to another. "Is Kevin the family dog?" she asked and started scanning the room herself.

Sniffing sounds and a warm breath on her leg distracted her. She glanced down and jumped. A little boy with brown hair as thick and tousled as his dad's was down on all fours and smelling her ankle. He was as cute as button. He was also as naked as a jaybird.

"Stop it, Kevin, you pervert," Sean yelled.

"I'm not a p'vert. I'm a puppy and she's a..." He paused and looked up at her, the serious frown on his face giving way to a triumphant smile. "She's a fire hydrant."

"A what?" P.J. asked, just as the little guy raised his leg.

"No, you don't." Chet scooped the child up into his arms. "Only house-broken puppies allowed in here. Brittany, take your brother upstairs and put some clothes on him."

"How about a collar?" the girl said, taking the tyke by the wrist and pulling him from the room.

Flasher snapped off at least a dozen more pictures...all of them back shots, as promised.

"I really didn't know parenting could be so...so..." P.J. stammered.

"Dangerous?"

"No. Humorous. I just thought that was your writing style. Now I see it's real life."

"Yeah, it's a zoo. Any TV sitcom would kill to be this entertaining."

"Well, you certainly have things in hand, Mr. Greene," she said as he led her through the kitchen and into the adjacent family room.

He certainly had a hand on her, she thought, feeling the pressure of his palm on the small of her back. The spot tingled and began shooting sparks to other, more intimate body parts. What was wrong with her? Was she short-circuiting, or something?

The sooner she got this interview under way, the sooner she could hightail it back to Chicago.

She glanced up and caught Chet looking at her. His eyes were the same brown as his hair, a rich coffee with the perfect mix of cream. A few faint lines fingered the corners. There weren't many, just enough to convince anyone that Chet Greene had been around for a while, but not overly long. She'd bet young girls still looked twice and swooned.

Well, she was no young girl nor was she prone to swooning. She was here to do a job, one that would secure her position with the magazine. She knew better than to mix work with...with...other things. As a woman, she had to fight doubly hard to prove herself. She wouldn't let a flash of attraction compromise her professional demeanor.

But then Chet smiled, that same lopsided, apologetic smile and P.J. felt a surge of desire undulate through her. *You do not swoon,* her inner voice chided. Still something pulled at her and that darn something felt as powerful as a strong undertow.

DARN. Chet shook his head. He wanted to blame the photographer for getting on his nerves, except he knew better. Sure the man's shutter release was set on automatic, but the whiz snap sounds had long ago turned into white noise. He couldn't even blame the strobe for distracting him; in the bright family room, Flasher wasn't using one.

One thing and one thing alone had him so off balance. P.J. West. As though her voice wasn't trouble enough, here she was in the flesh, sitting on his couch. Well, Ann's couch, but that wasn't the point. P.J. West was the point. No, not point. Curves. The woman was all curves.

Now that she had discarded her shapeless jacket, he could finally appreciate what she'd been hiding. He could see there was way more lying beneath her knit top just waiting to be appreciated.

Even so, he would have preferred a lot less fabric. The neckline rode too high to expose anything except the hollow at the base of her neck, and the capped sleeves didn't even offer him a peak of shoulder. But at least the thing hugged her well-formed breasts.

He watched the rise and fall of her chest and imagined resting his head there. He could feel himself ride the wave of her breathing. Yes, all curves. Perfect curves.

No, no, no. Think curveball not curves. P.J. West was a curveball, as in an unexpected twist, a kink in the mainspring. As in someone who could fire him if she discovered anything amiss. That thought sobered him. He jolted upright and sat with his spine straight as an arrow.

His head cleared. Unfortunately, his body was still skipping down passion's lane. He took a deep breath and waited for the loud swish of blood that pumped in his ears to quiet and the tight pull of his jeans to ease.

"Are you feeling all right, Mr. Greene?" P.J. asked.

He nodded, not trusting his voice.

"You ask me, I'd say he looks a little pinched. Like his clothes are too tight or something," Flasher said.

Trust a photographer to notice the obvious.

"The fall. A delayed reaction," Chet said.

Flasher squinted at him and grunted. "Uh-huh. If you say so."

Then he snapped a few pictures. Chet hoped the

proof sheet wouldn't show exactly where his clothes were straining.

Think professional. No matter how high his libido revved, P.J. West was off-limits. Anything beyond a handshake was a no-no, and handshakes like the one he had given her earlier were well within taboo territory.

What had he been thinking? He'd held on to her as if he'd never touched a woman before. Obviously, he had let too much time elapse between his last relationship and now, but he would remedy that. As soon as this interview ended and P.J. was out of his hair, he would start going out again. He'd call a few friends, hit the hot nightspots. Until then, he couldn't chance intimacy. At least not with P.J. West.

Then he looked into her eyes. Yes, they were blue with tan flecks. The swish in his ears got louder. He was going to have a hard time fighting this…attraction. Then again, maybe he could use it to his advantage. Sure, an all-out come-on would get him slapped and possibly fired, but a bit of measured flirtation could have some benefits.

A charmed woman tended to overlook flaws. Heck, women were gullible that way. They bought into that romantic fairy-tale stuff. So much so that any number of them would kiss a frog and not even see his green warts.

Yeah, he could do that. He could be the kind of frog Ms. P.J. West was looking for. The dedicated bachelor dad, sensitive, caring with a sense of humor. Of course he couldn't be *perfect*. No, he had to be the man he portrayed in his articles. He had to be Chet Greene, a stumble-along, learn-by-my-mistakes type of guy. Make that charming guy.

"If you prefer, Mr. Greene, we can skip that subject for now," P.J. said.

"What?" Chet snapped back and focused. "I'm sorry, I missed your question."

"Your late wife. What was she like?" She leaned forward as though she were about to hold his hand or pat him on the knee.

Ah-hah!

If a charmed woman tended to overlook flaws, a sympathizing one would deny they even existed. Chet took a deep breath. "She looked like Brittany."

He gave P.J. a brave smile. Oh, yeah. He would charm the pants off her.

No, no. Not the pants off her. He would charm all the suspicions out of her.

3

DARNED IF HE WASN'T charming, P.J. thought. She
gazed at the man sitting next to her and sank one
inch deeper into the folds of the cushy couch. Thank
goodness it was one of those expanded sofas and
not a love seat, but still she felt a need for more
space between the two of them. What was it about
this man? She'd been exposed to shy smiles and
soulful eyes before and hadn't been a sucker.

"So what else do you want to know about me?"
Chet's question startled her.

"Yeah, let's not forget why we're here," Flasher
said, and thankfully didn't take a picture. She could
only imagine how totally disorientated she must
look.

Yes. The interview. So far it had proven exactly
what she'd argued all along, that Chet Greene was
a caring single dad. Unfortunately this particular
single dad was not only attractive in an unassuming
way, but with a mere hint of a smile he could send
her heart skittering.

Flasher leaned down and whispered in her ear,
"The interview."

P.J. looked over at the oak coffee table where the
tape recorder sat. For the past hour and a half the

small machine had been documenting her conversation with Chet. Now it recorded her silence.

P.J. reached over and punched the stop button.

She played back the last comments, then rewound the tape again. A stall tactic.

All in all, the ploy had gained her only five additional seconds to gather her wits. Not enough time. The heat licking around her insides hadn't gone away.

Think professional. There was a time and place for everything. Smack-dab in the middle of an interview, an interview that held the key to her professional future, was not the time to succumb to the budding itch of an attraction.

Not unless she wanted to become a laughingstock among her colleagues. She hadn't spent the past six years pretending to be a tough cookie to become the joke of the industry.

She took a deep breath. Time to get the show back on the road and get the heck out of Dodge.

"I remember your bio mentioned you were a professor. How did you get into writing?" she asked. She noticed a muscle in his cheek twitch. It deepened his dimple, but did no more than that. She wasn't sure how she should read that.

"I needed a change." He shrugged. "How'd you get into publishing?"

"By following in the old man's footsteps."

"Oh. Is that who gave you the nickname P.J.?"

"They're simply initials, Mr. Greene."

He squinted. The way he looked at her through his narrowed eyes made her certain he could see inside her. He could look and see her years of struggle, years spent trying to please a father who refused to be pleased, years spent trying to prove she could best any son he could have had.

P.J. shook her history away. Time to focus on the present, and the present was sitting across from her looking much too appealing. Yes, she'd better wrap up this interview quickly.

"We've covered a lot of ground," she said. "In fact, I think we've touched upon just about every important topic."

"Everything except his sex life." Flasher wiggled his eyebrows.

P.J. caught her breath. "Yes, well..."

She'd had no intention of going there, but then her curiosity got the better of her.

"What about your sex life?" she asked. *For the readers' sakes,* she told herself.

"If you have open exploration in mind, you can forget it," Chet said. "Besides, I don't think your readers would be interested."

"On the contrary. They'd like to know how Chet Greene juggles work and kids and a social life. They'd be disappointed if we didn't discuss your...social life."

"Then I'm afraid they'll be disappointed. The content will be sparse."

"You're not trying to tell me you have no social life?"

He smiled the little-boy smile.

"I find that hard to believe," she said. "Surely you date now and then? The ratio of women to men certainly puts the guy at an advantage, like fishing in a stocked pond. Women can search a lifetime and only find preyers and perverts, but men—''

"How about some cold water?" Chet interrupted.

"What? I beg your pardon." P.J. blinked.

"You seem a little worked up...hot and bothered. I could get you something to cool you down," Chet said.

"No...thank you. It's just that—"

"You're single, aren't you?"

"Uh-oh," Flasher said.

She opened her mouth to protest then stopped. Now why was she getting so defensive? Think professional, she reminded herself then nodded, being careful to keep a polite smile in place.

"And do you date?" he asked.

"Well, yes. I—"

"How often? Every evening? Once, twice a week? Or is it a monthly thing like PMS?"

"Mr. Greene—"

"What about tonight? Say dinner? A drive around the waterfront?"

"No, I don't have a date tonight." She was close to shouting.

"Thought not. Would you like to go out?"

She gave a little squeak of a laugh. "You mean, you and me? A date?"

That smile again. She'd been fooled by what she had thought was shyness and openness when in reality he was merely making a pass. Given enough time, he would probably revert to the typical male-in-heat behavior she knew all too well. Served her right for pursuing the subject.

"That's very nice of you to ask, but I—"

"Uh-huh. The proverbial *but*. Few women would want to date a single dad with three children."

"That's not why I can't date you."

"Doesn't matter, really. The answer is still 'Thank you, but...'"

"Well, under the circumstances, I think we should keep our relationship...well not *relationship*." She laughed. "I mean our *association*. We should keep that strictly professional. Excuse me for babbling, but you took me totally by surprise when you asked me out."

"I wasn't asking you out."

"Excuse me?"

"I was making a point. Women will come up with lots of reasons why they will or will not date a single dad, but I've already made a choice. Believe me, the one marriage I had was enough to last a lifetime. I'm not actively seeking anyone."

P.J. sat on her end of the sofa and stared. Heat crept up her neck. She reached into her purse, pulled out an antacid and popped it.

"I tend to agree with the feminists," Chet continued. "No one needs to be matched and mated in order to be happy. I have my work, my house...the kids. I don't need to be seeing someone, to be involved romantically, in order to be fulfilled."

He had stolen her speech, ripped a page right out of her private code book.

"You're a man after my own heart, Mr. Greene."

He leaned back into the cushions and lowered his chin so that his gaze took on a discerning look. "And you'll have to decide how closely you're going to guard it," he said.

Seconds, minutes, hours seemed to pass while he sat there staring, his gaze intense. She felt her hormones squirm.

Flash. The camera's strobe blinded her. P.J. blinked her way back to earth.

"Oops, out of film," her friend announced.

"Maybe this is a good time to take a break," P.J. offered.

"I could use some strong coffee," Flasher said.

"Fine with me." Chet gave a palms-up, anything-you-say gesture. So accommodating, so charming.

She followed him into the kitchen. Her spine straight, her shoulders square, she struggled to salvage her professional persona.

"After our coffee break, I'd like to abandon the formal interview-question-answer format. I want to capture you in your day-to-day routine, follow you around while you go about your business."

There, she was already back in control. She slipped onto a counter stool. Things were again on track.

"I'll show the readers what Chet Greene's life is really like. I want them to know the man behind those articles. I want the readers to know Chet James."

"So you want to blow my alias?" he said.

Darn. That smile again. P.J. swallowed hard.

"I don't intend to blow anything," she said, but her voice was shaky because she couldn't guarantee she wouldn't eventually blow her cool.

BRITTANY SAT cross-legged in the middle of her bed and took in the long faces of her brothers.

"Bummer," Sean said and leaned against the dresser. "She's going to be here four more hours."

"She's not that bad. For someone old she dresses real rave," Brittany said. "Anyway, you weren't complaining when Uncle Chet promised you two new CDs."

"Yeah, but that was before I realized how long a six-hour interview really was. And we have to act nice the whole time."

"Yeah," said Kevin.

"Even the two of you can fake being human for six hours," Brittany said.

"Well I know why you're not complaining. You're gaga for Flasher. Flasher, Flasher," Sean teased.

"You're such a moron," she said, throwing a pillow and hitting him in the face. "Anyway, you can't back down now."

"Yeah, I won't get my candy," Kevin said.

"Forget the candy and the presents, Uncle Chet's counting on us," Brittany said. "If we blow it, he'll lose his job."

"Then he'll stop writing those articles and we won't be in that dorky magazine anymore."

Brittany had to admit Uncle Chet had gone overboard recently, giving too much detail and getting way too personal, but causing him to lose his job wasn't the way to fix that problem.

"We can work on that later," she said. "After his editor leaves, we'll call our own family meeting, but right now we've got other things to worry about."

"Like what?" Kevin asked

"Like watching out for Uncle Chet. It's up to us to make sure he doesn't goof."

"He practically lives here. What's to goof?"

"Lots," Brittany said. "Take now, for instance. They've been down there talking forever. Every minute is possible goof-time. The longer the two of them talk, the more likely Chet will say something wrong, right?"

Both boys nodded, and she continued.

"We have to make sure they aren't left alone for too long. We're going to have to create a distraction."

"What's 'stractions?" Kevin asked.

"Like in my Beast Warrior video game," Sean explained. "The blue monster is jumping up and down, breathing fire and weirding-out the hero while the green slime monsters are creeping up behind, ready to annihilate our guy."

"Oh, yeah," Kevin said. "And then the orange monsters jump down from the ceiling—"

"There're no orange monsters in Beast Warrior."

"Are too," Kevin said.

"Forget the stupid game," Brittany said. "We need a real distraction right this minute, and I think I have a perfect one."

"What?" both boys asked.

"Nothing gets a grown-up's attention like a sick kid," Brittany said, then looked at her younger brother and smiled. "Kevin, I think you're beginning to look a little ill."

"Me?" His eyes stretched open wide.

"Yeah," Sean said, quick to jump in. "You don't look so hot. You should be in bed."

"I'm not sleepy, I'm hungry. It's almost lunchtime."

"Not for you, kid," Sean said. "If you ask me, you're looking kinda green."

"Am not," said Kevin. "Frogs are green."

"And so are sick little boys. Sean's right. You should get right to bed. And I'll call Chet...I mean Dad."

"I'll even put my Quarantine sign on your door," Sean offered.

"And your Toxic Dump sign, too?" Kevin's eyes sparkled.

"Sure."

"Cool," Kevin said, and hopped out of the room chanting, *"Rib-bit, rib-bit."*

Brittany could hear his Kermit impression all the way down the hall. Good. All that hopping will get Kevin good and flushed. That ought to fool anyone, but she would stick the thermometer under the hot water tap just to make sure.

COFFEE.

Good idea, Chet thought as he rummaged through the pantry. Anything to get the focus off his personal life when all he could think of was starting something very personal with his editor. Focus on coffee and not P.J.'s voice or her blue eyes or full lips.

He moved to the cabinet over the stove. Salt, pepper, spices. No instant coffee.

"So tell me about your discipline methods," P.J. said. Her voiced licked his ears.

"What methods?" he answered, and moved on to the next cabinet. Opening door number three proved equally futile. Ann always made fresh coffee from beans she would grind on the spot. He wasn't even sure she had instant.

"You've read my articles. I'm what you'd call a seat-of-the-pants type of guy."

"Your basic backside slider, if I remember correctly," Flasher said.

"Don't forget the quarter turn, frontal finale," Chet responded, then turned his back and addressed P.J. "I've read the latest child psych books, but I think it all boils down to one thing." Chet did another scan of the kitchen.

The fancy European coffeemaker sat on the counter, an elaborate cappuccino machine next to that. He couldn't be bothered with filters and whole beans, and grinders. All he wanted was a jar of instant, a few spoons, cups and the microwave. Add water and milk, and voilà. So where was the stuff?

He was all too aware of P.J. standing off to the side watching him undo the neatly arranged shelves. He was all too aware of the knot in his stomach, also.

"And what's that one thing, Mr. Greene?" P.J. asked.

Finally he opened the last cabinet. *Eureka.*

"Respect," he said.

Coffee. The darn shelves were crowded with all types of java and fixings. But no instant coffee, he discovered after he'd pushed the cans and assorted filters aside.

"Kids are people," he said, and gave the shelves another once-over. "Just like us, they have their own feelings and hopes and frustrations."

His frustration was working its way up to a scream. No, he couldn't do that. Stay calm, breathe.

Surely Ann had at least one jar of instant in the house. It was un-American not to. It was certainly unhelpful.

"Sometimes grown-ups forget that," he continued as he searched. "Sometimes we treat children like objects or property and not like people. There's no crime in asking for your child's opinion and there's no crime in compromise. But when all else fails, the most important thing to remember is—"

He came to the last jar. Something small was hidden behind.

Please let it be coffee. If it is, I promise from now on I'll eat every vegetable Ann puts on my plate.

He pushed aside the last jar on the very top shelf and almost sighed with relief. Instant coffee, decaf, but acceptable. He snatched his find from the shelf and clutched it to his chest.

"—the bribe. Never underestimate the power of

a well-timed bribe.'' Chet looked at the baffled expressions on his guests' faces and smiled.

"Coffee coming up," he said, and took down three cups and filled each from the tap.

"Oh," P.J. said. Disappointment registered in her voice.

"Something wrong with the cappuccino machine?" Flasher asked. "Because if there isn't, I could get some shots of you working all those gadgets. Coffee flowing, milk foaming."

"What a great idea," P.J. said.

Chet looked over and caught the hopeful expression on her face. He felt his heart sink. Yeah, great idea if he knew how to operate the darn thing. That machine was Ann's pride and joy. She never let him touch the contraption for fear he'd break it. Which wasn't a bad idea. He could simply tell them the machine was broken.

He cleared his throat. "Well, you see—"

"Dad," Brittany's voice called down to him. "You'd better come up here. I think Kevin's sick."

"Right," he said, setting down the cups and breezing past P.J. and Flasher.

Never underestimate the power of a bribe, or the timing of urchins.

P.J. WAITED IN THE COZY family room just off the kitchen. She crossed her leg and pivoted the swivel recliner so she faced Flasher but could still watch Chet and the children as they did the dishes.

Sean cleared the table, and once Chet finished scraping the plates, Brittany loaded the washer.

Even Kevin, miraculously cured by a combination of fatherly TLC and applied psychology, had a role. The little tyke examined each dish, giving the final approval before handing them over to his sister.

The four of them worked as a team. That took practice, definitely not something that could be faked for a onetime performance. And they laughed and talked while they worked.

As happy as Snow White's dwarfs, she thought, and wished she could pull up such memories from her own childhood. She couldn't. Her parents, or rather her father, all too often forgot she was a person.

Enough of that. She gave herself a mental shake and glanced at Flasher.

"What do you think?" she asked.

"Well, he's attractive, charming, available—"

"That's not what I was asking you."

"Of course not. You already know all that."

"I'm serious, Flasher."

"Okay. In that case...I think you're a goner."

She rolled her eyes. "I think everything is copacetic. The house is real, the family is real. The kids are his...their relationship is wonderful, and there's no sign of any mystery woman or wife."

"Not even a picture. Don't you think that's odd?"

"Odd, but not unrealistic." Her own mother had died when P.J. was only ten. She remembered how her father had removed every photo of her from the house. The only one he didn't pack away was the miniature P.J. kept inside her own locket.

"What do you think about his bribery policy? You think he was telling the truth?" Flasher asked.

"Hard to say, but that's one aspect of Chet Greene the readers don't really need to know about. For the reader's sake," she added.

"Hide the truth, fan the myth. Definitely, a goner."

She cut Flasher a side glance.

"All done," Chet said, drawing her attention.

The four of them stood in the doorway and faced her. All of them were as wet as the dishes they'd just loaded. All of them wore grins, but only Chet's was electric.

P.J. felt the sparks clear across the room.

"And so are we," she said. "I think Flasher and I have more than enough material. After I report in to the office, we'll pack up and leave."

She gave one of her brightest smiles in spite of the lump in her throat. What was with her? Earlier, she couldn't wait to wrap up this interview and be on her way. Now the time had come and she was boiling over with mixed emotions.

Flasher's words echoed in her head. *A goner.*

No, she insisted. The only *gone* she would experience was walking out the door. But first to call The Reaper with the good news.

Five minutes later, P.J. sat in the family room, gripping the cordless phone and shaking her head.

"We can't do that." She almost shouted into the receiver. "I already have enough material," she insisted, then listened while her boss spoke.

"What's he saying?" Flasher whispered.

P.J. turned to her friend and mimicked a scream.

"Does that mean we didn't win the lottery?" Flasher moved closer and perched on the arm of the overstuffed chair where P.J. sat, sinking and sinking.

"Well, sure," she said into the phone. "The readers would love that, but... Yes, they'd eat it up...but... Yes. But—" She jumped up from the chair and paced. Pacing helped her think. Pacing and gnawing her nails. She chewed her pinkie.

Flasher slapped her hand from her mouth and whispered, "What? What?"

She covered the receiver with her hand. "He wants us to stay longer."

"Another hour? Two hours?"

"One week," she said.

"What?" The voice came from across the room.

P.J. spun around and saw Chet, the expression of surprise on his face was fast turning into panic. She wanted to give him a reassuring look. She wanted to tell him, "Don't worry, I have this under control," but the truth was, she felt about as panicked as he looked.

So she gave him the only honest thing she could, a frown and a shrug, then turned back to the man on the line.

"Yes, I understand how important this— No, I don't want to lose my— Of course. Yes."

She rang off, placed the phone on the coffee table, and stared at the thing as though it were to blame. After a few seconds, she shifted her focus first to Flasher then to Chet. Both men hovered, mouths agape, eyes large. They looked as though they'd been stung by a swarm of bees. If she weren't feeling so shell-shocked, she'd have laughed.

4

P.J. TOOK A DEEP BREATH. Sickness churned her stomach. How was she to sell this bag of baloney when she was having a hard time swallowing it herself? Easily. She would stick to the logistics and only the logistics. Emotions would settle once a simple plan of action was in place and everyone realized how smoothly this could be handled.

"He said we should have our respective roommates ship any necessary clothes or personables via overnight courier." She looked at Flasher.

"Well, that solves the toothbrush and clean underwear problem. What about the broken dates and previous commitments?"

"What about my privacy?" Chet asked.

"I'm sorry about that, Mr. Greene, but I couldn't say no."

"A little negativity challenged, are we? I'll show you how it's done." Chet framed his lips with his hands, made elaborate facial gestures then shouted. "No."

P.J. jumped.

"See, it's easy. Just put your tongue at the roof of your mouth and say *No*. Call him back, I'll tell the man myself."

"Won't work," she said. "My boss sees the potential in turning this into a series spanning three issues of the magazine. Money and increased readership are involved. The man won't budge."

"Then I'll call him. Maybe he can restructure your life, but he can't toy with mine."

"He threatened to pull the plug on your column unless we agreed. How much more restructuring do you need? Both our livelihoods are on the line."

"He can't do that," Chet said. "Who is this guy, anyway?"

"The Grim Reaper," P.J. and Flasher said in unison.

"Trust me, the name fits. One week," she pleaded. "We'll be out of your hair in six days."

"You originally said one day. No *six hours.* You wouldn't believe the trouble I went through arranging—I mean..." He paused then smacked his palm against his forehead. "I mean rearranging schedules...my schedule, the kids' schedules. I can't believe this."

P.J. felt sorry for him, but he wasn't in this alone. He wasn't the only one backed into a wall. She was being backed right up beside him and the promise of six more days of closeness was making her nervous.

"You have only your own popularity to blame, Mr. Greene," she blurted, and felt silly. So much for sticking to the logistics. So much for calming emotions.

Chet shook his finger at her. He opened his mouth then snapped it shut.

"Okay, okay," he said and turned a tight circle. "We can deal with this. Yeah. I just have to be resourceful."

He turned a few more about-faces then came to a halt in front of her. "There's a nice inn a mile or so down the road. Small, but comfortable. Historic, even. I'm sure they have a few vacancies. If not, there's a decent motel nearby. You'll have to drive back and forth, but...hey, a bed's a bed and at this short notice, you take what you can get."

His look of relief was almost painful to witness, and there was that smile again. She felt a stab of guilt. She was about to burst his bubble. P.J. cleared her throat.

"Mr. Greene, I'm sorry, you've misunderstood. My boss wants me to cover a week in your life. To do that I need to shadow you. I have to stay *here*. In your house."

"Here?"

He paled.

"Don't worry. I'll be as unobtrusive as possible. My being here should pose no problem."

She had almost convinced herself of that fact, but then Flasher whispered in her ear.

"You're a goner."

"A WHOLE WEEK?"

His niece's shriek drilled through Chet. He held up his hands to settle the unrest spreading among the ranks. "Six days. We can do that."

The four of them sat in the living room, Chet on the couch, Kevin in his lap and Brittany beside him.

Sean sat cross-legged on the floor with his elbows on his knees and his chin nesting in his hands. The air was sodden with gloom.

"I don't see why she can't stay at a hotel or someplace. Who can be normal with a camera always in your face?" Sean asked.

"I told you why they have to stay here, and as for the camera, Flasher promised not to take any full face shots of you three."

Chet had made a point of reemphasizing that rule. He couldn't have neighbors or friends identifying any of them and writing letters to the editor. Yep, he would definitely destroy as many rolls as possible, just to be on the safe side.

"Being taped is just as bad as being flash-blinded," Sean said.

"P.J. won't be using it full-time, only when the two of us sit down for a formal interview. You have nothing to worry about. Just act nice and call me...what?" Chet held his hand to his ear and waited for their response. And waited.

"Come on, guys," Chet said. "This wasn't my call, but I know we can pull this off."

"But a whole week," Sean moaned. "*Somebody's* bound to goof up." He looked at Kevin who stuck out his tongue.

"What about Mom?" Brittany asked.

"Taken care of. The spa didn't mind extending her stay and your mother was ecstatic. If nothing else, we'll be doing this for her. She could use a long vacation. So what do you say?" Chet looked on as each child nodded.

"I could use some more gummies," Kevin said.

"Blackmailer." Yep, time to review the bribe policy, Chet thought, then he tickled his nephew until the boy squealed.

P.J. LEANED AGAINST the island and watched Chet move around the kitchen. He seemed lost at first, opening and closing cabinets as if he didn't know where he'd put things, but now with the linguini boiling, the aroma of garlic-spiced tomato sauce filling the space, the man looked quite at home. A bit tense and tight around the mouth, but a tight-mouthed, tense man who knew how to cook. Still, she couldn't ignore that tweak of guilt she still felt.

"I wish you had let me take you out to dinner tonight."

"You must like chicken nuggets and burgers?"

"Aren't there any nice restaurants in town?" she asked.

"Not when you're dining with kids."

He turned toward her, spoon in hand, red sauce dripping on the floor and moisture dotting his forehead. A small smile turned his lips and she thought how wonderful it was to have someone care enough to cook for you.

"When you were a kid, did you like going to fancy restaurants with your folks, eating food you didn't like and having to sit up straight the whole time?"

Something close to a pinch grabbed her inside. She wished she did have such memories. P.J. held her hands together and pulled at her fingernails.

"I'm only saying I feel like we're putting you out. I wish I could do something to make up for that."

He raised one brow and flashed a mischievous smile.

"How about if you and Flasher pack up and go back—"

"Something other than flying back to Chicago," she said.

"Can't shoot a man for trying." He shrugged, then turned to check the pasta.

Again, the garlic smell tickled her senses. Her stomach growled. "Who taught you how to cook?"

"My sister, and she still worries that I'll starve to death. That's why I have a standing invitation at her house."

"You mean, since your wife died?"

P.J. watched the color drain from his face before he busied himself lifting and clattering tops. *Still suffering after three years.* Her heart thumped a little harder for him.

Chet cleared his throat. "Look," he said, the lopsided smile in place. "Everything's under control in here. Why don't you get a beer or something and take it easy. Go prop your feet up in the living room. Turn on the television or something."

"In other words, get out of my kitchen."

"For honorable reasons. I'm a messy cook. You don't want pasta sauce all over your clothes." To demonstrate, he whipped the spoon in the air. Red droplets rained down, and missed her by inches. He dipped the spoon and raised it again. The grin on his face looked downright devilish.

"I'm going. I'm going. But tomorrow I'll cook and *you'd* better watch out."

P.J. slipped from the kitchen and moved down the hall. She entered the living room and walked around, taking in the space and the decor. Flasher was right. The place was country enough to make all three Dixie Chicks homesick, or perhaps just sick.

And no family pictures. She hated to think his pain was so raw that he'd removed every reminder of his wife. Perhaps he had a portrait in his bedroom. That was a more comforting thought, she concluded, and walked out into the center hall.

A clicking sound caught her attention. She moved through the dining room, following the noise as it grew stronger.

"Yeah. Take that," came a voice from a room to the left of the china closet. "And that, slimeball."

P.J. stopped in the doorway of what looked like a media room complete with computer, stereo and large-screen television. Sean sat in a game chair, controller in hand, and his focus locked on the screen.

"Beast Warrior?" she asked.

Sean whipped around and stared at her. His mouth hung open and a guarded look crept into his eyes.

"Watch that green Orkman," she said, pointing to the screen.

Sean spun around, back at the controls, back fighting the beast.

"What level are you?" she asked.

"I'm on four now, but I've made it up to five. I can't get past the fire hole though."

"Did you try using the sword? No, no. Not as a weapon. That's the secret. If you throw it into the fire the flames will part."

"Cool." Sean squinted at the screen, maneuvered his warrior past a flying boulder. "You want to play?" he asked, peaking at her from under his lashes. "I've got an extra controller."

"Sure." P.J. sat down and took up the other instrument.

It sure beat sitting alone in the living room with her feet propped up. She looked over at Sean and winked. The boy smiled up at her, shyly at first, then broadly and welcoming.

A pleasant tweak stirred in her chest. She could really grow fond of these kids, she thought, then scooted closer to her partner. P.J. gave him a nod and the two of them started slaying beasts.

BY NINE O'CLOCK, a definite calm had settled over the house. A tinge of violet had seeped into the sky and the crickets had come out for the evening.

Chet walked down the stairs congratulating himself. Aside from a few minor glitches, the day had gone well. Dinner had been a breeze thanks to one of Ann's frozen pasta sauces. Okay, he had scorched the stuff, but no one had complained. Luckily, none of the kids had slipped and called him Chet, but the best part, the thing that had him breathing easier, was that P.J. hadn't asked any let's-trip-up-Chet questions.

This daddy charade was a doable deed, especially if the next six days proved as easy as this one. Now with the kids off to bed and Flasher retired to the attic guest room, he could finally relax.

Not quite. P.J. awaited him downstairs, probably with hopes of continuing her interview. She hadn't turned out to be the tough cookie he expected. Still, he knew better than to lower his guard. Maintaining his defenses would be difficult after such a tiring day. He had better escort Ms. P.J. West straight to her room, then retreat to the safety of his own.

Chet rounded the corner and entered the living area. Music greeted him. Soft jazz floated through the air and around his head. P.J. stood by one speaker, her eyes closed, her head tilted toward the sound. Her lips moved, mimicking the words. It was a Brazilian song, and he wondered if she actually knew the lyrics. She knew the beat. Her body moved ever so slightly to the slow samba.

If she had been any woman other than his editor, he would have been across the room swooping her into his arms. Staring was the best he could do under the circumstances. Staring and aching in places he preferred would remain dormant for the next six days. Suddenly a particular, strong impulse curled its way south. He groaned.

P.J. opened her eyes, her focus dead on him. For the longest time, she didn't blink. Chet imagined she was listening to his heart. It was beating loudly enough.

"I hope you don't mind. I took you up on that offer of a beer," she finally said and raised her half-empty glass.

Chet swallowed.

"I got you one, too." She lowered the volume and walked over to the sofa.

No, not walked, swayed. Why hadn't she found something less sensual to play? A loud polka, for example.

"I thought we could relax and talk," she said.

"I was thinking more along the lines of calling it a day."

"But there's so much more the readers would like to know about you."

"Forever working. What are you doing, bucking for a promotion?"

She colored. "Fine. Sit down. We'll finish our beers and go to bed."

He couldn't decide which was worse, being interviewed under the influence or sharing a sofa with P.J. while seductive music played in the background.

"Okay. Interview away," he said.

"Tell me why you quit the university?"

She'd started off with a stomach punch, but he wasn't about to spill his guts.

"Your readers want to know that?"

"No. I do."

"Ah." He sipped his beer and said no more. Neither did P.J. She smiled at him from across the stretch of sofa. Police used that technique, ask a question and let silence wring the answer out. He wouldn't fall for it, though.

That territory had a No Trespassing sign as big as day. Nope, he wasn't going to revisit that particular nightmare. Simply thinking about it made him uncomfortable and angry.

He would sit and wait her out. He'd simply concentrate on the music, but soon the CD had switched from the first samba to an even steamier number, and answering her question became the least of his troubles.

He imagined he held P.J. in his arms. He imagined he slow-danced her around the floor, in perfect rhythm, bodies a perfect fit. He tried hard, but couldn't block the images. Dangerous, dangerous. Talking couldn't be worse.

"Academia and I had a conflict of interest," he blurted. His voice sounded like one of Kevin's pull-the-string-and-talk toys.

"Your interest, I take it?" she said.

He nodded, intent upon saying no more, but the music picked up tempo and so did his imagination.

One, two and dip.

"I headed up a team. Ten years of research, interviews, follow-up, analysis. When it was all over, I had to use a magnifying glass to find my name on the final paper. Let's say I was more outraged than smart."

"Ah, don't tell me...you complained and got fired."

"And once betrayed you never forget the bite."

"The publishing world isn't any different. Ideas

whispered in the wrong ear get stolen. That's why the successful editor keeps her professional and social lives separate.'' Something dark passed over her face. Her mouth slipped into a rueful smile. *And who betrayed you, Ms. P.J. West? A friend? No. A lover.*

''Well, I've turned my bad luck around, resourceful guy that I am,'' Chet continued. ''My research was about the one-parent household. The original paper is collecting dust while 'Living and Learning' is helping many a harried single dad.''

Telling her had been easier than he thought. He didn't know why. He'd talked about his experience with Ann, but their discussions never relieved the bottled-up emotions that stewed inside him. Telling P.J. had been different. Suddenly, all the old tension eased.

''You're smiling,'' she said.

Yeah, he was. He was smiling all over. For some reason, he felt like a giddy drunk. Must be the beer, he thought. Or maybe he should blame that damn bossa nova.

BRITTANY SAT CROSS-LEGGED on the braided rug in her room and stared out into the hall where Sean manned the look-out station. She was aware of Kevin stretched out on the rug and glancing up at her, waiting for her to get the show on the road.

''Well, what's going on?'' Brittany whispered out into the hall.

''Nothing. They're sitting on the sofa,'' Sean answered, his voice as hushed as hers had been.

"They've been sitting there doing nothing since forever."

Shee. Boys were so slow. If she'd been kneeling there on the landing for the past five minutes with her forehead pressed against the railings, she would have more to report than that.

"Well, how close are they sitting?" she asked. "And what else are they doing beside talking? Like are they smiling or anything?"

"He's on one end and she's on the other. And, no, they aren't smiling. They aren't doing anything, except she keeps moving her hands around a lot."

"Nervous. Mom does that hand stuff, too, when she's nervous. That's a good sign. She likes him."

"Yuck," Kevin said. "I hate girls."

"She's not a girl, silly. She's a grown-up and if she likes Chet...I mean, *Dad,* then maybe this will work out."

"I think you're nuts. Chet says weddings give him the hives. He's never going to get married," Sean said.

"Of course he won't...not without some help. And that's where we come in." She beckoned to her brother and watched as he crawled commando-style back to her bedroom. She waited until he joined them on the rug before she continued.

"You don't want to be in Chet's articles forever, do you? I mean, just think of it. The whole world will read all about your first date, and your first kiss, and your first—"

"Okay. I get the picture," Sean said.

"Good." She knew that little example would do

the trick. "The only way we'll ever get out from under the microscope will be if Chet has kids of his own to write about. And to have kids, he has to get married."

"What makes you think he even likes her?" Sean asked.

"Didn't you notice the way he was staring at her all goo-goo eyed? And that handshake. I mean, he held on for days. Don't tell me you didn't notice that."

"Yeah, so?"

"Duh." She rolled her eyes. "Trust me, the chemistry's there. All we have to do is stir things up a bit."

"Donny Taylor drank some chemicals," Kevin said, "and he got real, real sick."

"Well, Chet and Miss West are going to get sick, too. Lovesick. And all because of us and Operation Cupid. Are we all in on this?" Brittany asked, holding out her hand palm-down on the rug.

The two boys placed their hands atop hers. "Sure," both said.

"Good. All we have to do is make Uncle Chet look like he needs help."

"Get real. Who'd want to marry a doofus?"

"I'm not talking about a doofus. Look, I read up on these things. Women like men who have faults, not big faults, just small things they can help fix."

"That's stupid," Sean said. "I always knew women were dumb."

"Would you want to spend the rest of your life

with someone perfect?'' Brittany asked. ''That would be creepy.''

Sean shrugged and Kevin aped his gesture.

''Trust me. This is the way to go,'' she said. ''They'll never know what hit them.''

5

"I REALLY AM SORRY about the way we've invaded your house," P.J. said as Chet led her up the stairs.

They stopped in front of the linen closet where he removed towels and sheets that smelled clothes-line fresh, not tumbled in a hot drier. She reached for the pile, but he didn't hand it over.

"You must want that promotion pretty bad. Why?" he asked and waited.

That made the second time he'd mentioned a promotion, but she knew better than to discuss *maybes*. Besides, she was the interviewer, not the other way around. The less he knew about her, the easier it was to keep their *association* on a professional level.

P.J. folded her arms, and looked first left then right down the door-lined hall. Her room hid behind one of those doors so she asked, "Which way?"

Chet said nothing. Seconds passed. Standing there facing this man made seconds seem like hours. She bit her nails.

"I know what you're doing, you know." When he didn't respond, she felt obliged to tell him. "You're deliberately not speaking because you think that will force me to spew out my life confessions.''

"It worked on me. You now know why I'm not locked away in some ivy-covered building teaching sociology. I want to know what's pushing you.''

She chuckled and began nibbling on another fingernail.

"I'll give you two more minutes,'' Chet said, pointing to her hands. "You'll either tell all or draw blood.''

She snatched her finger from her mouth, placed her hands on her hips, then finally hid them in the crook of her crossed arms. "I want to initiate some changes that only a woman can make.''

"So did Joan of Arc. Look what happened to her.''

"Yeah, well I'm not ruling that out, but I still have to try.''

"What's so important you'll burn for?''

"Harmony.'' P.J. paused. "My mother died when I was ten. My father knew nothing about women, let alone little girls. He tried to remake me into a son, which would have worked except I got older and discovered my talking *genes*.'' She finger-gestured quotation marks around the last words. "After a while,'' she continued, "discussing last night's ball game wasn't enough for me anymore.''

Though she didn't expect that bit of information would ever come back and bite her, she still hadn't intended to share so much personal data.

"You wanted to *communicate*.'' Chet mimicked her finger gesture.

"And express *feelings*. I scared the poor man silly. I see it happening today. A lot of men are afraid of women simply because they don't understand where we're coming from."

"Venus, I've been told," he said.

P.J. rolled her eyes. "If I'm senior editor I can introduce a woman's perspective to the magazine."

"What makes you think the readers want anything other than sex and sex and more sex?"

"Your popularity."

"You're going to burn at the stake because of my column? How do you think that makes me feel?"

"Swollen-headed, no doubt. I am really sorry about all this, though. My crusade shouldn't drag *you* through the fire."

"Hey, I'm in this to keep my job, too...my very lucrative job. Let's just say our goals overlap."

"And how do you *feel* about that?"

Chet flinched.

"Gotcha," she said and chuckled.

Chet shook his head and smiled. "Feelings don't scare me. I get them all the time. Take now, for instance."

"What about now?"

"I sense you'd rather be anywhere but here. Unfortunately you started this bear hunt and now you find yourself trapped in his den. How's that for feelings?"

"Not quite what I had in mind, plus that you're wrong. I can think of worse places to spend six days. My high-school reunion, for one. A periodontist's office, for another. Anyway, I'm not hunting bear. I want to prove you are no fraud.''

"I'm touched. I had this notion that you were going to be a female steamroller out for number one and the hell with anyone else. I was prepared to dislike you. I mean, really dislike you.''

"I hope you've reconsidered.''

"I'm a writer. I'm an ace at making changes.''

She'd hoped for more than that. The collapsed feeling in her chest told her so. "Then we won't spend the week at war.''

Darn. He flashed that glimpse of a grin again. She held her breath and waited for her flutters to stop.

"No war,'' he said. "I feel lucky that this isn't another conflict of interest situation.''

Me, too, she thought but didn't say so. No telling how he would interpret that, especially given the way she was staring at him and how he was staring back.

"I've got one more question,'' he said. "What does P.J. stand for?''

"Family secret,'' she answered, her fingertip to her lips.

Suddenly the space separating them seemed smaller. Had he moved closer? She stepped back into the wall.

She didn't realize she'd put her finger in her mouth, until Chet removed it. He held on to her hand and rubbed his thumb over the heel of her palm. She knew what was coming next, knew it by the darkening of his eyes.

And how do you feel about that? The heck if she

knew. Everything was tumbling around inside. Before she could sort it all out, Chet was leaning over his bundle of sheets and she was tiptoeing to meet him.

"Mommie." The word was no more than a soft mew.

A small thump landed on her thigh. P.J. looked down on Kevin's curly head. She was about to answer when Chet pushed the linens into her arms and swooped the boy into his. The little guy's eyes were closed when he said, "I have to go potty."

"Sure, champ," Chet said and then threw her another of his shy smiles. She couldn't mistake the look of relief she saw there. Maybe her expression was similar. She knew she was relieved to be breathing again even though the deep drags of air she took could in no way be called normal.

"Second door on the left." He pointed with his chin then carried Kevin in the opposite direction.

P.J. waited until the bathroom door closed behind them before turning toward her room. He had called her Mommie. A warmth spread over her. She didn't know how she would have felt about kissing Chet, but she knew how she felt about Kevin.

THE MORNING SUNLIGHT glared through the glass front door, heating the hallway in spite of the air conditioner. So this was summer in the South? Did people really adjust to this kind of heat? Fanning herself, she rounded the corner and entered the kitchen.

"Good morning, Miss West," Brittany and Sean sang out.

"Hey, Sleeping Beauty," Flasher said.

She couldn't believe it. It was six o'clock on Saturday morning. She thought she'd gotten up early, but Brittany and Sean were in the kitchen busy as bees with Flasher recording every moment. She wanted to be alone to sort out last night, but that was not to be. The kitchen bustled.

The aroma of coffee tickled her nose. The smell of bacon assaulted her stomach.

"What's all this? Are you expecting more company?" she asked.

"Sean and I thought you'd like a real Southern breakfast. We're fixing grits, bacon, scrapple, and biscuits—just the heat-and-serve kind, but they taste all right."

"Mmm-mmm, yummy." Flasher grinned at P.J. He looked far too amused. He knew she was a loyal bagel and coffee woman.

She'd never seen that much food on a breakfast table. Her eyes were half closed, her body not fully awake. She hadn't the energy to tackle this feast. Just thinking of it left her feeling...bloated. She could feel the pounds inch on to her thighs and hips.

"We were waiting for you to come down before we did the eggs. How do you want them?" Brittany asked.

"Not only is this little lady a looker, she can really cook." Flasher gave Brittany a wink plus one of his best smiles. P.J. watched a deep blush tint the girl's complexion.

"Aren't you hungry?" Sean asked.

P.J. noted the expectant looks on the children's faces and forced a smile.

"Shouldn't we wait for your father?"

"There's no telling *when* he'll wake up," Sean said. "Sometimes he forgets breakfast altogether."

"So you have to cook for yourselves?"

"We don't mind. He works real hard, sometimes late into the night," Sean said.

"He won't admit it, but I think it's too much for him, working and taking care of us and the house...all by himself. It's not easy doing all that...alone," Brittany added.

"I suppose not," P.J. said. The single-parent trap, trying to be all and do all, but unable to see that was an impossible setup. Even Mr. Living and Learning wasn't immune. Again, that little twinge pulled at her heart.

"So how about if I help out today?" P.J. asked. "When everything's ready, we'll surprise him."

The kids exchanged looks and nodded. "You can do the grapefruit."

Flasher slipped up beside her. "This is an interesting segment in A-Day-in-the-Life. Man sleeps until noon, leaves his children to fend for themselves."

"Obviously he won't win the Super Dad award." To her surprise the words came out with enough acid to burn her tongue.

"I'm sorry." P.J. stroked her friend's arm. "Guess I got up on the wrong side of the bed."

"Doesn't matter which side you get out of if the bed's empty." He winked. "Goner."

"Am not," she said as she grabbed a knife and stabbed the first grapefruit.

IF THE SMELL OF COFFEE hadn't clued Chet that things were amiss, the chatter coming from the kitchen certainly did. He hitched Kevin up piggy-back style and made his way down the hall.

"I smell food," the boy said and sniffed the air. Wrestling and kicking, he made his way to the floor and ran. "Mommie's home."

"Wait." Chet grabbed for the speeding urchin, but came up with air.

The barefoot tyke pity-patted toward the kitchen. Must be a racehorse today, Chet thought, as he gave chase.

"Wait, Kevin," he said, his sock-clad feet offering zero traction on the polished floor. Chet slipped, then skidded on his backside the rest of the way, and came to a crashing halt in the doorway.

"Ah. Another photo moment," Flasher said, snapping away.

"What's going on?" Chet struggled to his feet.

"Breakfast," P.J. said.

"For whose army? Don't tell me this is the way they eat in Chicago?"

"No, the South. That's what your children told me. They wanted to make breakfast since *you* usually forget."

"I usually forget? Sean? Brittany?" Chet looked

at each of them, at their downcast faces. A chilly feeling drifted over him.

"May I be excused? I'm not hungry anymore." Brittany smiled at Flasher and slipped from the room before Chet could answer.

"Me, neither," Sean said and followed his sister. Kevin sniffled as he plodded after them.

P.J. and Flasher watched the children leave then turned and glared at him.

"What? What did I do?" Chet asked.

"Oh, nothing," P.J. said. "You didn't get up on time. You didn't see that your children had a decent breakfast, and after they did your job for you, you didn't even say thank-you."

Brittany and Sean never got up earlier than nine unless it was a schoolday. And as for breakfast, toast, yogurt and juice qualified as a large meal. Anything more would require force feeding. Those two were up to something, but he couldn't tell P.J. that. Not without exposing his own scheme.

"All right. I blew it. Minus five daddy points for today."

"Ten," she said, "but that's okay."

Her smile was soft. Her mouth turned up in the cutest manner. She had forgiven him. She had seen him at one of his nonstellar moments and hadn't condemned him. He was glad about that.

He felt something grumble like a hunger pang, but instead of emptiness he felt warmth spreading throughout his body. Suddenly he realized he wanted her to like him, and not because of the magazine. He wanted her to like him, Chet James, not Chet Greene.

"Thanks," he said.

"No, really, it's okay. This will be great for the article. The readers will relate to you better knowing that you can be as clueless as the next guy."

She couldn't have been more effective if she'd thrown a bucket of ice water in his face. Chet shivered himself back to reality.

"Then they're in luck. Today's chore day. I do the laundry, the cleaning, the cooking…lunch and dinner only, but you already know that. So stick around, there's plenty of opportunity to relate to your everyday-average-clueless Joe."

He left P.J. and Flasher exchanging wide-eyed looks and marched out of the room. He would do the laundry first, and while that was going through the cycles, he would attack the cleaning. He would show her. He could out house-daddy the best of them.

"I CAN'T IMAGINE what brought that on," P.J. said.

"Another case of the empty-bed blues if you ask me." Flasher walked over to the stove and surveyed the breakfast offerings. "You two are circling each other like Adam and Eve. I say forget all this caution and bite the darn apple." He selected a bit of scrapple and popped it into his mouth. "Or some of this stuff. It's good, too. What is it?"

"Fried heart attack," P.J. said. "And I'm not being cautious, I'm being professional. I'm here for a story, remember, not a man."

"Who says you can't get both, and change your life in the process?"

"The senior editor job will change my life."

"You going to help me eat some of this or what?" Flasher moved on to the bacon. Next he dug a spoon into the buttered grits.

"I'll have my regular coffee and antacid. It's healthier."

"Forget regular. Step out, take a chance."

"Not with my career and not with Chet Greene."

"You must dislike the hell out of him."

"Of course I don't. He's kind, and open, and honest. Certainly intelligent and funny." All the things she'd been looking for in a man.

"And available," Flasher added.

Yep, he was that, too. Which pinpointed the problem. She would never again get involved with a man she worked with. She'd come too far to commit professional suicide. Besides, she would never make the first move, and Chet hadn't indicated he was making anything beyond a home for his children. He hadn't shown the least interest in her.

Then she remembered their first handshake, and the incident in the hallway. And she remembered those coffee-brown eyes that jolted her with a punch more powerful than caffeine.

"I don't get it," Flasher said in between bites. "You're tough as steel with those macho mules at work. You're confident, poised...the works. But put you in the same room with a genuine nice guy, you're scared silly."

She mimicked a laugh. "I'm not scared."

"Then go talk to the man. Go on, after him."

"And why should *I* go after *him?*"

"Because you're supposed to be interviewing him. He's the story, remember?"

"Oh. Yeah, well…" *That darn article.* She tossed her head and left Flasher smirking and stuffing his mouth at the same time.

BRITTANY AND HER BROTHERS sat on the bottom basement step. Not wanting to chance detection, they had left the electric light off and huddled around the flashlight she had taken from the broom closet. The illumination was minimal, but she could still examine her face in the hand mirror she'd also confiscated.

"If you ask me, they sounded mad," Sean said.

"That's good. You only get mad at people you like," she said. "Trust me, it's working, so stick with the plan. Do you think my nose is too big?"

"What? What does your stupid nose have to do with anything?" Sean asked.

Brittany rolled her eyes then went back to inspecting her face.

"What if she gets real mad and leaves?" Kevin asked.

"Hey, I like that even better," Sean said.

"That's no way to marry Chet off, Ditwit. We'll be stuck in his stupid articles forever," she said, then grabbed a handful of hair and piled it atop her head. "You think I look older this way?"

"You look like an upside-down mop," Kevin said.

She scowled at him. "Flasher said I look mature for my age, and very photogenic."

"Oh, brother." Sean rolled his eyes. "Forget Flasher. We've got an operation to carry out, remember?"

"You two can handle that alone for a while, can't you?"

"I guess we have to since you're off in La-La Land. Anyway, I have a few ideas. I suppose we can make Chet look helpless enough."

"Not too helpless, okay?" Brittany made sure they both agreed, but she didn't know why she bothered. They were kids. They couldn't possibly come up with anything beyond a harmless juvenile joke. And here she was with really important things on her mind. She pressed the mirror to her chest and sighed.

6

CHET OPENED the washer and found it filled with clothes. The dials were turned to the proper levels—warm wash, full load, regular cycle. Ann must have loaded it for him. All he needed to do was add detergent, softener and boot that baby up. He measured out enough for a large load then added a bit more for good measure.

Flash. The strobe left him blinking.

"That stuff is concentrated, you know," Flasher said.

"Makes them blinding bright, something like your strobe light."

"You don't have to impress her with your housekeeping skills. She already likes you."

Chet jerked. He felt his face heat. He knew his mouth gaped, but he didn't have time to recover. Flasher, the fastest camera alive, caught him again.

"My, my, my. This place is full of goners," Flasher said, shaking his head and walking out.

Goners? The man was imagining things, but then, he was a creative type. Chet didn't have time to worry about Flasher's fantasies. He had chores to do.

By the time he'd finished cleaning up the kitchen, the washing machine had run through all its cycles. Apprehension gripped him as he entered the laundry room. The way things were going, he half expected to find the floor covered with water and suds. He heaved a sigh when he discovered everything as it should be. At last something had gone right.

"Need help loading the dryer?" P.J. leaned against the door frame. "Or aren't you finished sulking?"

"I don't follow you," he lied. He still felt the sting of her words—"it would be great for the article." The *article*. The *readers*. And he'd been foolish enough to believe she'd been thinking of him.

"You stalked out of the kitchen. Seems to me you were angry about something."

"Just busy. Chore day, remember. This clueless guy can't stand around flapping his jaws."

Chet opened the washer, stared for a second. The wash. Nothing had turned blinding white. Everything was either spotted or streaked with a drab blue.

He slammed the top closed, hoping P.J. hadn't seen, but knowing she had. He felt her beside him. Her breath warmed his neck as she peered over his shoulder.

"Would you believe me if I said I meant to do that?" he asked.

"And you're also going to tell me those are white?"

"They are...bluish white." He reached around inside and pulled out an indigo T-shirt. *Who put that in there?* "Damn." He slapped the side of the washer then grabbed his hand and howled. *Double damn.*

"I'll just leave. You look like you have more sulking to do."

Chet grunted. Sulking? He wasn't sulking. He was having a hard time making this house-dad role appear easy, but he wasn't sulking. He grunted again as he added more detergent. This time he added non-chlorine bleach and restarted the machine.

With the laundry going, Chet focused on house-cleaning. He pulled the vacuum from the closet. It was one of those heavy-duty models whose advertisements boasted enough suction to pick up a bowling ball. He'd purchased the machine for Ann a few months ago. Aside from the bowling ball test, she had put it through its paces and had nothing but praise.

This should be a breeze, he thought. Once around the room and he'd be finished. And with no screw-ups.

"I can do that."

Chet turned and blinked. The voice sounded like his niece's and the girl somewhat resembled...*Brittany? Was this Brittany?* Her hair was pulled into a lopsided French twist and she had on lipstick and *rouge? That couldn't be rouge!* And *that outfit* showed way too much of *everything*.

"Wha...wha...wha—" he stammered. "Where'd that getup come from?"

"You bought it for me after that last article, remember?"

He remembered giving her money and sending her shopping. No way would he have picked out something as skimpy as that. "Has your mother seen that?" he whispered.

"Really. I'm not a baby," she whined, then marched over and took possession of the vacuum. "Anyway, I'm here to help. We grown-ups have to share the workload."

"Right, and afterwards I know one not-yet-a-grown-up who's marching upstairs and putting on some real clothes." And he didn't care how much she rolled her eyes.

Chet walked over to the wall outlet. He plugged in the cord. Brittany turned on the switch and screamed.

Dirt, and dust and brown nameless stuff swirled around them. The darn machine wasn't sucking up anything. It coughed out a dust storm. Powdery trash billowed into the air.

Brittany ducked into a corner, screaming. The vacuum hissed and howled. Chet closed his eyes and groped his way to the machine. Once there he felt around for the power switch.

Someone touched his shoulder. He felt a hand brush his. *Click.* The vacuum wheezed and died. He let a few more UFOs pelt his face before he opened his eyes. When he did, he found P.J. standing beside him, frowning.

"Please don't say you meant to do this, too."

"Only if you're gullible," he said and looked around. Debris was still settling, but he didn't have to wait to declare the room a disaster. Furniture, lampshades and plants were coated in fallout. The once-peach rug was now volcanic ash-gray.

The boys rushed forward and froze at the doorway, expressions of awe on their faces. No doubt anticipating Ann's reaction, while at the same time relieved they weren't responsible.

Or were they? Chet studied their faces. He saw surprise, apprehension, and something else he couldn't pinpoint.

"I say call in the cavalry." Flasher snapped away.

P.J. nodded. "A professional cleaner can have this room looking brand new in no time."

"Forget brand new. I'll be happy if it looked like a room again instead of a giant ashtray."

He had the sinking feeling the days to come weren't going to get any easier. His only consolation was the soft look in P.J.'s eyes and the warmth of her hand on his forearm.

"Is that all you care about?" Brittany shrieked. "Forget the stupid room. Look at me."

"Goodness, it's a talking dust bunny." Flasher chuckled and snapped.

Brittany screamed, then shot past them and out of the room. In an instant she charged up the stairs, leaving behind a dust cloud and the echo of her door slamming shut.

"SHE WON'T TALK to me and she won't come out of her room," Chet said as he walked down the stairs.

He leaned against the banister. P.J. stood next to him but he couldn't look at her. Some Super Dad *he* was. He felt so inadequate. All the advice he'd given his readers and he couldn't even talk a thirteen-year-old girl out of her room.

"Well, of course," P.J. said. "She's completely embarrassed. No one wants to look like a fool in front of her crush."

"What crush?"

"Flasher," P.J. said.

"Flasher? How can she have a crush on someone ten years older than she is?"

"It happens. So what are you going to do?"

Panic swamped him. What could he do? His textbooks would be of no help. They touched upon the subject, but they offered no practical advice. Calling Ann was out of the question. Even the mention of a hangnail would have her worried. A crush on an older man, one who also happened to be a houseguest, would propel Ann back home in record time.

"How in the heck am I supposed to handle this? I couldn't even figure out my own love life. How can I help Brittany figure out hers? I'm not prepared for this. She needs to talk with her mother."

Chet froze. What did he just say? He felt his stomach cringe and blood drain from his face.

"If her mother were here, I mean."

"I can talk to her...woman to woman." P.J. reached over and touched his hand.

Chet looked down. Her fingers seemed so pale

and delicate, and yet they sent a powerful current through him. His heart stopped then kicked over double-time. He swallowed.

"Sure. Why not? *Modern Man*'s editor to the rescue. There's irony in there…somewhere." He tried to sound casual, but he felt too choked and anxious. An inner churning pushed his feelings upward and out in the form of words he half whispered. "You probably have a pretty low opinion of me right now."

"On the contrary, it takes a brave man to open up the way you have. A brave and honest man. I admire you a lot, Chet Greene." She patted his arm then walked up the stairs to chat with the lovesick teen.

Admired? His lack of parenting skills grew apparent with each new trial, he was lying to her, still she admired him. Where was that suspicious, big city attitude he'd expected, had planned and prepared for? Charmed away? He could congratulate himself on his abilities, but somehow his heart wasn't in it.

P.J. RAISED HER HAND to knock on Brittany's door, changed her mind and stuck a finger in her mouth. She hadn't a clue what to say to a brokenhearted youngster. How did she get into this position?

Chet. The look on his face, the agony, the worry, had filled her heart. The man wore his emotions on his sleeve. No macho posturing from him. And that touched her. She at least had to try to help. She liked him too much to abandon him.

Her breath hitched. Yes, she liked him. She admired him. Her heart did a quick pity-pat. P.J. swallowed. *Like. I only like him.* And she liked Brittany, too, so she chased away her unfounded worries, knocked on the door and entered upon the girl's muffled invitation.

The girl lay face-down on her bed. Two pillows covered her head.

"Hey, there," P.J. said.

Brittany sat up and blinked. "Oh. It's you. I was expecting—"

"Your father. Yes, well, we talked and decided you probably didn't want to see any men just yet."

"Never's too soon," Brittany said and wiped her eyes.

"Never wish for never." P.J. should know. *Never* was what she faced in terms of finding her Mr. Right.

"But they're so stupid."

P.J. sat on the edge of the bed. "Don't forget careless."

"And stuck-up and selfish."

"I don't know why we waste our time with them. Some of them are so gross. Take Flasher for instance—"

"Flasher's not gross." Brittany stared wide-eyed at P.J., then pulled back and frowned. "Oh, I get it. You're trying to trick me into saying I overreacted."

"No way. If it'd been me, I would have punched him."

Brittany laughed. "Why didn't I think of that?"

"Because you're too nice. And you haven't run across as many frogs as I have. You're young, yet."

"I'm no baby."

"No, you're not, and Flasher's no teenager, either. He's a bit too old to appreciate you. But I bet he's feeling pretty embarrassed and guilty right now."

"You think? Good." Brittany pouted then sighed. "I guess he is kinda old."

"Very. He's still a nice guy," P.J. said gently. "Just...ancient. You've got years ahead of you, lots of interesting guys to meet and date."

Brittany stared at her. P.J. held her breath. No one had helped her through her first broken heart. Or her second, or any of the others, for that matter. She wasn't sure she'd said the right things. She wasn't sure she'd helped at all.

Suddenly Brittany smiled. "So you're telling me there's life after Flasher?"

P.J. nodded. Relief flooded her. She'd done it. Helped a tender youth through a crashed crush and left her with hope. Time to leave. P.J. stood.

"Why aren't you married?" Brittany asked.

The question drew her up short. Married, with a family of her own. She immediately thought of Chet. Impossible. She tried to laugh, but the sound she made was forced.

"I will," she said, "as soon as the perfect man walks into my life. You know any?"

"Perfect? Tommy Johnston in my class. He does everything right. He's so perfect, I can't stand him. He makes me feel...I don't know...subhuman or something. You can't really go with someone perfect. Besides, all the magazines say men with flaws are sexy.'' The girl blushed.

''Sexy, huh?'' *Like Chet*. P.J.'s heart vibrated like a plucked bow string. She sat back down.

FIFTEEN MINUTES LATER Chet still sat on the steps, no wiser...definitely stiffer. The bedroom door opened and the two women emerged. Brittany had scrubbed her face and changed her clothes. Though he'd still label her outfit outrageous, at least now it was age-appropriate outrageous. He noticed a distinct bounce in her step as she walked by.

''She's smiling,'' Chet said to P.J. ''Whatever you did up there was way above and beyond the duty of an editor, but it worked. Thanks.''

''You have a wonderful family. My liking them has nothing to do with my role as an editor.''

He could tell she spoke the truth. He had seen her expression when she watched the kids. Almost a longing, as though that promotion wasn't the only thing Ms. P.J. West wanted.

She had hubby, home and hearth written all over her. No doubt she had her eye on his kids. Ann's kids. He swallowed. And he was to blame. He'd manufactured a perfect family with the perfect single dad and he'd waved it under her nose.

Guilt gripped him. He would have to set her straight. He couldn't watch her slip into the pit he'd dug.

Whoa. He pulled himself up short. Best keep his mouth shut. Stick to his original plan, charm her, but keep his distance. She'd be gone soon. Once she returned to Chicago, both of them would be safe. And so would his livelihood. All he had to do was maintain his masquerade and his distance for a few more days.

"Just for future reference, what in the world did you two talk about?" he asked, and tried to sound like a concerned parent.

"Frogs."

"Green, slimy, frogs?"

Her smile looked downright impish. "Warts and all." She leaned over, kissed him softly on the cheek and left him there tingling from head to toe and turning a question over in his head. Exactly who was charming whom?

P.J. PERCHED on the edge of her bed, staring cross-eyed at her notes. She'd shuffled them around for the better part of the day when she should have been shadowing her subject. This week-in-the-life story would flop if she didn't get on the job, but here she sat, holed up in her room, and all because of a kiss.

Get over it, girl. You pecked the man on the cheek. That didn't qualify as an act of reckless passion...unprofessional, but not lustful.

She sighed. Rationalize as much as she pleased, she still felt embarrassed. Embarrassed not because she'd kissed him, but because that little peck left her longing for something more. She closed her eyes and again felt his early stubble scratch her lips. She inhaled the slight sweat he'd worked up doing his house chores. She imagined her head on his chest, his arm around her, and his kiss, a real kiss. And she imagined more...lots more.

No. There could be no more. She'd better come to terms with that fact. She was simply seduced by the cozy family atmosphere. Chet was a wonderful father, the kind she'd longed for as a child.

She admired him as a parent, not as a man, a lover. That was all there was to it, so why dwell on something as harmless as a little kiss? She would act as though it never happened.

And I'll make darn sure it never happens again.

"OKAY, KIDS. Family meeting time." Chet herded the group out back onto the screened porch. How would Ann handle this, or Chet Greene, Daddy Extraordinaire, for that matter? He hadn't a clue so he plowed ahead blindly. "You three are up to something and I want to know what."

The children exchanged looks. "It was Brittany's idea," Sean said.

"I didn't tell you to ruin the laundry by putting that dyed shirt in the wash. I certainly didn't tell you to make the vac explode," she said. "I only told you to make Chet look helpless...just a little helpless."

"But why?" Chet asked.

"'Cause she thinks women like doofus guys," Sean said.

Chet felt that prickle run down his spine again, and was almost too afraid to ask any more questions, but he had to get to the bottom of their scheme. He took a deep breath. "Let me get this straight. You decided to make me into one of those doofus guys so women will like me.''

"Nope." Kevin grinned. "Just her."

"Ah." At least they had good taste. If his job weren't on the line and he weren't so busy maintaining his masquerade, he'd probably pursue P.J. on his own. "You wanted Ms. West to like me so I can keep my job."

"Not exactly," Brittany said. "We wanted her to really like you."

"Really, really like you," Sean added.

"Look, kids, that's very sweet of you, but I think it best if I find my own girlfriends, don't you?"

Kevin made a face. "Not a girlfriend. Uck."

"We were kinda thinking more of something else," Sean said.

"Like what kind of something?"

"Something like a wife," Brittany said.

CHET SAT ON THE TOP STEP of the basement landing. The dim light cast the staircase in shadows and made it hard to see down into the gray and gloomy space. It certainly didn't help him see his own situation any clearer. Nothing would.

Wife. Chet shook his head. "Had one of those. That was enough."

How could the kids even think he would ever marry again? He'd told them often enough that he never would.

Even if he ever changed his mind, he would never marry P.J. True she was nothing like his ex, a woman so consumed with give-me, give-me, give-me, that she started talking divorce a month after his illustrious career in academia went belly-up. Still, P.J. was his boss. He couldn't even date the woman without risking everything he had worked for in the past months.

Besides, P.J. would never let him get close enough. She kept that shield of hers up and ready to deflect any incoming emotions. It was a shame she felt she needed that protection, but he understood her reasons.

Like him, P.J. knew all about betrayal. That more than anything made her different from his ex-wife whose disguise was soft velvet over steel. P.J.'s was the opposite.

And he loved every time P.J.'s steel gave way and the velvet touched him.

Yes, if he ever married—

Married? Wife?

Confirmed bachelors, lovers of slipknots, did not get married.

Never.

BRITTANY SAT on the porch swing and curled her legs underneath her. As far as lectures went, Uncle Chet's hadn't been all that bad. He hadn't gotten half as mad as she'd expected.

"Okay, brains, now what?" Sean asked.

She took a deep breath. "Simple. Now we change the plan."

"But we promised we would stop meddling."

"Correction, we promised to kill the make-Chet-look-helpless plan. Which is a good idea. You two went way overboard.''

"So." Sean pulled back, his lips tight, his forehead puckered.

Boys. They were so defensive. She hoped that was something they outgrew.

"So, now we have to do damage control. It's time for a new plan," she said.

"Are we going to get in trouble again?" Kevin asked.

"How can we get into trouble doing something nice? We're going to make Chet look awesome, like a real live hero."

"Cool," both boys said at once.

7

CHET HANDED OVER a check for ninety-seven dollars to the gristly looking woman in charge of the cleaning crew he'd hired. In less than two hours, she and three other women had transformed the dustbin back into a living room. Now, he watched as they packed their arsenal of cleaning supplies and marched out.

"Call if you need us again," the leader said.

"I won't," Chet promised. From now on everything would run smoothly. He had to impress P.J. No, he had to impress his editor. Any more disasters and he'd become the deposed daddy specialist. That meant dinner had to be perfect.

Thanks to the heat-and-serve entrées stuffing Ann's freezer, that would prove a no-boner. The hardest thing he had to do was select the meal of the day. He walked into the kitchen and opened the chest. A welcoming cold front greeted him as he riffled through the neat stacks of white-wrapped blocks.

Lima beans, black-eyed peas, okra. *So, where's the meat?* He rummaged around some more. Vegetable lasagna. Vegetable soup. Catfish fillets. *Ah, close, but no prize.* He pulled out an odd-shaped package and read the label—roast chicken.

Perfect. Fried chicken would have been more regional, but a roasted bird would do. He ripped off the paper then dropped the chicken into the sink. It landed with a dull *klunk*. It was frozen, all right. Frozen and raw.

He planned to serve dinner at six-thirty, seven at the latest. So how much oven time did a frozen block of meat need? Chet pulled out a cookbook and studied the time table. Given its weight, the bird had to roast for two and a half hours at three-fifty. He checked his watch, five forty-five. So much for a quick heat-and-serve. There was only one thing to do.

He turned the thermostat to four-fifty, put the chicken in a pan and threw it in the oven.

"Mr. Resourceful strikes again," he said, wiping his hands and heading for the newly cleaned living room. Yep, he had everything under control.

That thought left him the minute he stepped into the hall and heard voices coming from the media room. Curiosity and dread pushed him in that direction. The space was small, windowless and usually lit by the television. Now with the set off, the overhead spots washed select areas in a warm intimate light.

P.J. and the kids, huddled together in one chair, sat bathed in just such a glow. She was reading to them, a Harry Potter, and the kids sat enraptured.

The power of the scene knocked Chet off balance. He swayed then leaned against the doorjamb. They looked so...comfortable, in a Norman Rockwell way. P.J.'s face shone. Home and hearth fit her better than that study in black she tried to project herself as. She was beautiful, and soft, and caring. And he ached with longing.

Then he noticed Flasher, camera in hand, lurking in the corner. Chet shook himself out of his cozy dream, plastered on what he hoped passed for a neutral expression, then announced his presence with a loud cough.

Everyone turned in his direction. P.J.'s eyes seemed to smile when she looked at him. Could he be misreading things, or was she as pleased to see him as he was her?

"P.J. likes gummies," Kevin said through a mouthful of candy.

"P.J.?" Chet looked at the children then her.

She smiled. "Ms. West seemed too formal for friends."

"Yeah," all three of the kids answered.

"Actually they were explaining about the blue laundry and the vacuuming accident," she said.

Chet jerked. Had they revealed their matchmaking scheme and if so what did P.J. make of it?

"We told how we kinda made a mess and all," Brittany said.

"On account of we wanted you to look like a normal guy who botches things up a lot," Sean added.

"They thought you'd lose your column if you seemed too perfect," P.J. added.

"No chance there." The past days had proven just how flawed he was. He may be a good writer, but he was no actor. He couldn't fake disinterest in P.J. no matter how hard he tried.

Brittany cleared her throat and shot P.J. a glance. "That makes him just right," the girl said. "We think he's great."

And all this without a single bribe. He looked into each young face, but saw nothing suspicious.

"You are really lucky to have kids who love you so much. Of course, that speaks well of you."

He did his best modest grin, hoping to leave the subject behind as quickly as possible. "I do my best."

"According to the children, your best is something indeed...close to superhero status."

"I bet you keep your cape and tights in the basement," Flasher said.

Chet looked at the three munchkins. Whatever they'd fed her, please make it something benign, like getting tickets to sold-out games or rescuing cats from trees. "I'm sure they've exaggerated."

"Helping the police capture that bank robber, and saving your neighbor's life when she had the heart attack. How could they exaggerate that?" P.J. asked.

Easily, he thought, and groaned to himself. "I trust you won't put any of this in your article."

"Mr. Modest. The children warned that you would dismiss your heroics. We can leave out the details, but we should mention the award."

"Award?" Chet held his breath.

"The good Samaritan award from the mayor,"

Brittany said, nodding her head, encouraging him to follow along.

"No. No mention of that. Not even a hint." He never realized he could sweat so heavily outside the gym.

"And why not?" P.J. and Flasher both asked.

"Awards are no big deal around here. I think last week, the dog catcher got one for the most mutts captured in a single day. The mayor gives awards out as freely as campaign kisses. Good photo op, you know."

"Which reminds me. I've been dying to see some of your family photos," P.J. said.

"Fa...fa... Family photos?" Chet could feel his color drain.

"They're packed away," Brittany said.

"Way away," Sean added.

"Lost, even," Chet said.

"No, they're not. I know where they are." Kevin bounced off the chair and was gone before anyone could stop him.

For several seconds silence held the room. Chet tried to think, but his mind had turned as cloudy as buttermilk. He looked to Brittany and Sean for help. They stared back, blank and helpless.

"Go help your brother," he finally said.

"Right. We'll catch...I mean, help him," Sean said.

Both kids stood, but before they had a chance to move, Kevin lumbered into the room, struggling with an album large enough to hold the photo history of the entire world.

"Here it is," Kevin said.

"I'll take it." Chet, Brittany and Sean lunged at the same time.

Klunk. Their three heads knocked. The sound echoed in Chet's brain. The pain momentarily stunned him.

"I have it." P.J. settled the book in her lap and Kevin beside her. "And you can tell me all about the pictures."

She opened to the first page, a hospital scene—mom, dad and newborn. Brittany's debut. Chet knew the photo. He'd taken it.

"Who's this?" P.J. asked.

"Nobody," Kevin said. "Let's turn."

Thank goodness for young egos.

Kevin grabbed a handful of pages and flipped. Ann would die if she saw how he manhandled her treasure, but Chet wasn't about to intervene. The boy flipped again and again until he reach the last fourth of the book.

"This is me," he said.

Chet hesitated then peeked at the two pages. Both featured a zoo trip, the one he'd taken the children on. A few of the pictures had been taken by strangers and pictured him hugging all three kids. Relief made him dizzy. He could have kissed the lad for turning to these photos.

"And this is me, and this, and this," Kevin continued.

Chet relaxed. Shots of the zoo dominated four more pages, he remembered, followed by pictures of the circus trip, and the state fair, all events he had arranged. Chet appeared in all of them.

But after that came shots of Kevin's last birthday party. Photos of Kevin blowing out the candles...pictures with Ann. He couldn't let P.J. see those.

"Let's put the album away now," Chet said. His voice sounded higher than normal and he detected an uncharacteristic tremor. He reached for the book, but the little guy huddled over the open pages.

"Yeah, Kevin. You're going to make us all brain-dead. This is so boring," Brittany said.

"I'm not bored. I'd like to see more." P.J. fluffed the tyke's hair and smiled.

"Me, too," said Flasher. "Amateur photography is so Grandma Moses."

Chet was trapped. He couldn't rip the album from Kevin's hands and end the matter, not without looking like a complete fool...a mean fool, to boot. So he stopped breathing and waited. Kevin lifted the next page and turned.

"And this picture is— Hey."

The room went dark.

Chet sprung into action. He grabbed for the album, but netted both the book and the boy. No matter, two birds in hand were better than none in the bush, Chet thought as he made his getaway.

When he reached the doorway, the lights flicked back on. He got a glimpse of P.J.'s face, her eyes wide, her red mouth open. He hesitated a moment then dashed to safety.

P.J. LOOKED AT FLASHER. For once her friend was caught by surprise with his mouth agape and his camera dangling from its strap. She looked at Brittany.

The girl shrugged. "He has this thing about old family photos."

"So it appears. You care to explain?" P.J. asked.

Brittany hung her head and mumbled something P.J. couldn't understand. She was about to ask the girl to speak up when Sean burst into the room. He was breathing hard. Smudges marked his cheek and cobwebs clung to his hair.

"And where have you been?" P.J. asked.

"Playing with the circuit breaker, no doubt," Flasher said.

Red crept up the boy's neck. He, too, hung his head.

"Okay. Which one of you is going to explain?" P.J. asked.

"It's pictures of Mom," Sean said.

"He doesn't want to see them and he doesn't want us to show them," Brittany quickly added, then hung her head again.

Poor man. And here she was, Simon Legree about to torture him. "Why didn't he say something?" P.J. asked, then answered her own question. He had tried...subtly, but he'd tried nonetheless.

She felt the pull in her chest again, but this time it was stronger. This time it was accompanied by stomach jitters. The same kind of jitters she got while sitting in airplanes that barreled down the runway right before takeoff. P.J. let out a weak sound.

"He'll be okay," Brittany said, and Sean seconded her with a nod.

Before she could question them further, the two hastened from the room.

Flasher walked over and squeezed her shoulder. "You couldn't have known," he said, then he, too, walked out.

P.J. sat there alone feeling twisted, pulled and tumbled all at the same time. She was still sitting there when Chet reappeared. Kevin and the photo album were conspicuously absent.

Chet's features were drawn with tension and his complexion was pale. His eyes looked as if they were set back into hollows. They were still the deepest, warmest brown she'd ever seen. She couldn't help but stare, and as she did she felt a warmth rush from her toes upward. Her head felt like a balloon.

She hadn't been this dizzy since the New Year's Eve when she'd had more than everyone's share of champagne. She wasn't drunk now, but she was definitely floating, on her way...somewhere.

Or was she already gone?

CHET TOOK ONE STEP into the room, then another. Was it the lighting or was P.J. looking exceptionally inviting all of a sudden? Her eyes looked misty. And the way she was smiling at him...no, not smiling. She was doing something else with her mouth that he couldn't define, something that made him want to touch her lips. Kiss her.

No. He couldn't touch. He could look and he

could imagine. Boy, could he imagine. He fantasized all kinds of things as he watched her catch her bottom lip between her teeth. If ever he'd seen a pair of lips that needed kissing. If ever there existed a man so eager to accommodate.

He walked toward her. She stood. Was it nerves that made her clench and unclench her hands?

The phone rang before he reached her. The loud bell jarred him like an alarm clock. He stopped, a foot from her. He could smell her perfume—light, as faint and enchanting as a single rose petal.

The ring persisted. The kids obviously weren't going to pick up, so he reached for the cordless phone on the end table.

"About time. I was beginning to think you all had been kidnapped by aliens," his sister's voice came over the line.

"Ann?" Chet threw a look in P.J.'s direction, then turn his back and walked out into the hall. "Why are you calling?" he whispered.

"Can't I call my own home? What's with the third degree? Uh-oh. Something's wrong, isn't it? Who's sick? Kevin?"

"No one's sick. Everything's fine."

"Then why are you whispering?" Ann asked, whispering herself.

Chet glanced at P.J. A new expression clouded her face. She held her mouth differently. Gone was that soft inviting look, replaced by a tension that pulled her lips into a fake smile, so fake it looked painful.

Did she think the caller was his girlfriend, or did

she simply resent the interruption? Whatever the cause, he wanted to rush over and envelop her into a reassuring hug.

"What's going on, Chet?" Ann drew his attention.

"Nothing. Really. It's just…let me call you back later."

"No need. I was calling because, well you remember when I was leaving, I kept thinking I'd forgotten something. Well I remembered what it was. I forgot to tell you that on Sunday the kids are—"

A shrill sound blasted through the house. P.J. gave a small cry. Chet dropped the phone and covered his ears. The receiver dangled and twirled in space while the cord wrapped around his arm.

"What's that noise?" P.J. asked.

"Fire," Flasher shouted as he rushed past the door and headed for the kitchen.

Shit. The chicken.

"Chet. Chet."

He could hear Ann yelling even before he put the receiver to his ear.

"Everything's under control. I'll call you back." He slammed his end onto the cradle then rushed for the kitchen.

8

CHET HUNCHED OVER the kitchen sink, coughing and blinking. Smoke stung his eyes and tickled his throat. Through the blue-gray haze, he stared at the charred carcass sitting under the running tap. Everyone had gathered around him.

"A moment of silence for the bird that would have been dinner," Flasher said as he snapped off a few shots.

Chet wondered how quickly and at what temperature film burned. He would have to experiment on that and the other rolls. Right now he had bigger problems, he realized as he surveyed yet another room to clean.

Ann's white lace curtains looked charcoal gray. Fire extinguisher foam covered the stove and floor, and the sink overflowed. Greasy brown water had spilled down the cabinets and onto the tiles.

"What are we going to eat, now?" Sean asked.

Yeah, he had that problem, too.

"How does pizza sound? My treat," P.J. said and received a shout of approval from Brittany and Sean.

"I'm a snake," Kevin said. "Do snakes eat pizza?"

"I can't let you do that. I destroyed dinner, I'll fix something else," Chet said.

The kids groaned.

"I don't think you'll win an election on that platform. Besides, I'm suddenly in the mood to eat out, and since I don't like fast-pressed burgers and prefer to pass on anything that used to cluck, pizza seems to be the only option. So what's the problem? You disapprove of pizza for dinner or of me treating?"

"Does rescuing disaster victims come under your job description?" he asked.

"Hardly. I make it a rule never to turn my back on a hungry man." She laughed, a warm chuckle that made him smile all over.

A pang hit him low and mercilessly. He felt a hunger, all right, but it had nothing to do with food.

"I'm a snake. Do snakes eat pizza?" Kevin asked again.

Chet swung the boy into the air then held him to his chest. "Every chance they get."

"Good. 'Cause I didn't want any of that," Kevin said, pointing to the burned chicken.

P.J. STOOD in the kitchen, listening to the sounds coming from the foyer. She could hear Chet giving Flasher directions even though the children's excited voices occasionally drowned his out.

She didn't know how Flasher had convinced Chet to let him and the kids pick up the pizza. The move had been a blatant maneuver to get her and Chet alone. Why hadn't Chet seen that?

She heard the youngsters clamor out of the house.

A few minutes later, she heard the motor start, then grow faint as the car drove away.

Everything fell still. The silence of the house closed around, giving her a glimpse into her future. *Solitude.* Would she spend her life in solitude? Suddenly she felt achingly alone, but not for long. The sound of Chet's approaching footsteps reminded her that she wasn't.

Something kicked around in P.J.'s stomach. Nerves? No, she was no teenager like Brittany. She was P.J. West, not Patty Jean the Unsure. She was too old and too professional to let an infatuation intimidate her.

Still the kicking persisted and when Chet appeared in the doorway, her whole body flushed. He managed that sheepish grin of his, almost undoing what little composure she had left.

Professional. Think professional. She snapped to attention and gave a sharp salute. "Private West reporting for K.P. duty, Sir."

Chet's grin widened. She struggled to keep her rigid position, afraid if she relaxed the quivers that raced around inside her would become visible shakes, rattles and rolls.

"I know cleaning kitchens isn't in your job description. So it must be a new way to succeed in business and get promoted," Chet said.

Try, how to keep busy. If she stayed busy, she could be alone with a guy she shouldn't be attracted to and not go to pieces. "I'm being a good Samaritan, here. Your role is to thank me and point me to a mop."

Chet pulled open the broom closet, removed the cleaning supplies, and gave her what she'd need. "We'll tackle the sink and cupboards first, then swab the deck."

"Yes, Sir," she said, but not as snappy as before. *Professional.* Think professionally, she told herself even if the profession happened to be Cleaning Engineer at present.

Ten minutes later she was deep into her task, swinging her mop in time with the tune Chet whistled—the seven dwarfs' work song, she believed. She swiped her mop and joined in with the lyrics.

Housework. She hated housework. A week ago she would have laughed if someone suggested singing while she worked. Maybe every experience improved when shared with someone you liked.

P.J. stopped, leaned on the handle and watched Chet. The muscles in his shoulder flexed under his shirt. She itched to touch them. She couldn't help wonder how they would feel. She couldn't help wonder how his arms would feel wrapped around her.

Nor could she could help imagining being in her own kitchen with her own husband and her own children. In spite of herself, she imagined that man as Chet and the children the three youngsters she'd grown so fond of.

Suddenly she felt cozy and warm. *So this is what it's like.* She gave a sigh and leaned more on the handle. The mop moved. P.J. slipped and landed on the wet floor.

"Sleeping on the job can get you a week in the brig, Private," Chet said.

She pushed herself partway up, then stopped. A damp chill spread over her bottom. P.J. flopped back down on the floor.

"Need help?"

She looked up and saw Chet standing over her, offering his hand. She felt flushed. She couldn't move. Wetness soaked through her slacks. The telltale spot would show, even on black.

Chet didn't wait. He grabbed her under the arm and pulled her to her feet. "Anything broken?"

Pride. She shook her head.

"Can't be too careful. Rotate your head, move your shoulders, twist your back...slowly."

She followed his instructions. "Anything else, Doctor?"

"Turn around and—"

"Why?" She stiffened.

Chet tilted his head and pointed behind her. "So you can pick up the mop. Of course, if you have another method..."

She moved backward, stepped over the mop and with a curtsey, swooped the thing up in one fluid motion.

"Very nice. I'll remember that the next time my behind gets wet." He winked and turned to retrieve his mop.

He knew. Without thinking, P.J. hoisted her own mop, jousting style, and charged. She didn't expect the impact to be as strong as it turned out to be. The sponge end connected with Chet's rear and knocked him forward a few feet. A big wet spot decorated his jeans.

Slowly he turned. A look of devilment filled his eyes.

She swallowed and backed away. "Would you believe that was an accident?"

He didn't answer, but he continued to approach.

"Then would you believe I'm sorry?"

"I'm sure I will, but not just yet," he said when he was standing in front of her.

"I am, you know."

He took the mop from her hand and rested it against the sink. The mischief had vanished from his eyes. They were dark and dangerous in a different way now. She couldn't take her focus away even when she felt his thumb trace her chin line. Not even when he rubbed it back and forth over her bottom lip. She felt hypnotized.

She parted her lips and felt her breath passing over them in shallow puffs. When he used his thumb to pull her bottom lip down and traced along the inside, she stopped breathing entirely.

She grabbed hold of his waist and steadied herself. He brushed his mouth across hers, retreated then swooped down for business. She gave herself up to her senses. She tasted the salty flavor of him and explored the texture of his tongue. She smelled the odd mixture of smoke and lemony cleaning spray that clung to his clothes and she heard—a ringing in her ears. She fought to ignore the sound.

A sharp ring pushed through to her consciousness. The phone. Chet swayed a moment before he pulled away. Then he was gone.

"Yeah?" he said into the receiver. He sounded as breathless as she felt.

Suddenly he stiffened and turned his back to her, closing her out. She felt a freeze cover the room and swallow her. A girlfriend? The same one he'd spoken to earlier?

Again her chest twisted, but this time it really hurt.

CHET RECOGNIZED ANNE'S VOICE.

"I waited by the phone," Ann said.

"Sorry. Things got crazy," he whispered. He could kick himself. How could he have forgotten to call her back?

"I heard. What was that noise?"

"I burned dinner. You know, you have very sensitive smoke alarms. Anyway, the house didn't burn down, and we won't starve. The kids and Flasher are picking up pizza."

"Who's Flasher? What kind of a name is that?"

"A nickname. They'll be home in a couple of minutes. I'll have the kids call you."

"You let my babies go out with someone with a name like that? How does someone get a nickname like that? Does he wear a trench coat? What does he go around flashing?"

"Cameras…only. I know him. He's very reliable, responsible"—*annoyingly observant*—"and he's… uh…"

The front door opened with a welcome sound of

laughter. Chet could hear the voices of all three children.

"And they're here. How's that for reliability?" he said, then covered the mouthpiece and shouted into the hall, "Aunt Ann is on the phone. Why don't you take the call in Brittany's room?"

"Aunt who?" Sean said.

"*Annnn*, stupid," Brittany said.

Chet held his breath and listened to their footsteps trump up the stairs. Chet gave a whale-size exhale and turned, only to find P.J. staring at him. The expression on her face was a cross between hesitation and curiosity.

"Ann," he said.

"*Aunt* Ann." P.J. nodded, but the look in her eyes said something he couldn't understand. He could read her voice though. Suspicion curled around every word.

How much had she heard? "She's younger than I am, but the way she hovers, you'd think I was her baby brother."

P.J. blinked and blushed. "Your sister? I thought..." She clamped her lips.

"We covered that subject earlier, remember. I haven't gone out in ages. I certainly haven't kissed anyone, not that way. Not like with you."

He wanted to do it again. He held his focus on her as he moved closer. Her chest heaved. The vein on the side of her neck pulsed. When she parted her lips, he was ready. Slowly he lowered his head.

"Pizza. Or have you folks decided upon a different diet," Flasher called from the doorway.

"Well, don't let it get cold. That goes for the pizza, too." With that he slipped back into the dining room.

"Sorry," P.J. said and hastened away.

Sorry? What did that mean? He would have to find out, and soon.

P.J. SAT IN THE MIDDLE of her bed, her knees up and a pillow balanced on top, supporting her head. She'd kissed him. A real kiss, not a peck on the cheek, but a passionate, full-abandoned sort of kiss.

The taste of it, the pressure of his mouth on hers, remained. So did the burning desire building within her. She wasn't supposed to kiss him, but she had. Now she was sorry. Sorry the moment had stopped there. She craved more.

Well, she couldn't have more. She was on assignment, she had to be professional. Yeah, think professional. The argument was getting old especially now that for the first time she really understood what she was missing. Especially now, given how she felt about Chet.

Her feelings had grown beyond the mere physical attraction. She felt respect, and empathy and...safe. Her tough facade had slipped so many times and Chet hadn't taken advantage. Yes, she could trust Chet.

But what if she was wrong? She had misjudged so many times before. She was tired of kissing frogs and ending up with no prince. How could she be sure this time was different? She couldn't. Best she maintain her distance. That was the true safe thing…distance.

Besides, if The Reaper got wind of her feelings, he would label her findings tainted by bias. He would probably discontinue the column because he didn't trust her judgment.

She would have to remain professional, for Chet's sake as well as her own.

CHET PUSHED HIMSELF through the morning rituals, showered with his eyes closed and brushed his teeth with his mouth open in a yawn. He couldn't believe how tired he felt. Staying up all night cleaning the kitchen had done him in. Juggling all his lies wasn't helping. If he got through this, he wouldn't tell another. Well, he had to keep his Chet Greene guise, but he'd tell no new lies at least.

He donned his usual uniform—jeans and cotton shirt—indulged in one final stretch and headed downstairs. Silence greeted him. Even the air smelled innocent. Not a hint of last night's disaster. Not a hint of cooking of any kind.

Good, no breakfast surprises today. Maybe this was a sign of things to come, smooth sailing, no goofs, and no ambushes waiting around the veggie bin. He would have everything under control again…for real.

In no time Chet had set the kitchen table with bowls, spoons and glasses. He clustered cereal boxes into a haphazard centerpiece, which he bookended with the milk and juice cartons. For good measure he tossed a stack of paper napkins onto the table then stepped back and admired his creation. Quick, efficient, goof-proof. It was even attractive in a plebeian sort of way. P.J. would appreciate that. *Martha Stewart, eat your heart out.*

Summoning the troops proved more difficult, but after a bout of door pounding and repeated shouts of "Come and get it," everyone finally started filing down the stairs. Chet waited at the bottom, ready to usher them toward the kitchen.

They seemed as tired as he felt. The kids had never been morning people, so their sleepwalking condition didn't surprise him. However, he thought P.J. would be…what? Not the get-that-promotion, catch-the-first-worm hustler she had tried to make him think she was. No, after last night he expected her to look like he felt. He expected her to be…glowing.

But here she was, dressed in a black T-shirt and slacks, no makeup, no smile. She looked as though she'd spent the whole night wrestling something. Thoughts of him, perhaps? He'd like to believe so.

Thinking of her had made him restless. He imagined he wouldn't have slept at all if he hadn't worked himself to exhaustion with his night-owl cleaning campaign.

"Good morning, Mr. Greene," she said when she hit the landing.

Chet froze. His insides spiraled out of control.

Mr. Greene? After last night in the kitchen with the mops and all? Hardly appropriate for someone you were on fanny-bopping status with. Hardly appropriate after the kiss they had shared.

"Did I miss something?" he asked.

"If so, I hope it's not the coffee. I can really use some this morning. I've lots of work today."

"It's Sunday. You plan on working?"

"Today's still a day in the life of *Modern Man*'s most popular contributor, is it not?"

Chet nodded. That clipped tone had invaded her voice again. And he'd thought she'd stayed awake thinking of him. If anything she'd had nightmares about losing that promotion.

Flasher looked at him and shrugged. "She gets like this occasionally. Something to do with the bed."

P.J. glared at Flasher. A blink of pink colored her face. Then she zipped past both of them and headed for the kitchen.

"What's wrong with the bed? Am I missing something?" Chet asked.

"Uh-huh. That's the point. You're missing out big-time, but you aren't the only one," Flasher said.

Chet waited for an explanation. It never came. The chime of the doorbell came instead.

"I'll get it." Brittany sailed down the hall.

No. I'm suppose to get the door. Me, the grown-up. He rushed to beat his niece to the foyer, but arrived too late. Brittany opened the door and stepped backward, a look of pure shock on her face.

"Dad," she squeaked.

"Yes?" Chet answered.

So did the voice on the other side of the door.

9

DAD?

Chet's blood pressure took a bungee jump. His head swam and so many prickles raced along his spine he thought he'd landed butt-first on a colony of fire ants.

He willed his muscles into action, nudged Brittany aside, then stood blocking the entry.

"Uncle Bill," he said, stressing the "uncle" and winking at the blond man who had one foot over the threshold and was about to add the other.

"Uncle who?" Sean and Kevin chorused.

In the background, he heard footsteps shuffle toward him. The troops were massing for a look-see.

"What a surprise!" Chet pushed forward.

Thanks to all the hours he'd spent in the gym, plus the element of surprise, he managed to back Bill, all six feet two inches of the man, out of the entryway and onto the porch.

"What are you doing here?" Chet asked, stepping outside and closing the door behind them.

"It's my Sunday with the kids. What are you doing here? Where's Ann? And why are we out here on the porch?"

So that's what Ann had forgotten to tell him.

Chet took a deep breath, steadying himself. Already he was formulating a plan.

"It's a long story," he said. "Bear with me."

P.J. STOOD by the living-room window, watching Chet say goodbye to the children. Odd that he hadn't remember the arrangements he'd made with his brother-in-law. Her visit had created more stress and problems for him than she'd originally anticipated.

Certainly more than she had bargained for on a personal level. How was she to know she would fall so completely for this family or that she would be so drawn to Chet? She never dreamed, never dared hope that the man she came to know through his articles would be even more wonderful in person—so honest, and caring, and...perfect. And now she feared she was in love.

Darn The Reaper for extending her assignment.

Who was she fooling? She was more to blame than her boss. Her ambition, her push to be the first woman senior editor of a major men's magazine had gotten her here. And her own ambition was making a muck of her personal life.

She took a deep breath and shook her head. Did it have to be like that? Did she have to choose between a career and love? With someone as open and understanding as Chet, maybe she could have both. *And risk him losing his job?* No, she couldn't do that.

She watched Chet make his way up the walk, his face creased and worried. The parent look, forever concerned about their offspring's welfare. Would she ever know the feeling? Hope budded in her chest while despair crept through like a fall frost.

She left the window and met him on the porch.

"Well, this won't be a typical day in my life. I guess your work plans are blown. So now what?" he asked.

"What do you usually do when you're alone?"

"Write."

"Let me rephrase that. This is probably the first free day you've had in ages. What would you *like* to do?" If she were back in Chicago, she would go to a museum, or down to the lake, or listen to a live concert.

"Go bowling," Chet said.

She blinked. "You bowl?"

"Not in ages, but I bet I can still throw a few strikes. Afterward, I'd go for barbecue down at Dixie Wings then I'd hit the state fair. You know, eat cotton candy and get stuck at the top of the Ferris wheel."

His face was as bright as Kevin's had been the other night when she'd offered the boy strawberry gummies. No, brighter. P.J.'s heart squeezed in a new way. Excitement tickled her stomach. She, too, would like to do those things, simple things made fascinating because of the company.

"Then let's do it," she said. "Let's go bowling, and eat cotton candy. We can ride the Ferris wheel."

"We?"

Surprise and disappointment jolted her. "Well...I

just assumed…'' she began, then tried again. This time she fought to keep her expression neutral and her voice natural. "You're right. Enjoy your day off."

"I don't get it," he said. "This morning you were as formal as a funeral announcement. Now you want to gallivant around town with me. I can't figure you out, unless…"

He looked askance at her. The muscles around his mouth twitched. "Unless this is another story angle for your readers. A *day-off*-in-the-life-of. Or is this about last night? I thought we were—"

"Let's not go into that. Let's forget the whole thing, all right."

"There you go again. Suppose *I* don't want to forget?"

"Then I'm sorry."

"Yeah, you said that last night…right after I kissed you. Are you sorry about that, or sorry you let your guard down?"

"Technically, I'm your boss. What happened could be classified as sexual harassment."

"Sexual," he said, "but hardly harassment."

He moved closer. He looked so tempting with his coffee eyes focused on her as though she were the only thing in the world that mattered. Too tempting. P.J. placed her hands on his chest and held him back.

"You shouldn't forget why I'm here," she said.

"Yeah, for your promotion." To her surprise, he backed off.

"No. You don't understand. Things have gotten very complicated."

"You have no idea exactly how complicated things really are." He laughed, then looked away and exhaled. "Okay, let's do your 'Daddy's Day Off' story, but you can forget the cotton candy and the Ferris wheel."

"Why?" No cotton candy, no ride on the Ferris wheel? She had looked forward to that.

"The state fair isn't until September, but don't worry I can come up with a couple of alternate adventures."

"Count me out," Flasher said.

He stood in the doorway, car keys and camera bag in hand. How long had he been there? His neutral expression suggested he hadn't heard much of Chet's and her conversation.

"This day is a work wipeout, I'm going to do some sight-seeing, visit some *old* battle sites," he continued, then dug into his pocket and pulled out a handful of something P.J. couldn't see. He grabbed Chet's hand and pressed the items into his palm.

"What is thi—" Chet peeked. He choked on a cough. He looked at her and choked again, then he balled his fist tight and rammed Flasher's gift into his back pocket.

"Don't thank me. See you sometime tomorrow morning," Flasher said. He pick up a duffel bag and bounded down the steps.

"Tomorrow? You can't stay out all night." Did her voice sound desperate, terrified?

"Sure I can. I'm over twenty-one." Flasher waved and kept walking, heading for the rental car they had parked out front.

She scurried down the walk and caught up with him at the car. "I can't stay here alone with Chet."

Flasher crossed his arms. "Why not? You're over twenty-one, too. That makes it legal, even down South. Here's your chance to make something blossom."

"That's not part of my assignment. You want me to ruin my career?" No sense letting him in on the truth, that she was less afraid for her career than her heart.

"When are you going to stop letting your professional life rule your personal life?"

"This is professional. I'm writing a story, remember?"

"So there's a little crossover. Work-related romances happen all the time. Twenty-five percent of them result in marriage."

"You made up that statistic."

"So? Anyway, that's not the point. You like him, he likes you. You even like the kids."

"I love the kids." If it were simply an issue of the kids, she wouldn't be worried. Chet—available, handsome, angry Chet—complicated the situation.

"There you go. It's perfect. Do you think any of the men you work with would balk at that equation?"

"No, but they're—"

"Men. Anything they can do P.J. West can do better. But your hesitation has nothing to do with your career. I think you're afraid. How will you ever find Mr. Right if you run when opportunity knocks? This could be it, *Patty Jean*. Chet is everything you've been looking for, right?''

Right. But he wasn't looking for a love-struck editor whose judgment, or lack of judgment, could ruin him financially. She pressed her lips together and frowned.

Flasher gently shook her shoulders. ''Relax, loosen up and see what happens. You can do this. Think of it as a challenge. And stop biting your nails.'' He slapped her hand before it reached her mouth.

''Stop bullying me,'' she said.

''I'm not suggesting you do anything drastic, just drop the No Trespassing sign you wear across your chest.''

Instead of her nail, she bit her lip. She wanted to deny what her friend had said, but couldn't. She couldn't follow his advice, either. P.J. shook her head. ''It would come back to haunt me.'' *Or Chet.*

''Doll, missed opportunities haunt. Everything else is a learning experience and when it comes to you and sex, you're back in grade school.''

''I'm not that bad.''

''Prove it,'' he said, then climbed into the car and sped off.

No children. No Flasher. Just Chet and her for the entire day...and night. P.J. felt an odd swell of anticipation building inside her, so strong she almost screamed. Instead she put her pinkie in her mouth and started some serious nail chewing. She had to stick to her guns. She had to keep her distance.

She glanced over and found Chet walking toward her. Heat rushed up her neck and into her cheeks.

"You look a bit flushed. If you want, we can bag the bowling," Chet said.

"Wouldn't think of it." In fact she would suggest as many side trips as she could imagine. Anything to prolong their day out and postpone their evening together in an empty house.

CHET LOOKED AT P.J. as she stood holding her bowling ball and facing down the pins. She was as tense as she had been during the drive over when she'd sat beside him, stiff and silent. Every time he'd glanced her way, she'd pulled herself straight as a pole and had popped a finger in her mouth.

He studied her now. If she didn't have her fingers stuck in the ball at that moment, he suspected she would have one in her mouth. The thought made his heart hitch.

Who was she trying to fool? He knew what was wrong, he knew what was happening. Every pinched muscle of hers was clamped around last night. Her tension, her attitude, and especially her sudden barrier were all about last night…and him.

Good. If he was the cause, good. She was having a physical effect on him, too. She was under his skin.

What was it about this woman? What captured him? Her lie—the way she tried so hard to appear tough when she was really soft and caring? And fragile. He longed to touch her, get closer to her. Now that he'd kissed her once, he couldn't imagine not kissing her again. And he wouldn't stop there, either.

First he had to work on that barrier she'd rebuilt overnight.

He watched her march up to the line and hurl the ball. As with the four previous times, the ball landed with a thud then rolled down the gutter.

"I'm not cut out for this," she mumbled.

"You're too serious. This isn't work, this is supposed to be fun. Try relaxing more."

"If one more person tells me to relax, I'll deck him. Anyway, I don't see what's fun about tossing a thirty-pound ball down a trench."

"You will once you start killing a few pins."

"Killing pins? This is definitely a guy game, isn't it? In that case..."

Chet watched her picked up another ball, and fix her stare. She inched her shoulders up to her ears and held her breath. *Some relaxed.* She was about as stiff as a poker.

"Hold it." Chet walked over and faced her. "Do you approach everything with this much intensity?"

"Only competition."

"I'll let you in on a little secret. We aren't bowling for dollars and I couldn't care less if you outscore me or not. So relax."

"What makes you think I'm not?"

"This," he said, and pushed her shoulders down. "And this." He started massaging her neck. Upon his touch, her muscles bunched even tighter. He didn't give up, but kept kneading until he felt her tension ebb and her muscles yield beneath his hands.

Her gaze locked on to his. An instant later her eyelids fluttered closed. P.J. tipped her head backward, exposing her throat.

Chet stared at her neck, so long and too pale. Did she spend all her hours working indoors? She would fry under their Virginia sun. He imagined himself spreading sunscreen over her throat, her shoulders, her breasts.

The tingles attacked him again. This time they ignored his spine. This time they concentrated front and center. He clenched his teeth and held back his groan.

"What's wrong?" P.J. asked. "Why'd you stop?"

Chet jerked. His daydream scattered. She was staring at him, a cryptic expression on her face.

He could only imagine what showed on *his* face. His aim was to get rid of her hang-ups, not let his lust hang out. Embarrassment chilled him.

"You're relaxed enough," he said.

"Are you patronizing me? You want relaxed, I'll show you relaxed. How about this?"

P.J. shook her head, then she shuddered all over. She took two deep breaths and let out a throaty sigh. That sound snaked deep down inside him.

Her shoulders drooped. Her head rolled and she swayed. She seemed to go limp. Damn. She was fainting? Chet caught her right as she leaned toward him.

Thump.

He let out a howl.

Her bowling ball landed on his left foot.

SOUTHERN EMERGENCY ROOMS didn't offer any faster service than the few P.J. had visited in Chicago. Half the day had passed by the time she and Chet exited the hospital. The way he leaned on the cane the doctor had given him, he looked as though he needed her help. She walked as close as she could without actually touching him. She dared not get closer. She didn't know if she could stop at just a touch, and after this morning, she didn't know how he would react. Perhaps he would reject her.

She glanced over at him. He looked solemn, preoccupied. She knew she should leave it at that, but the silence choked her. She had to be certain he wasn't angry.

"You do know how sorry I am," she said.

"Ah...that *S* word again. You know, you're pretty dangerous. You should come with a warning label."

"You're the one who wanted me to relax," P.J. said.

"There's a difference between relaxed and catatonic."

"At least nothing's broken, and that shoe thing looks comfortable." She pointed to the blue foam bootie the doctor had insisted he wear.

"You like it? When my two weeks are up, it's yours. Add it to your shoe closet. It doesn't match my wing tips."

"What wing tips? You don't wear wing tips."

"There's a lot you don't know about me."

"Well, that's why I'm here."

"Correction. You're not here because you want to learn about me. You're here for your readers."

"That doesn't mean I'm not interested, too."

His devilish smile crept into position. "How interested?"

"Now you're teasing."

He shrugged, then turned and hobbled away. Even with a cane, he moved fast. She had to hurry along behind.

"You're still mad, aren't you?" she asked when she caught up with him.

"You ask that of a man who's promised you his *shoe thing?*"

"Okay, you believe in bribes. What can I do to make up?"

He stopped and faced her. The corners of his mouth turned up, as did his left brow. She didn't like the glint in his eyes. He moved closer. Darn, she could feel his heat, or maybe it was her own.

"You want to make up?" His voice sounded husky.

P.J. nodded. His gaze swept her face, her neck, her chest. She stopped breathing.

"Ice cream."

"What?"

He dangled the car keys in her face. "I know I promised you barbecue, but that was before I learned what a dangerous person you are. Bowling balls are nothing compared to rib bones. I can't chance you stabbing me with one of those, so we'll have ice cream. It's softer...and safer."

She blinked a few times before taking the keys. Safe had her vote. Ice cream was a whole lot safer than what she had just been imagining. Safer, but not as filling.

"It's almost six o'clock. Aren't we going to have dinner first?" she asked.

"Let's skip the preliminaries and go straight for the dessert. Where's your sense of adventure?"

There goes that shy grin again. Coupled with his raised eyebrow, it made him the perfect picture of naughty.

"We'll pick up ice cream *after* we get some take-out barbecue, and we'll eat dessert last."

"Got my vote. Nothing wrong with building up anticipation."

"I'm not talking about anticipation. I'm talking about hunger, Mr. Greene."

"So am I, Ms. West. So am I."

"I mean food," she shouted at his retreating back.

"Uh-huh."

She stood there with her mouth open, watching him lumber toward the car. She did mean food, didn't she? At this point, with her head singing one tune and her body sitting in on a different jam session, she couldn't say what she meant.

BY THE TIME Chet and P.J. pulled into the driveway, black clouds dominated the sky and the promise of a thunderstorm hung heavy in the air. The two of them rushed for the house as the first raindrops started falling. Chet unlocked the door and ushered her inside.

He noticed her shiver. He would have loved to pull her close and warm her, but didn't. She still seem too tense and reserved. He had to disarm her deflector shield first.

"Hope you don't mind eating in the kitchen. Walking back and forth to the dining room won't help my foot," Chet said as he headed for the freezer with the package of ice cream he carried.

"The kitchen's fine." P.J. followed him into the area and put the bags from Dixie Wings on the counter. She flicked the light switch. Nothing. "Power outage?" she said.

"Can't be. The freezer is running. So's the air conditioner."

"Sean?" she asked.

Bless his eleven-year-old heart. Chet nodded. "That means dinner by candlelight, unless you want to crawl down in the basement and check the circuit breaker. I can't," Chet said, pointing to his injured foot.

She shuddered. "Maybe the storm will pass quickly and the sun will come out."

Chet grinned and shook his head.

She shrugged, but he could tell she was feeling anything but nonchalant. She held her shoulders much too stiffly and her smile was too wide and tight to be natural.

She moved about the kitchen with ease, however. Chet watched her pull plates and flatware from the cabinets. He was amazed how quickly she'd learned the layout of Ann's kitchen. He spent hours in this house and still had to hunt down the dish towels.

That was no fluke, though. He was domestically challenged by design. Women loved men who looked like they could be housebroken. Women smelled such men from miles away and hunted them down, but he had no intention of being tamed, penned and branded for a second time.

Still, his philosophy didn't stop him from admiring P.J. In no time she had the table set and stood waiting for him to take his seat. He slid into his chair and gazed at her from across the table.

Soft candlelight bathed her pale skin. Her eyes sparkled in the glow. The shadows that played across her face made her smile seem downright mysterious. Even with his empty stomach pinching, he thought P.J. West looked more tantalizing than a whole platterful of barbecue ribs.

She stared back at him. Darn those candles and their romantic effect.

"You're staring."

"You have sauce on your chin," he lied.

She touched her napkin to the spot he indicated then looked questioningly at him. Chet pointed to the left. P.J. wiped there, also.

"Lower," he said. She obeyed, running the cloth down her neck in a slow deliberate manner. Chet watched, mesmerized. Again he pictured himself spreading lotion over her...all over her.

"You're still staring."

"You missed a spot." He pointed to her nose then bit into a rib and smiled.

P.J. reached up, but stopped mid-action. "I thought getting messy was part of the experience," she said and raised one eyebrow.

"It is. Just seems odd on you. Me...I can slap sauce every which way and never cause a stir. We used to have barbecue feast just to see who could get the dirtiest."

"You and your wife?"

Chet paused mid-bite. His stomach cringed.

"You ever think of remarrying?" she asked.

He shook his head, then continued to eat. He'd better get her off that subject before she spoiled the mood.

"The children seem intent on matchmaking."

And she seemed intent upon making him nervous. "They know if I'm married I can't write my single dad articles with them as my starring cast. How's the barbecue?"

"Is that so bad? I mean, you don't plan to write 'Living and Learning' forever, do you? The kids will grow up, leave home. You'll be too old unless you want to switch to giving grandfatherly advice."

"Thanks. Bring on the rocker and the shawl. Anyone ever tell you what an ego buster you are."

"Too often." She looked down, then continued in a softer voice. "It's something to consider. Anything could happen. What would you do without the column?"

"Should I be worried? Are you trying to break bad news?" He was losing his appetite.

"No, I was simply interested."

She looked that, all right...interested and concerned, and lovely. That's what he liked about her. That and the way she interacted with the children, the way she listened when he talked. It all touched him. Chet swallowed.

"I'm writing a book," he said. "A collection of tales and confession from single dads. My experiences, but I'll also use material from the fan mail I get."

"You've saved them?"

"Every one. They're treasures. I didn't realize how much good I was doing until I started receiving those letters. They're the most reward I get out of writing the column."

"More than the paycheck?"

Chet gave a start. He hadn't thought about that, and didn't want to. Hadn't his university experience taught him that the money and the security it bought came first?

"Well, is it?" P.J. asked again.

"Is *Modern Man* cutting its pay rate?"

"Your position's secure, even more so after my feature on you comes out."

"Yours, too. You'll get your promotion. Here's to security," he said and raised his beer in a toast.

Her face clouded. She stared at her plate. "Have you ever worried about getting what you wished for?" Her voice had dropped to a whisper.

She seemed so small, so wistful. He wanted to collect her and her dreams in his arms and hold her, rock her, love her worries away.

"Doesn't happen enough to cause concern," he said. "Take now, for instance. I want you. I shouldn't—bad career move and all that—but I do. Unfortunately, you've got this shield, painted the severest black I've even seen. Every time I think you've tossed it, you drag it out of storage and slam it back into place. So getting what I wish is one worry I'm not troubled by…not the way you mean, at least."

"I'm sorry."

"So you've said." Chet stood, picked up his plate, and walked to the sink. Damn. He'd blown it. He shouldn't have gone for a direct attack. He could just imagine her now, reinforcing her barrier while she neatly ate her barbecue.

"I did it again, didn't I? I made you mad." P.J. walked over and stood beside him.

He could close his eyes and feel her. "I'm not mad." But he was, at his own clumsiness.

"Sure you are. The vein by your temple is pulsing."

She touched the side of his head. A fairy touch, but it had the impact of a cattle prod. He felt short-circuited. His head buzzed, his heart pounded. He was coming undone. He grabbed hold of her hand and pressed it palm flat against his chest.

"Do I get my wish or do I get a *so sorry?*"

"You don't want me, Chet, not really. You're only interested in me because I'm available…I mean, because I'm here. You said yourself that you don't date. Well, you need to go out. Resurrect your social life."

"That's what I thought I was doing. I get the sorry speech. Your proposal doesn't fit our current needs. Your basic form letter.''

"That's not fair. All I'm saying is you need to get out. Focus on having a social life.''

"There's not a thing wrong with my social life.'' He couldn't believe this. This was his speech. How did she steal it? He was supposed to tell her this, not the other way around.

"Right. You're a typical workaholic, holed up in the office, avoiding life. Hiding. Will the real Chet James please stand up?''

What was this? She was hitting too close to too many truths. Plus she had him—*him*—backed into the sink.

"Don't be ridiculous,'' he said. "I'm not hiding from anything. My career is important to me, that's all.''

"That's exactly how I would answer, too, if I weren't involved with someone. When *was* the last time you were in a relationship?''

"Oh, come on. The next thing, you'll be asking when was the last time I had sex.''

"Well?''

She jutted out her chin and placed her fists on her hips. She looked downright brazen, but he could tell the question embarrassed her. Even in the dim light he noticed her blush. He looked into her eyes and saw tenderness there, and vulnerability...and longing.

"You really want to know,'' he said.

"I'm not sure.'' Her voice was as small as a kitten's, but her gaze was steady and searching. She shook her head. "Oh, darn. This isn't supposed to be happening. We're business associates. We can't get involved, I don't care what Flasher says."

"What does he say?"

"That we're crazy about each other."

Trust a photographer to see the obvious. "Anything else?"

"That he can see both of us are too to scared do anything about it."

Chet's hands shook as he reached out and touched her shoulders. She moved closer, so close her breasts grazed him. He felt her hardened nipples against his chest. He let out a low moan as his breath caught.

She looked up at him then, her blue eyes glistening. He tipped her chin even higher. Her lips parted.

"Who's scared? Remind me to tell Flasher he's shooting with his lens cap on," he said and slowly lowered his mouth onto hers.

10

EVER SINCE THAT FIRST time, P.J. had longed for another of his kisses, but she wasn't prepared for the softness of this one. She had expected something fierce, intense and demanding. Instead he rubbed his lips over hers, tasting and coaxing until her desire tightened itself into a coil that begged release. She pressed into him, tiptoed and pushed her hips hard against him.

He pulled away, took her hand and walked backward. He led her out of the room, his focus never wavering from her face. When they reached the stairs, he stopped and smiled the crooked grin that made her stomach flutter.

"I want to carry you up, but I don't think my foot will hold out."

Her heart hammered. She placed his hand on her chest. The heat of his palm rushed over her. "Stop stalling. I don't care how we get up there, as long as it's fast."

"Fast." His voice rasped and he crushed her to him and kissed her with tongue and lips.

She couldn't say who carried whom. She could swear she floated. They reached the top of the stairs in each other's arms, kissing and caressing. The sound of their breaths was a chorus of hoarse puffs. They crashed against a door—her bedroom door. She could feel Chet fumble with the knob. The door banged open. The two of them stumbled sideways into the room and up against the dresser.

They explored each other with hands and tongues and lips. Her boldness surprised her.

She rubbed her hand across the stubble on his chin and shivered. The scratchiness tickled her palm. She buried her nose in the hollow of his neck. He smelled of barbecue. With the tip of her tongue, she traced circles along his collarbone. He tasted salty. He groaned, a primal sound that undid the last bit of reserve she still had.

She wanted to touch him, all of him. She pulled at his shirt, his pants. He took over, ripping at his clothes until he stood naked before her. Then he helped her, pushing the straps of her blouse off her shoulders and down to her waist. He stopped and stared. His hand trembled as he reached up and cupped her breasts.

Longing corded from her tight nipples down between her thighs. She placed his hand there and moved against him. She throbbed with need. She gasped. Did he know how long she'd waited? Did he know she never believed this could ever happen, that she would find this, find him? She trembled with happiness and need. She'd waited forever, and she couldn't wait any longer.

She kicked off her sandals, shimmied out of her pants, her panties. She leaned against the dresser and pulled him to her.

"Wait." His voice was raw and scratchy. Scooping his jeans from the floor, he searched the pockets and came up with a foil-wrapped packet. "Compliments of Flasher," he said, sheathing himself.

He seemed to have sensed her need, her desperation. He lifted her and dove deep inside her.

Her cry came as a mixture of surprise and pleasure. She wrapped her legs around him and drove him deeper. All of him, yes, she wanted to feel all of him. She had thirsted too long to hold back now.

They clung to each other. Their hands explored, their tongues tasted. Their bodies were spurred on by a primitive rhythm. The beat drove them on in frenzy. P.J. had never imagined she could feel so free yet so possessed.

She lost herself in the experiencing of him, her senses finally jarred alive from too long a sleep. Loose. So this was loose and relaxed. She knew that only with this man could she have let that happen.

"P.J.," he said. He stared down at her, his eyes hazed with passion.

She touched his lips and whispered, "Patty... Patty Jean."

"Patty," he whispered, his lips brushing her ear. Never had it sounded so right. Soft, strong, honest.

He repeated her name, over and over with each slow, teasing thrust. She wriggled and moaned, her flesh tingling, her body on the edge of explosion, until she could barely stand it. Then she ached and urged him into a faster dance.

Passion consumed her, building inside her, wave upon wave cresting atop the other until she erupted in a wild release of pleasure. Chet stilled, then moved hard inside her. Her second cry of pleasure was answered by his. Together they quivered, holding on to each other, rocking and breathing as one.

SUNLIGHT FILTERED through the sheer lace curtains and made delicate patterns across the bed. It warmed Chet's face, but not as intensely as the presence of P.J. sleeping beside him or the memory of their night together. They had loved, fiercely at first, driven by need and desire they had too long tried to deny. Later, as they lay in bed they had loved one another with unhurried kisses and slow strokes and long looks into each other's eyes as each climbed and soared into climax.

He wanted to love her again. He wanted to pull her close from behind, mold her body to his and wrap her in his arms as he lost himself inside her once again. But he had done that so many times throughout the night, sometimes as initiator, sometimes following her lead, that now he knew she needed rest. They had time. If he had his way, they would have forever.

He turned onto his side and watched her. Her face was turned away so he rose up on one elbow for a better view of the mouth he had so thoroughly kissed. Her lips were parted and slightly swollen. Her cheeks were still pink where his beard had rubbed. Looking at her filled him with desire and warmth and contentment.

She rested on her back, one arm above her head, the other just below her chin. Open and trusting.

The urge to protect overwhelmed him. *Protect,* but from what and from whom? Himself? His lie?

Guilt burned in his chest. This woman was in for a major betrayal from him, the man who personally knew the anguish it would cause. From him, the man who had fallen deeply in love with her.

Panic ripped him. Chet felt as though strong hands squeezed his chest. He couldn't breathe. He sat up in bed, knowing he had to tell her the truth. He was lying to *Modern Man Magazine,* not her. Would she understand? Somehow he had to find a way to make her understand, or he would lose her.

I can't lose her. The truth of that rang through him.

Slowly, he climbed from bed. P.J. stirred. She tossed her head on the pillow and murmured something Chet couldn't understand. Then she smiled and turned onto her side. Her blond hair fell across her eyes as she settled back to sleep.

Chet didn't realize he hadn't been breathing until he exhaled. Quickly and silently he slipped into his clothes and stole out of the room. He headed for the kitchen. He did some of his best thinking there. Some of his best material came to light while he sat at Ann's table listening to the kids' latest escapades. Hopefully he would find a solution to his own predicament there, also.

P.J. WOKE feeling warm and sated. She couldn't believe how relaxed and free she felt...and all because of Chet. She turned and reached for him. He wasn't there. P.J. bolted upright. Had she dreamed last night? No. His side of the bed was still warm. She was still warm...all over. Then she smelled the coffee and fell back on the mattress, smiling.

He was making her breakfast. Probably just cereal and toast, but she knew whatever he fixed, he would prepare it with love. Love. Belonging.

Yes, she had found her perfect man. She belonged with Chet. She had sensed that from the moment they'd met, but she tried to deny it. Fear and conditioning were powerful enemies. She had overcome them. With Chet's help she was no longer afraid to be herself...to be Patty Jean.

She understood what she had been missing, hiding behind the steel armor that was P.J. West. No more. Thanks to Chet and what he'd shown her about herself, she no longer needed her armor—her false persona.

She gladly laid it down, and for the first time she realized how heavy it had been. Heavy and restricting.

Then she remembered. In less than a week she would return to her world. Well, from now on things would be different. Patty Jean was just as strong and capable as P.J. She was finished with antacids and nail biting. She was a damn good editor, the best, and she would be the best even without panty hose of steel.

Chet had shown her that. He'd shown her his own strengths as well as his vulnerabilities. He wasn't afraid to reach out, to help as well as be helped.

Could she ease his pain over the loss of his first wife? She wanted to. There was so much she now wanted, and none of it had to do with *Modern Man* or the promotion or proving her worth.

CHET SIPPED his second cup of coffee and tasted nothing. He paced from one end of the room to the other. His body was getting exercise, but his brain remained as dormant as a potato. He sat his coffee on the counter and faced the refrigerator.

"Listen, P.J., I've something to tell you," he said to the appliance, then shook his head.

No, no, no. Too stark. That wouldn't do. He took a deep breath and started over.

"P.J., sometimes a man has to say something that...that... Damn." Too preachy.

He took hold of the handle with both hands, flexed the muscles in his face then assumed what he thought was a sincere expression.

"P.J. I...I..." Emotion. He needed an opener that would grab her and hold her attention and her heart.

Chet grasped the sides of the refrigerator as though they were shoulders, her shoulders. With as much passion and earnestness as he could muster he said, "I love you."

"Should I be jealous?" P.J.'s voice came from the doorway.

Chet jerked. The refrigerator shook, its contents rattled. He spun around and leaned against the door, steadying himself more so than the appliance.

She had donned a jersey nightshirt, black like the rest of her wardrobe, but she needn't have bothered for all it covered. The thing hemmed-off mid-thigh and the too-wide neck opening exposed her left shoulder and part of her breast. And darn if he didn't want to rip it off her.

"P.J. I didn't know you... I didn't hear you..."

"But I heard you. Wooing another and so soon after loving me?" she said, a teasing lilt in her voice.

She crossed the room and stood in front of him. Her face glowed.

"No, I was, um, practicing." He kissed her.

She kissed him back with such force, he heard a humming in his ears loud enough to deafen him. His stomach tightened to an ache. He hardened with renewed need. He wanted her there in the kitchen pressed against the darn refrigerator, but he couldn't. He had to tell her now, or he never would.

He broke the kiss, grasped her shoulders and held her at a distance. At first she laughed, then she looked at him and frowned.

"P.J." He opened his mouth to say more, but squeaked instead. His throat tightened.

She looked stricken. "You do love someone else. Please tell me it's the refrigerator. It's fat and ugly. I can deal with that."

He could have laughed and hugged her, but he knew if he did they wouldn't talk. He would stop communicating...with words at least.

"P.J., we have to talk."

"Talk? Why is this making me nervous?" She took a deep breath that made her breasts ride high and inch further out of her nightshirt. "Okay, let's talk. We didn't do much of that last night, did we?"

Suddenly his palms were clammy. His throat felt as if he'd swallowed glue. He pried his tongue from the roof of his mouth and began. "I have to tell you something so you can understand that I—"

A loud thump cut him short. The noise came from outside and sounded as though something heavy had fallen on the front porch. The doorbell chimed, once, twice, three times in rapid succession.

The kids weren't due back for hours, nor was Flasher. Chet decided to ignore the interruption. Whoever it was would go away. He coughed and started anew.

"Sometimes a man says or does something he later regrets—"

"Oh. This is one of those, let's-forget-last-night-ever-happened speeches. I see." She bit her thumbnail.

"No. You don't see. I'm trying to tell you that—"

The chime rang again, this time nonstop as though someone's finger was permanently affixed to the bell.

Chet sighed. "I'd better answer that. Wait here."

Perhaps the interruption wasn't a bad thing. He could use a few extra minutes to get his speech polished.

He walked down the hall unbelievably buoyed by his good fortune. The feeling evaporated when the front door swung open, pushed by two suitcases...two familiar-looking suitcases. Suitcases that were supposed to be vacationing at the spa with their owner.

Every muscle in his body double locked. He couldn't move. He couldn't breathe.

"Don't just stand there, help me," Ann said as she struggled to slide her luggage into the room.

"Ann." He half squeaked, half cried.

She looked up from her task. "Chet," she said, mimicking his voice, then tugged on her bags.

"What are you doing here?"

"Struggling. Alone. Come and help me before I get a hernia."

Chet lifted both cases and set them down by the stairs, then turned back to Ann. "Why did you come back?"

"I live here. I'm allowed to come back. And don't give me grief because I came home early. I missed the kids. And I couldn't stop feeling guilty about leaving you here with all that responsibility while I idled away the hours doing mud baths and drinking cucumber cocktails."

She walked over, patted him on his cheek then looked around the room. "Besides, I wanted to make sure you really hadn't burned the place down."

"I didn't. I, uh, uh..."

"Did you wreck my kitchen? Oh, no, let me see."

She started past him, but he jumped in her path and pulled her into the living room.

"You can't go in there."

"Why not?" Her voice climbed a few decibels.

"Shh," he said, fanning his hands in front of her face.

"How bad is it? What have you done to my kitchen, Chet? And why are you shushing me?" she shouted even louder.

"Chet? Are you okay?" P.J. stood in the doorway, gripping her deadly mop with both hands. Her little black nightshirt hung like a gladiator's tunic. She resembled a warrior princess.

Chet groaned.

The two women eyed each other, then bore into him with their individual gazes. "Ann, P.J. P.J., Ann," he said by way of introduction.

The two women nodded to each other then again fixed their stares upon him. Sweat dotted his forehead. Dread pounded through him as strong as his heartbeat. He wanted the carpet to rise up and swallow him, but carpets weren't known to perform such acts of mercy, especially not peach carpets that had recently had the life steam-cleaned out of them.

"I'm his sister." Ann broke the stalemate.

"Ann? Oh, yes, of course." P.J. colored. With one hand she grabbed hold of her neckline and pinched it closed up around her throat.

"I take it you're his..."

"Editor." P.J. squared her shoulders and looked his sister in the eye.

The tough-as-steel woman rides again, even half dressed. Chet had forgotten she existed, but this reincarnation was different. This time she was all spunk and dignity, without a shield. He warmed with pride.

"So editors do housework these days?" Ann said, pointing to the mop.

P.J. gave a weak laugh and set the mop against the wall. "I heard the shouting. I assumed there was trouble."

"Don't dismiss that theory too quickly," Ann said and turned toward him. "Chet, what's going on? Where are my kids?"

"Your kids?" P.J. said. "But...but they're Chet's children."

"His ex-wife would die laughing over that. The woman hates kids," Ann said.

"She's already dead." P.J.'s voice lost its strength.

"Chet's wife is alive and living well, thanks to his alimony payments. Brittany and the boys are mine and as you can see, I'm alive, too. Although another day of alfalfa sprouts and tofu probably would have done me in."

"But he said..." P.J.'s voice sounded so small it made Chet ache.

Her eyes widened and she gasped. Her face seemed to crumble through hundreds of expressions, each more painful-looking than the one before. When she turned toward him, her expression was stony, the look in her eyes shadowy and distant.

Chet felt a kick slam into his gut, his chest. "I can explain."

"You've got my attention," Ann said.

But P.J. pivoted and marched out of the room. Chet stood frozen listening to P.J.'s footsteps ascend the stairs. He should follow her, make her listen while he explained, but he couldn't move his feet. Then it was too late. He heard her bedroom door slam with the finality of a period at the end of a sentence.

Suddenly his muscles collapsed. He sank into the closest chair and let gravity pull him deep into the cushions. Maybe the chair would swallow him since the rug refused.

"Okay, Mr. Resourceful, explain," Ann said.

Chet took a deep breath, steadied himself then told all. All except the details of the night before. When he finished he felt no better. Indeed he felt worse and expected his spirits would plummet even further as the days, the weeks, months went by. *Alone.* He was alone.

"If P.J. doesn't kill you, Chet, I will. What were you thinking?"

"I was trying to keep my job."

"Guess what?"

"I know. I've lost both of our jobs." And P.J. wanted that promotion. Again guilt took a huge, raw bite out of him.

"And you used the children in your little scheme. Wait until I finish talking to them."

"Don't be hard on them. It's my fault. If anything they've learned a valuable lesson—lying doesn't pay."

Ann considered, then took a deep breath. "You've proven *that,* all right, but they still get a lecture."

He slumped and hung his head. He would have to find a way to make up to the kids.

"And you… I'd make you do major penance, but I think you're going to be doing that, anyway."

And then some. He suspected penitence would become a regular dietary supplement.

He pressed the heels of his hands into his eyes. The blackness he saw seemed so cold, so infinite. He was looking into emptiness.

Get used to it, Mr. Living and Learning.

11

P.J. THREW HER BELONGINGS into her bags, packed them down and zipped the suitcase shut. She picked up her notes and stuffed them into the trash can along with the cassette tapes she had unwound and tossed in earlier.

"Lies, lies." He had lied to her. Pain and disappointment ripped at her insides. And she had believed him, trusted him. And he had betrayed her.

"He's no better than the rest." No, he was worse, much worse. His disguise and deceit were well practiced. His knockout punch guaranteed to keep her down long past the count.

She remembered last night, how she had lost herself so completely in his arms, his warmth, his love. No, not love. Passion, pure carnal lust. That's all Chet Greene was capable of. That's all he sought, a quick roll in the sack with the boss woman.

"Greene," she said with a snort. Even that was a lie.

How could he? How could *she?* "Stupid, stupid, stupid." She knew better than to mix business with pleasure and now she would pay the price.

The realization of all she had lost sucked the air from her lungs. She leaned against the bedpost. The

Reaper would delight in firing her, but not before he made a spectacle of her.

She wouldn't give him the chance. Nor would she resign then slink out the back door in secret. No, if she was to get axed, she would lower the blade on her own neck. She would announce the fraud tomorrow, at the next staff meeting. She'd accept responsibility and resign in front of them all. Any jokes and snide comments, they could make to her face. She was ready for that, her skin had been toughened enough to withstand the ridicule of her colleagues.

What she couldn't withstand was the bitter ache Chet had wrenched into her heart.

"But you must," she told herself. And she would.

P.J. pulled her cell phone from her briefcase and dialed information. She wouldn't wait for Flasher to return with the car. She'd order a cab to take her to the airport, then she would dress and wait in her room.

CHET WAS STILL SLUMPED in the easy chair when voices and laughter boomed in the hall. It sounded as if a herd of elephants was about to charge into the house.

"Who left the door open?" Brittany called.

"Chet? Hello?" Bill's heavy footfall and deep voice filled the room. "We're back early."

The early bird special. Why not? The more, the merrier. Chet didn't have the energy to answer.

"That was Kevin's fault. He jumped in the fountain in the park, twice, so he didn't have any more dry clothes,'' Sean said.

''I'm a fish. Fish don't need dry clothes.''

''In here,'' Ann called.

''Mom.'' All three children screamed at once, ran into the living room and surrounded their mother with hugs.

''I missed you, too,'' she said after the kids gave her breathing room.

''Wait a minute. What are you doing back?'' Brittany shot a glance at him then back to her mother.

''I never should have gone. I see you three...*four*,'' she said with a squint directed at him, ''can't be left alone.''

A car horn beeped outside. Chet glanced out the window and saw a taxi parked in front of the house. P.J.'s escape vehicle no doubt. His heart sank into his shoes.

''It was Uncle Chet's idea,'' Sean said.

''Of course it was. And whatever bribe you finagled out of him gets donated to the homeless shelter.''

Kevin hiccuped. ''I already ate my bribe.''

''Then we'll think up something else just for you, Mr. Guppy.''

''I'm no guppy. I'm a shark.'' Kevin bowed his head, did a mimic swim around the room that ended with a nosedive into Chet's stomach.

Pain fired Chet's insides, but he would take that over the slow persistent squeeze that was choking the life out of him.

"So, where is P.J.?" Brittany asked.

"She's leaving." P.J. dropped her bags in the hall and entered the living room. She didn't give him a glance, but focused on Ann. "I apologize for any disruption my visit caused your family."

"No," Chet said, springing to his feet and rushing to her. "*I* apologize. I know you think I lied to you, but I didn't. I lied to the magazine. Everything I said to you was the truth."

"You deceived thousands of readers on a regular basis. Once you get into the habit, I doubt one gullible editor—*ex*-editor—matters."

"Yes, you do matter. I want you in my life like I never wanted anyone before. I don't want to lose you. I love you."

P.J. blinked. She stared at him. A frown creased her forehead then melted away as her eyes misted and her mouth parted. Her expression softened for a moment, for a very short moment, before she clamped her mouth into a hard, unforgiving line.

"Yeah, right. So you'll sulk for an hour. But guess what? You just lost something that you really love. You lost your job, Mr. Greene. The kicker is, I lost mine right along with you."

"That doesn't have to happen. I can make things right. I'll do one final article…a farewell message. I'll say I'm giving up the column for…oh, personal reasons. You keep your job and I'll ride off into the sunset. I'll concentrate on writing that book we talked about."

"The book about family relations from a *single dad's* perspective?"

"Yeah. Well, a man's perspective. It will work. Everyone will be happy. You may still get that promotion."

"If I keep my mouth shut and go along with your story. That's another one of your bribes, Chet."

"Like I said, never underestimate the power of a well-timed bribe." He stepped closer. His hands shook when he reached up and grasped her shoulders. He felt her tremble at his touch. So she still had feelings for him. Everything would be okay, after all. She understood he hadn't meant to hurt her, that he really hadn't lied to *her*.

He smiled down at her, at her open face and her clear blue eyes. "What do you say, Patty Jean?" he asked.

The look in her eyes hardened. The brown flecks in her eyes turned red and sparked a warning. He heeded too late.

Whoop.

Her fist slammed into his gut with the force of a wrecking ball. Chet's breath whooshed out in one painful cough. He doubled over and gasped.

"It's *P.J.* to you." With that she turned, picked up her bags and left.

12

LIFE HAD NEVER SEEMED blacker, Chet thought as he wheezed and coughed.

"Wow. Did you see that punch?" Sean said.

"Aren't you going after her?" Brittany's voice rasped with disbelief and reproach.

"I don't think he can," Ann said. She and Bill took hold of Chet's arms and led him back to the chair.

He fell into the cushions and sank even deeper into despair. "It's over. I tried, she wouldn't listen."

"Good for her," Ann said. "If you tried that let's-make-a-deal routine on me, you'd be dead now."

"But P.J.'s real neat, Mom, and Chet likes her. And she likes him." Brittany looked like a little street lawyer.

"Not anymore," Bill offered.

"He didn't try hard enough. Come on, Uncle Chet, don't let her go. We like her, too." Brittany pulled at his arm, trying to dislodge him from his seat.

"Kids, go up to your rooms," Ann said.

"Good idea," Bill said. "Best you not see this.

Your mother's going to take a switch to your uncle.''

"Bill.'' Ann gave her ex-husband a stern look.
"*You* go home. Chet and I want to talk...alone.''

No he didn't. If anything, Chet wanted to go
home and lick his wounds. If he stayed, Ann would
pour salt on them in the guise of one of her lectures.
Unfortunately, he hurt so much, he couldn't stand,
let alone make an exit.

Ann started in on him the minute everyone left.
"So you love her.''

Point already established, but he simply nodded.

She folded her hands and sat on the arm of his
chair. "I'd say by the way she rushed into the room
wielding a mop and ready to do battle on your be-
half, that she loves you too.''

"Did,'' Chet said.

"Does,'' Ann countered. "Why else would she
have been so mad? I read that you only get truly
angry with those you love.''

"Don't believe everything you read. Most writers
don't know what they're talking about and the rest
are lying. I should know. Anyway, P.J. is looking
for Mr. Perfect and I blew it. I proved just how
imperfect I am. She'll never settle for a defect like
me.''

"And neither should you. I'm not saying be in-
fallible, I am saying, like the rest of us, you can
work on a few things. Clean up your act.''

"And where do you suggest I start?'' he said. In
the past few days he'd cleaned more than enough

rooms, but he was willing to add one more item if it meant getting P.J. back.

"For one thing, you've lost sight of what's important. It's not money, Chet. You think the more you have the more you can buy your way out of trouble and buy yourself happiness? You think that's security?"

Something like that. He had to admit he'd been operating under that principle. Hearing Ann say it, though, made him sound... Shallow?

"Well, wise up, little brother. You can own a king's ransom and still be miserable if you don't have that one person who means something. The only security you'll find in this world is through love and family. That's what will see you through life's tough moments."

Ann was right. Didn't the two of them stick together? Didn't they help each other out whenever crisis struck? How could he have been so stupid? He was so focused on becoming a financial success he'd lied to thousands of people even though he knew that was wrong. Worst of all, he lied to P.J.

"So now what?" he asked.

Knowing the error of his ways didn't change much. He felt as bad as before. The pain in his chest throbbed with the same intensity. He still felt as if he were spiraling down a tight rabbit hole.

"So now you're going to set things right." Ann wagged her finger in his face. "And I don't mean by bribing your way out of it. If you really love P.J., you won't let her walk out of your life. Not without a fight, anyway. Go after her, Chet. If you don't, I'll never forgive you. Better yet, if you ever want to eat dinner here again, you'll do it.''

"You said no bribes."

"*I* can bribe, you can't. Chet, if you don't go after her, you'll never forgive yourself."

"I know. I'll be so miserable, I wouldn't be able to stand myself."

"Neither will anyone else. So, what are you waiting for?"

Suddenly a weight lifted. Breathing proved easier, still difficult thanks to the slam into his diaphragm, but he'd settle for any improvement.

"You're right. I love her. I'm going to try and get her back."

An eruption of cheers came from the second-floor landing.

"Kids, I told you to go to your rooms, not listen on the stairs."

"We're going." The noise of stomping feet filtered downstairs. Only a fool would think they'd actually moved from their sentry post.

Chet laughed. He felt hopeful again. He'd call. No, he had to talk to her in person.

Chicago wasn't that far away. He could fly there in no time. When he arrived, he would track down her apartment and camp out on her doorstep until she let him explain. No. *Until he made amends* and made her see he was ready to change.

He may not be perfect, but he was honest enough to admit it. And he would work every day to improve. How could she want perfection when she could have him, Mr. Resourceful? Better yet, Mr. Living-and-Learning-The-Hard-Way.

Chet grabbed the phone and dialed the airlines. He could catch the next flight out and get there tonight. Such a simple plan.

Correction, such a simple plan if there had been any unbooked flights, Chet thought as he hung up the phone. He'd spent hours listening to schedules and stopovers and optional routings without hearing the one thing he needed, a booking that would get him to Chicago that night.

"Well, you can always phone her," Ann said.

"She would only hang up. I have to go in person. She can slam the door in my face, but that takes more energy. She'll finally give up and listen just to get rid of me. Somehow I've got to get there."

"You can drive," Kevin yelled.

"Kids," Ann warned.

"No, he's right. I *can* drive. If I leave now and drive nonstop I could get there—"

"A total wreck, *if* you get there at all. You'll have to make a few rest stops and even overnight somewhere. You can't go straight through unless you had a second driver."

"Would you?" he asked, looking at Ann. He knew he was grabbing a greased pig, but it was worth a try.

"I just got home. Besides, what would I do with the kids?"

"Maybe Bill will join me." Chet rushed out of the living room. No doubt his ex-brother-in-law had already driven away, but Chet decided to check outside before he started phoning. He hastened down the hall, threw open the door and collided with the man standing on the other side.

"Ah-hh." Both Chet and Flasher jumped back.

"Goodness. What's the hurry? Is the kitchen on fire again?" Flasher said, his eyes wide as he fumbled for his camera.

"Flasher. Thank God you're early, too." Chet grabbed the photographer by the shoulders and pulled him into a bone-crushing bear hug.

"If I'd known I'd get this kind of greeting I would have been back before the cocks crowed," Flasher said.

"Excuse me." Ann stood in the hallway. A puzzled frown pinched her brow as she eyed both men.

"Ann, Flasher. Flasher, Ann," Chet said. "My sister."

"You really don't have a trench coat," she said.

"A what?" Flasher asked.

"Get packed. You're going to Chicago," Chet told him.

"I am? What about the story? Where's P.J.?"

"Gone," Chet said. "Don't worry, I'll explain on the way. In thirty minutes, I'll be back to pick you up. Be ready."

"You're flying back with me?" Flasher asked.

"No. We're driving."

"Yippee." The kids ran down the stairs shouting.

Confusion followed with the kids hopping and circling the adults. Chet kissed Ann on the cheek. He hugged each child, kissed each cheek and stopped short at Flasher's puckered lips.

"I'm taken," Chet said, and rushed out of the house. He had to get home first. There were a few things he had to pack, things that would help make his case. He hoped.

IN HER LITTLE CUBE of an office, P.J. sat behind her desk, holding the telephone to her ear and listening to Flasher. She felt guilty leaving him in Virginia and was glad he'd made it back to Chicago on his own. Still she wished he were in the office and not across town in his apartment, resting up from the all-night drive. At least he would get some sleep, though, which was something she hadn't managed to do.

She had tossed the night away and was now feeling the effects. Her eyes felt gritty, her head pounded and every muscle in her body screamed. Her stomach wasn't faring well, either, so she dug through the bottom drawer in search of her antacids.

Nothing compared to the ache in her heart, though. It suffered from a poisonous dose of bitterness and sorrow, grief fortified by a strong injection of embarrassment.

She shuddered, then unwrapped the tablets and popped them into her mouth. She held her hand over the mouthpiece.

"I hear chewing. Are you biting your nails?" Flasher asked.

"Nope. I haven't any left. I'm now on a steady diet of antacids."

"Mmm. No sleep, no nails, and the kind of heartburn no bicarbonate will cure. I can imagine how you look.''

''Imagine the worst. Too bad you aren't here to do my makeup,'' P.J. said.

''Do you have raccoon circles under your eyes?'' he asked.

''Terrible ones.''

''And does your skin have that sickly gray tone?''

''That, too, and my eyes are red,'' P.J. said.

''Forget makeup. Go home before someone sees you.''

''Can't. I have an important meeting in fifteen minutes.''

''If memory serves me, all this trouble started with one of your important meetings.''

''Well, it all ends with *this* one,'' she said. Her voice sounded flat even to her ears. ''I'm giving a full report, then I'm resigning.''

''Whoa. Back up. Number One, a staff meeting is no place for true confessions...professional or otherwise, if you get my drift. Number Two, resigning is out of the question...you're still this magazine's best asset. And Number Three—''

''Number Three, I blew it. I introduced our readers to a fraud and they bought the full package.''

''So they'll get over it. The few that don't will stop buying the magazine, but the majority will keep their subscriptions and live happily ever after. And you know why? They may have come to *Modern Man* because of the 'Living and Learning' column, but they'll stay for the sex and how-to-pick-up-women drivel.''

"In that case, I'm definitely resigning.''

"P.J., P.J., P.J. This isn't about the readers, is it? It's about you and Chet.''

Of course it was. "I let my guard down, Flasher, and it's come back to haunt me. If I hadn't been so infatuated, I would have asked more questions. I would have been more alert and—''

"And the only difference is, you would have found out earlier. So?''

I wouldn't have slept with him. I wouldn't have fallen in love. Pain gnawed at her. Tears swelled behind her eyes. No she wouldn't cry. She'd done enough of that and all she'd gotten out of it were two red, puffy eyes.

"He tried to bargain his way out,'' she said.

"Yep, he told me.''

"He told you? When?''

"On the drive up. It was a long drive, he told me a lot of things.''

"Chet's in Chicago?''

Suddenly her heart did a wild loop-the-loop. Chet was not miles and miles away. He was nearby. In spite of everything, excitement raced through her.

Sobriety hit just as quickly. He probably wanted to press his case, wanted to convince her to back up his story. Well, she wouldn't see him. "How could you, my so-called best friend? How could you bring him here? Don't tell me you're harboring the criminal, too?''

"No,'' Flasher said. "He dropped me off and

left. Said something about camping out on your doorstep.''

''You gave him my address?'' Was betrayal the virus of the new millennium? ''If I get home and find him there, I'll...I'll kill him.''

''He's really a decent guy, but I guess that won't measure up for P.J. the Pure and Perfect.''

''That's cruel. I never claimed I was perfect. I just—''

''Won't forgive Chet because he isn't.''

''He's a liar.''

''And so are you, Ms. Patty Jean. Every time you walk into the office and morph into P.J. West, Lady of Steel, you become a liar.''

''That's different. That's professional preservation.''

''Which applies to Chet, too. He came up with a unique concept for the magazine and did some 'professional preservation' to stay in business. How was he to know that you would show up on *his* doorstep?''

''Are you trying to blame me?''

''I don't like scattering blame around. There're too many pollutants in the air as it is. Anyway, did you know he's practically supporting his sister and her family?''

''Probably another one of his lies.''

''If it's a lie, it's Ann's.''

''I left you alone with them for only a few hours. How'd you get all chummy?''

''It helps if you don't go around socking favorite uncles in the gut.''

So he heard about that, too. She should feel ashamed. Instead she felt smug.

"So, what else did Chet tell you?" she asked.

"That he loves you. That he has some important things to discuss with you."

"I won't listen."

"Even with him camped on your doorstep? Be kind of hard to avoid."

"I'll get a room at the Hilton, buy a whole new wardrobe on credit. I won't have to go back to my apartment ever again." Right. Her cards would max out after three purchases.

Too bad that plan wouldn't work. She didn't want to see Chet. She wasn't sure she could face him and not feel that same tug in her chest. He was so right for her in so many ways. And now that was ruined.

No, she didn't have to face him ever again, but she did have to face the fact she would probably never find that special someone.

"Why did you have to bring him to Chicago?" she asked. Her voice cracked and she swallowed.

"Because you're in Chicago. He did something stupid...okay possibly a quarter millimeter shy of illegal. The Reaper's knickers will knot."

"Do you think the magazine will sue?" Why was that worried tone in her voice?

"More than likely they'll cover up the whole thing. Anything to avoid bad publicity."

Flasher was right. She sighed with relief. A suit would hurt Chet and his family. She didn't want that. Then what did she want?

She remembered Chet's kiss, his arms, the way she fit so perfectly with him. Her heart hitched, then beat wildly. A warmth spread from her center outward. Her gasp pulled her back to reality. Flasher was saying something. She focused in on him mid-sentence.

"—but that doesn't erase all the good things you saw in him. He made a mistake, P.J. Don't you make a mistake by closing him out. At least listen to him. And don't execute him for not being perfect."

"I wouldn't want someone perfect."

"Since when?"

"Since I've had my eyes opened by a thirteen-year-old."

Maybe last week she would have accepted nothing less than perfection, but that was before she took account of her own flaws and before her chat with Brittany. The girl was right. Goody Two-shoes made normal people feel subhuman.

Chet could never be labeled a Goody Two-shoes, still she wasn't sure she'd meet with him.

"Why should I listen to you?" P.J. asked Flasher.

"Because I have wisdom beyond my years and you know it."

Because he had her best interest at heart and he knew her soft side, she decided. Only one other person knew that about her. Chet. He hadn't used the information to hurt her, either. His scheme was in place long before the two of them discovered each other.

He had tried to tell her the truth. The minute their relationship became more than editor-writer, he had tried. But then he blew it.

P.J. took a deep breath. She understood how he could succumb to his ambition. She even forgave him that. She knew the power of ambition.

What she couldn't excuse was the way he'd stood there and tried to bargain his way out of accepting responsibility. And he had expected her to back up his story. She couldn't forgive that.

If only he had confessed and faced the music. That would have shown honesty and character. That's all she would have asked. She couldn't love someone who did less. Still she would hear him out even though being near him would tear at her and fill her with regret and longing.

"Fine. When I go home tonight, I promise I won't kick any animal I find curled outside my door." *I won't let him in, either.* The corner coffee shop would do. She would sit, listen, then say good-bye and point the buzzard south.

P.J. rang off then looked into her hand mirror and groaned. Red-veined eyes stared back at her. Her hair hung flat and lifeless and, yes, her complexion had turned grayish.

Talk about looking her worst, and for a meeting where she needed to look perfect. She wasn't even close to looking presentable and she knew no amount of makeup would help.

Her appearance didn't bother her as much as her attitude crisis. She needed to walk into that meeting exuding confidence, cool professionalism, and a this-magazine-is-going-to-be-lost-without-me pos-ture. Instead she felt as tired and lackluster as her hair looked. Fine time for P.J., Lady of Steel, to go AWOL. Well, it was high time she introduced her co-workers to Patty Jean.

She took a calming breath, squared her aching shoulders and marched out of her office. She maintained a clipped pace all the way down the hall. When she reached the conference room door, she didn't hesitate. She turned the knob and strode inside.

Three drawn and wary faces turned in her direction. "And I thought I looked bad," she murmured to herself as she glanced at each of her male colleagues.

"Where's Smith?" she asked when she noticed one co-worker missing.

"Erckkk." Jones drew his finger across his neck.

"Comforting to know things haven't changed," she said. Her legs wobbled, but she made it to a chair before they gave way on her.

Unfortunately, she didn't have time to compose herself. The side door swung open and in walked The Reaper gracing the room with his alligator presence. He sat at the head of the table, spared a glance at the men then locked his focus on her.

"You're supposed to be in Richmond getting that story on the daddy guy."

"I've finished. There was no reason to stay longer."

"I'd like to hear how you can finish a week-long assignment in less than four days." The Reaper's voice never boomed. It sliced through the air as hushed and lethal as a scythe.

"I don't just mean I've finished this particular assignment. I've finished my assignment with *Modern Man*," P.J. began. Her voice shook at first then grew steady. "You suspected one of our authors of fraud. You thought he was putting his name on articles penned by a woman. Some silly housewife, I believe were your words. You were wrong. And you were correct."

"I don't pay you to talk in riddles. I hope you've done a better job in your article," The Reaper said.

"I have no article. I went to Virginia expecting to find a single man dedicated to raising his children. That's what I found. If I had dug deeper, I would have found more. Unfortunately, Mr. Chet James, the man our readers know as Chet Greene, is—"

The conference room door opened with a bang as it slammed against the wall. Everyone turned at the noise.

"Is here. And I hope on time," Chet said.

He stood in the doorway and nodded at everyone present. When his gaze found her, he stopped and stared.

P.J.'s heart slammed into her throat. She couldn't breathe. Lack of air made her dizzy. She opened her mouth only to let out a pitiful pant.

One of her co-workers slapped her on the back. P.J. gasped, coughed, then filled her lungs.

"That happy to see me, darling?" Chet said.

How could he be here at her office, crashing her

meeting when he was supposed to be camped out on her doorstep? She stared back flabbergasted. She blinked. Something about him was different.

The suit. Chet wore a suit. She'd never seen him in one and decided he would look dashing if his jacket and pants weren't so wrinkled. Quite dashing, she thought as her gaze traveled down to his shoes.

Wing tips? She gawked, then shot her focus back to his face, to his coffee-brown eyes, now lined with red and surrounded by dark circles.

She couldn't believe how tired he looked, but then he and Flasher had driven all night. No wonder his cheeks were hollow and his hair was mussed and falling down in his bloodshot eyes. The dark stubble on his chin didn't surprise her, either.

He had driven all night and hadn't even stopped to change.

Her heart squeezed. Before she could stop herself she smiled.

He remained in the doorway as though walking any farther was more than he could manage. But he did manage to smile. That same slow lopsided apology of a grin that never failed to tug at her insides.

13

CHET COULD SENSE the receptionist behind him, tiptoeing, trying to see over his shoulders. The middle-age bulldog had hounded him all the way down the hall. He hadn't worried she could stop him, but he hadn't ruled out her biting his ankle. He wouldn't press his luck, so he stayed put and beckoned with his finger. "I won't stay. I've come to speak with Ms. West."

"I've nothing to say to this man." P.J. folded her arms.

"Shall I call security?" the bulldog asked.

"Yes," P.J. shouted.

"No." The Reaper shook his head. "Maybe our daddy expert can explain things in plain English since my editor can't."

Chet walked farther into the room. Curious stares followed him. He'd never felt so nervous. In the rush to get to Chicago, he hadn't prepared a speech and certainly hadn't planned on an audience. Now what?

Okay Mr. Resourceful.

He cleared his throat. *Show time.*

"I believe Ms. West was about to make an announcement—my announcement actually, so I guess it's fitting I break the news." He glanced over at P.J. She sat forward in her seat. Curiosity dominated her expression, but Chet saw something else hiding in the shadows of her eyes. Was it anticipation, hope?

"But before I do that, I want to tell you about this woman." He watched P.J.'s expression cloud with confusion. He gave her a smile and continued. "You work with her, you think you know her. I doubt you do. P.J. West is a professional extraordinaire. Thorough, caring and compassionate."

Chet took a deep breath. His heart was speeding, his thoughts flying.

"She's probably going to tell you she's resigning because she discovered I'm a fraud," he said.

Murmurs filled the room. The men shifted in their chairs. The Reaper sat back and frowned. P.J., too, wore a frown but hers wasn't as hard-edged as her boss's.

"Well, she's wrong," Chet said and watched disappointment wash over her face. She slumped back in her seat and stared at him. Ever so slowly, she shook her head. He hurried on.

"P.J. West is the best thing this magazine has ever seen, or ever will see. It took guts and creativity to rescue that first article of mine from the slush pile and turn it into something bigger than any of you dreamed possible. I don't know about circulation and how you media types measure a hit, but I know success and a good idea when I see it."

He walked to the table, hoisted one of the briefcases he was carrying, and dumped its contents. Letters spilled over the table.

"This is success," Chet said, and lifted the second case and repeated the process. Letters covered the surface and spilled to the floor.

"What in the... Call security," The Reaper said. One of the men sprang from his chair.

"Wait." Chet held up his hand. "Please."

The Reaper nodded. Chet waited for the man to sit back down, then he continued.

"This is fan mail. Little notes from single dads all over this country...and the world. If you're unimpressed, I have boxes of these back home."

"Now that you've redecorated my office, what's your point?" The Reaper glared at him.

"You don't have a single editor on staff with half the foresight of P.J. West. You'd be a fool to let her resign. Keep her. Keep the letters. They can be a new feature—dads writing in, sharing their experiences. You'll need a new angle since you won't have me. I won't be writing any more 'Living and Learning' articles...for personal reasons."

He heard P.J. sigh. Disappointment flashed across her face as she sat shaking her head at him. He continued, never taking his focus off her.

"Quite personal. I don't qualify. I'm not a widower, and I'm not even a father. I can tell you these things now because P.J. West taught me about honesty and integrity."

He paused. His heart beat so fast he thought it would race right out of his chest. She was looking at him, her eyes misty and soft. All the anger and regret had vanished from her face. Chet looked at her and felt a calm settle over him. He still hadn't said the most important thing, but that would be easy now.

"And I love her. I just hope she still loves me."

P.J. blinked. She opened her mouth, but no words emerged. Slowly her expression hardened.

Chet froze. All the blood seemed to drain from his head. This was not the response he expected. Where had he gone wrong?

The Reaper looked at both of them then grunted. "This discussion has no business in my conference room. Take it outside."

"Wait a minute," P.J. protested when Chet grabbed her elbow.

"Outside," The Reaper repeated.

P.J. glared at Chet, then stood, smoothed her skirt and let him lead her to the door. He could feel her anger ooze out of her pores.

"By the way," The Reaper said just as they stepped through the open door. "You're fired. Both of you."

"I've got news for you, too, you withered-up old fool. You don't deserve her," Chet said and closed the door.

As soon as the door closed behind them, P.J. shook free of Chet's hold.

"How dare you march in here, disrupt our meeting and then make my boss think there's something between us."

"Isn't there?"

He stepped closer and she raised her fist.

"No. You think because you made that little speech in there that everything is now hunky-dory? You lied to me, Chet."

"I know."

"What?" She didn't expect him to agree.

"I said, I know I lied. I lied to the readers. I lied to you, and I lied to myself."

She folded her arms and cocked her head. "You're up to something."

"Yep. I'm up to being a different person, one who doesn't count success in dollars and cents. I lied when I told myself that was true."

"And when did you come to this revelation?"

"The minute I realized I cared more about helping single fathers than I did about the money. The minute I realized I cared less about the column and the money than I cared about you and what you think of me."

"I'll tell you what I think. I think you're a jerk."

"That was yesterday. I've changed."

"You're right. Today you're an ass. How dare you come here and—"

"Declare I love you?"

She blinked. "What?"

"You weren't listening."

"Of course I was. It's just that...that..."

"You're overwhelmed. Me, too."

"Stop putting words in my mouth. I'm not overwhelmed, I'm angry."

"I'll let you sulk for a few days. You'll get over

that. Someone wrote that you only get really mad at those you love.''

''I don't trust authors. They lie.''

''Never about something that important. Admit it, you're crazy about me.''

''I hate you.''

''You'll get over that, too.''

He must have noticed the warning look in her eyes and changed his approach. ''Tell me what I have to do so you'll forgive me.''

P.J. said nothing, because that twisty flutter returned to her chest. He had already done all she could ask for. He'd admitted his mistake, accepted responsibility. He'd even sacrificed his column for the truth. What more could she ask? A little pain, perhaps?

Yeah, she wanted to punch him for putting her through such agony, she thought, glancing down at her fist. She could sock him in the stomach and give him one heck of a bellyache. But she had already done that, right before she'd left Richmond.

She sighed and looked up at him. Chet had his thumb in his mouth and was nibbling on his nail. Her heart fluttered. Darn she loved him...him and all his flaws.

''I'm sorry about your job,'' he said.

''Don't be.'' She kept her voice steady even though butterflies fluttered in her stomach, her chest, her throat. ''I'm a darn good editor. The best. Any magazine would scramble to hire me, but I'm not sure I'll even go that route. I may start my own

publication. The best way to get your message out
is to be in charge of your own crusade.''

''That's a big step. You need any writers?''

''Maybe.''

''I work for food these days.''

''That's about all I could afford.''

''I'd work even harder for forgiveness,'' he said.

That apologetic smile of his crept into place and
she knew how she'd answer.

''Please forgive me, P.J. Ann already has. The
kids are broken up, though. They miss you.''

The children. She missed them, too. She felt her
chest tighten. Her heart tripped over itself. She'd
never expected to grow so attached to them in such
a short time. And she had rushed from the house
without so much as a goodbye. Maybe she could
write to them later.

''The kids want us to make up. You want to be
responsible for breaking three little hearts?'' Chet
asked.

''You rat,'' P.J. said and tried to look angry.

''Nope. I'm a frog. A frog hoping for a miracle.''
With that, he puckered.

''What you did was reprehensible.''

''I can reform. Look, I used to be a confirmed
bachelor. Now all I can think about is being with
you...forever.''

He moved closer. P.J. stood her ground, not out
of defiance, but because her legs felt so wobbly. She
dared not take a single step even though she wanted
more than anything to walk right into his arms.

Chet solved that problem. He took hold of her

waist and pulled her to him. She could feel his heart pounding the same rhythm as her own.

"I'm a man on the brink of change. Plus that, I'm what every woman wants."

"Says who?"

"Brittany, she's an expert. I'm sensitive, vulnerable and have a whole lot of flaws that need fixing. So what do you say? You think you can kiss this frog, P.J.?"

"Patty Jean, to you," she said and tiptoed to meet his lips.

Three heart-stirring tales are coming down the aisle toward you in one fabulous collection!

LOVE, HONOR & CHERISH by SHERRYL WOODS

These were the words that three generations of Halloran men promised their women. But these vows made in love are each challenged by the test of time....

LOVE

Jason meets his match when a sassy spitfire turns his perfectly predictable life upside down!

HONOR

Despite their times of trouble, there still wasn't a dragon Kevin wouldn't slay to honor and protect his beloved bride!

CHERISH

They'd spent decades apart, but now Brandon had every intention of rekindling a long-lost love!

"Sherryl Woods is an author who writes with a very special warmth, wit, charm and intelligence."
—*New York Times* bestselling author
Heather Graham Pozzessere

On sale May 2000 at your favorite retail outlet.

Back by popular demand are

DEBBIE MACOMBER's

Hard Luck, Alaska, is a
town that needs women!
And the O'Halloran brothers
are just the fellows
to fly them in.

Starting in March 2000 this beloved series returns
in special 2-in-1 collector's editions:

MAIL-ORDER MARRIAGES, featuring
Brides for Brothers and *The Marriage Risk*
On sale March 2000

FAMILY MEN, featuring
Daddy's Little Helper and *Because of the Baby*
On sale July 2000

THE LAST TWO BACHELORS, featuring
Falling for Him and *Ending in Marriage*
On sale August 2000

Collect and enjoy each MIDNIGHT SONS story!

Available at your favorite retail outlet.

*Two complete novels by two of
your favorite authors!*

Wild
to Wed *by*
MURIEL JENSEN
JULE McBRIDE

*Sometimes the best-laid wedding plans
can go wildly wrong—
and end up with things going
perfectly right....*

Don't miss this charming
"2-in-1" value-priced collection from
two of your favorite authors!

Available May 2000 at your favorite retail outlet.

HARLEQUIN®
Makes any time special ™

Visit us at www.eHarlequin.com

PSBR2700